THE DICTATOR

Banker #2

PENELOPE SKY

Hartwick Publishing

The Dictator

Copyright © 2019 by Penelope Sky

Contents

Siena

MEN COLLECTED MY THINGS FROM THE HOUSE AND brought them to the three-story mansion in Tuscany. They took all my clothes and whatever essentials they thought were necessary.

I wasn't given a choice in the matter.

My house would stand there uninhabited. Landon would eventually realize I was missing and Cato was still alive. He would probably assume I was dead until he heard the rumors that Cato was expecting a child.

He would be relieved I was alright.

Until nine months from now.

My bedroom had a private bathroom, a small living room, and a balcony that overlooked the front of Cato's property. He owned acres of land and paid top dollar for a tall wall to surround his home, green ivy growing over the limestone. Anyone else would think they were in paradise.

I knew I was in a prison.

Cato hadn't spoken to me in three days. He stayed in his bedroom or left the house to go to work. Realistically, he couldn't avoid me forever, but if he had it his way, he probably would. He would just wait for me to deliver the baby nine months later without looking at me once.

I sat on the edge of the bed and pressed my hand over my stomach. It was as flat as ever with no noticeable changes. But my hand felt life growing inside, the son or daughter I never meant to make. My birth control was still active, but doctors said it was only ninety-nine percent effective.

Perhaps Cato was that one percent.

The most beautiful thing had happened to me, and the fact that I would never get to appreciate it broke my heart. My child needed a mother. More importantly, I needed a child. I would bond with them over the next nine months, get to know them so intimately. Once they left my body, I would be both sad and happy. But then that bliss would be taken away from me.

And I would be buried six feet under.

I would never be able to change Cato's mind. With his brother looming over his shoulder and the world thinking he was a fool, he couldn't take back his decision.

Feeling powerless was the worst part of all this.

My face looked better now that the swelling had gone down, but the area around my eye was still blue and my lip discolored. The pain was still there most of the time, but after a week, it should be gone.

My bedroom door opened, and Cato entered, dressed in a navy suit. He didn't knock the way Giovanni did. Just like he did at my home, he welcomed himself inside without warning. In this instance, this was his home…so he really could do whatever he wanted. With one hand in his pocket, he walked toward me, his eyes examining the bruises on my face. "Let's go."

"Where are we going?"

He walked out without answering me.

I slipped on my shoes and headed down the stairs to join him. He spoke to Giovanni quietly as he waited, both hands in his pockets. He towered over his butler and filled out the suit better than a mannequin.

Once I came to Cato's side, he walked out the front door to the car that was waiting for us.

A part of me was nervous he was going to shoot me in the driveway, but the car brought me peace of mind. I got into the back seat, and we left for Florence.

Cato looked out the window and didn't say a word to me.

"Where are we going?" I repeated.

His hand gripped his left knee, his fancy watch reflecting the summer light. He was a large man who needed a large car like this. He could barely fit inside my bed. "These nine months will be a lot smoother if you don't talk." He didn't even give me the respect of looking at me when he spoke.

"I'm going to die in nine months anyway. So I may as well do what I want."

He turned to me, his gaze vicious.

Now that a gun wasn't pointed in my face, my resilience had returned. I'd never been the kind of woman to take shit from anybody. As long as I was immune, I wouldn't take shit from him either. "Now tell me where we are going."

His jaw clenched harder. "Just because I won't kill you today doesn't mean I won't bust that pretty lip and blacken that other eye."

The insult washed over me with no effect. I'd never forget the relief I felt when Cato pulled Bates off me. His fist was cruel, and if he'd hit me one more time, he would have broken my nose or cheekbone. As it was, the pain had been excruciating. Cato could have done nothing, but he protected me instead. "We both know you won't. Don't pretend to be something you aren't."

He faced forward and shook his head slightly. "You don't know me very well."

"I do know you, actually. And you aren't a monster."

"No. I'm worse than a monster."

When the war began, he struck me in the car and made my head slam into the window, but it was a tame hit compared to what Bates had done to me. It was nothing in comparison. If that was the worst he could do, then I was in good company. "Cato—"

"I don't want to hear it." He must have picked up on the emotion in my voice. He must have predicted the words about to tumble out. "Save your apology. I don't want to listen to it."

"I wasn't going to apologize."

He turned back to me. Now he looked like he really wanted to hit me.

"You want to know where this scar came from?" I touched my left shoulder.

He followed my fingers but didn't ask the question.

"Damien broke in to my house, hunted me down, and when I refused to surrender, he shot me. Then he dragged me to Micah and told me they had my father. If I didn't bring you to them, they would kill him. And if I failed, Damien would get me all to himself—to play with his food before he ate it. It was nothing personal, Cato."

"And I've never taken it that way. You did what you had to do—and I'll do what I have to do."

"In the beginning, I didn't feel guilty about betraying you. I heard you were a terrible man."

"And I am." He faced forward again.

"It was when I got to know you that I realized you were a lot more than that. When it was just the two of us, you were charming, playful, and kind. The more time we spent together, the softer you became. I never expected to like you. I never expected to respect you. But once those feelings developed, I felt so terrible. I argued with myself for hours, trying to decide between you and my father. In the end, I turned that car around. I chose you."

He wore the same indifference, like my speech meant nothing to him. His hand remained on his knee, and he looked out the window as the city of Florence became visible. "Here's your answer. We're checking to make sure that baby is mine."

I ignored the insult that swept over my body. "It is, Cato."

"I think so too. But I learned my lesson. Never trust anything that comes out of your mouth."

2

Cato

THE DOCTOR HANDED ME THE RESULTS IN PRIVATE.

We were a match.

That baby was definitely mine.

"You're certain?" I asked as I folded up the paper and placed it in my pocket.

"These kinds of tests are never wrong, Mr. Marino."

I walked into the patient room and saw Siena standing there. She had put her dress and shoes back on now that the procedure was finished. Her brown hair was pulled back in a clip, and her eyelashes were thick with mascara. She'd done her best to cover the bruises on her face, but no amount of makeup could hide the damage.

I'd watched my brother beat her mercilessly, and despite my rage, I respected her for the way she handled it. Not once did she scream. Not once did she cry. She didn't allow any audible sound to give my brother satisfaction.

And when I pointed the gun in her face, she didn't piss herself.

She looked at me through those full lashes but didn't ask what the results were.

She already knew.

I'd had her tested for diseases just to make sure. Her results were clean. I tested myself and got the same results. Maybe that was overboard, but I didn't know this woman at all. I found it unlikely there was another man in the picture, not when I fucked her so well and so often, but I'd rather be safe than sorry.

Wordlessly, she walked out with me and returned to the car.

We left Florence and headed back to the house. Bates would meet me there so we could discuss the Beck brothers. They'd started drilling in a new location, but it didn't seem like they'd made progress yet.

I hoped I didn't have to kill his family.

She crossed her legs and sat quietly beside me, her hand resting across her flat stomach. Her gaze was directed out the window, and she wasn't as talkative as she was earlier. Her black dress fit her curves nicely, and the pearls around her neck made her look like royalty. Whenever she was at the house, she dressed conservatively, like a librarian, but I found the look strangely arousing. She commanded respect with her clothing, and that forced me to respect her—to some degree.

I hadn't had the chance to let the truth sink in. I'd been too angry to understand how drastically my life would change in nine months.

I would be a father.

I never wanted kids. I never wanted to be a father. This was the last thing I had any interest in.

But I would never forget how shitty it was not having a father. I would never forget how much it hurt me when I was young. Those abandonment issues followed me until I became a man and realized I didn't need him.

If I turned my back on my child, I would be no better than him.

Couldn't let that happen.

So now I was going to be a father.

A fucking father.

She turned to me, her pearl earrings catching the light. "How do you feel about this?"

The question made me angry enough to look at her. "I told you I didn't want a family. How do you think I feel about this? Now I'm having a kid I never wanted to have. All because you lied to me." Maybe that scar in her arm was old. Or maybe the implant had been deactivated over time. Or maybe it was a scar from something completely unrelated.

"I didn't lie—"

"Women don't get pregnant on birth control."

"Well, I did," she hissed. "I don't know how it happened, but it did. You must have super sperm or something."

I was too pissed to be pleased by that response. "We're stuck in this situation for the next nine months. I say you stop lying and just be honest. A real man and a real woman tell the truth boldly. They don't hide behind their lies. They have more balls than that."

Her eyes narrowed to hostile slits. "I'm not lying, Cato. I really didn't plan for this. When I kept getting sick, pregnancy didn't even cross my mind. I've been on this regimen for a long time, and it's never failed me."

"So you have let a guy come inside you." I should have known that was a lie too.

"No. That's not what I said."

"If you're using condoms, then how do you know it ever really worked?"

"Condoms break all the time. A responsible woman

always has a backup. And in case you forgot, you were the one who wanted to go bareback."

"Because you enticed me."

"Oh, that's my fault?" she asked incredulously. "Women entice you all the time. I never pressured you into that relationship. You basically demanded it and didn't give me a choice. So don't rewrite history."

No one ever stood up to me, and while it usually turned me on when she did it, right now it just annoyed me.

"It doesn't make sense for me to do this on purpose. My job was supposed to be to hand you over to Damien. How does getting pregnant help with that? Explain the motivation behind that."

I didn't have any theories. It really made no sense for her to do that. But then an idea struck me. "Inheritance." My eyes narrowed on her with a new sense of rage. "I die, and then our child gets everything. Which means you get everything."

The hatred on her face matched mine. "I don't want your money, Cato. I've never wanted your money, and I'll never want it."

"Right."

She pressed her lips tightly together before she spoke. "Not all people are obsessed with money, Cato. Not everyone needs overwhelming security like you do. Truly happy people can have nothing and feel perfectly content. Only sad people need a billion dollars to feel secure."

"I'm worth six billion."

She rolled her eyes. "Is that supposed to impress me?"

"Impresses everyone else."

"You know what does impress me?" she snapped. "The way your brother is so loyal to you. The way you're loyal to him. The way you smile after you tease me. The way you fuck me four times in a row like you haven't seen me in weeks even though it's been one day. The way you look far more powerful naked than in the $10,000 suits you wear. The way you take care of your mother. The way you pulled your brother off me when he almost beat me to death. The way you lowered your gun when you knew there was another life at stake. That's what impresses me, Cato. Not the size of your wallet. That's what made me turn around. Because I actually care about you."

———

I WALKED into the conference room downstairs and found Bates sitting with his feet on the desk, smoking a cigar while the Monet painting hung behind him.

"No smoking in here." I sat across from him and eyed the painting on the wall. It was impossible for me to look at it and not think of the woman who picked it out for me. The beautiful colors of the flowers made me think of the brightness of her eyes, and the quiet stream reminded me of her home…even though there was no stream nearby.

"Why?" He took another puff. "I always smoke in here."

I nodded to the painting on the wall. "Because of that."

He let the smoke rise from his mouth as he turned his head to look at it. "Looks like a piece of trash that trash picked out."

"It's Monet, and I paid ten million for it. Put out your fucking cigar."

Bates took another long puff before he smashed the cigar into the ashtray.

"Besides, with a pregnant woman around here, we can't have any smoke anyway."

"You just make me hate that bitch more and more…"

He interlocked his fingers behind his head. "I can't wait until we kill her. Executing traitors is one of my fetishes."

I opened the folder and read through the contracts.

Bates kept staring at me. "I'm guessing you're the father, then?"

"Yes." I clicked the top of my pen and added my signature to the bottom of the page.

"Damn." He shook his head. "We can still kill her, you know. We agreed we wouldn't have families."

I clicked my pen again so it wouldn't dry out and looked at my brother. "I know what we agreed on. But shit happens."

"Never fuck a woman without a condom." He held up a finger. "Rule number one."

I never should have broken that rule. "It is what it is, Bates."

"The baby is like a week old?" he asked. "Does that really count?"

"Enough, Bates."

"Come on, think about it." He pulled his legs off the table and sat up, his elbows resting on the surface. "You have the baby, kill her, and then what? You're changing diapers and reading bedtime stories? Having a kid isn't easy. Why do you think Father left us? Because it was fucking hard."

"Nothing is too hard for me. I can handle it."

"You say that now. Wait until you hear the constant screaming all day and all night. And how do you think this will affect your sex life?"

"I'll get a nanny."

"Doesn't matter. At the end of the day, that little brat is still your responsibility."

Regardless of my brother's argument, I would never take my unborn baby's life. "This way, we have a legacy.

We have someone to pass the business down to. It's not the worst thing in the world."

"What if it's a girl?" he countered. "She wouldn't be able to hold her own."

"If she's my daughter, yes she will," I said proudly. "I won't raise a princess. I'll raise a queen."

"I still think you should reconsider."

"Well, I never will. So drop it."

He gave me that knowing look, the same look he'd been giving me all our lives.

"What?"

"Why do I feel like this has something to do with Siena?"

"Because it does. She's the one who's pregnant…in case you didn't notice."

"Maybe you're more attached to this baby because she's the mother."

It was a ridiculous accusation. "If she weren't pregnant, I would have killed her. You know I would have." My finger wouldn't have hesitated to pull the trigger. She was a traitor, and she deserved a traitor's death.

"But when I was smashing my fist in her face, you told me to stop."

"Because you were going to kill her. And I'm the one who deserved to take her life."

He shook his head slightly. "I hope that's the truth, Cato. Because she's a snake in our garden. Never turn your back to a snake."

I looked down at the contracts then pushed them across the table toward him. "Trust me, I won't."

3

Siena

I SAT ON THE BALCONY AND CRIED.

Sobbed.

Now that the dust had settled, reality hit me hard.

My father was gone.

Both of my parents were gone.

The last thing I said to my father was harsh, so harsh it would haunt me for the rest of my life. He had been too stubborn to talk to me in five years, and I had far too much pride to go back on my word, so those were the final words that we would ever say to each other.

It's your fault she's dead. You didn't love her, and you don't love me. All you care about is money and power. You can't love things that won't love you back. You can't take those superficial things to the grave. All you can take is your soul—and you don't have one.

I'd left his house and never looked back.

Now I regretted how ferocious I was. He didn't come after me once in five years, so he obviously didn't care, but he's still my father.

He was my father.

In the back of my mind, I always thought we would

find our way back to each other. I always imagined we would have Christmas together again. I thought my father would realize he was wrong and beg for my forgiveness.

But now that wasn't possible.

I didn't even have my brother anymore. I would be dead in less than a year, and Landon would be the last of my bloodline.

Unless someone hunted him down.

My family had been destroyed by money. Had been destroyed by greed.

My hand moved over my stomach, and I feared for my child. They would be born into a wealthy family, having a father more powerful than any other man. But they would also be vulnerable to the same sickness.

Greed.

I'd always imagined raising my family differently, in a small house with a little money. We would have family dinners, game nights, and we would set up the Christmas tree on the first of December. Our lives would be simple and peaceful.

But now they would be born into a world of crime, violence, and greed.

I didn't want that for my baby.

The only way I could save them and myself was if I ran away. If I somehow found the perfect opportunity to disappear. I would run off to a new country, change my identity, and hide until Cato stopped looking for me.

That seemed just as impossible as turning him over to Damien.

But I had to try. It wasn't like he could kill me if he caught me—at least not while I was pregnant.

The door to the balcony opened, and Cato stood there. Wearing his gray sweatpants that hung low on his hips and no shirt, he spotted the redness in my eyes and the shower of tears on my cheeks.

I didn't even have a chance to fix my makeup. He barged in without notice. "You really should knock."

"It's my house."

"My room."

"I own this room and I own you." He shut the door behind him and sat in the lounge chair beside me.

I wiped the makeup from under my eyes and steadied my breathing. I wouldn't cry in front of him. Like I hadn't just sobbed my heart out, I pretended nothing had happened at all. I looked out into the darkness across his property, seeing the few landscape lights illuminating the plants and trees. "Is there something you needed, Cato?" He never visited me unless he had a reason. We didn't have chitchats, and we didn't have sex anymore. I wasn't required to do anything with him now that my plan had failed, but I did miss it.

He rested his arms on his knees and rubbed his hands together. "Giovanni said you skipped dinner."

"I wasn't hungry."

"I don't care. You need to eat."

I rolled my eyes. "I've been pregnant for a few weeks. Skipping a meal won't make a difference."

"I'm sorry if I gave you the impression this was a dialogue." He turned to me with a cold gaze. "This is me telling you what to do. You will eat all your meals—including this one. Defy me, and I'll shove it down your throat."

So he clearly didn't give a damn I was crying. "I'm fine, by the way."

"I couldn't care less if you're fine. Giovanni is gonna bring your dinner. If you don't eat it, there will be consequences. And I will know if you ate it or not." He rose from the chair and headed back into my room.

A life of obedience wasn't interesting to me. "You're more likely to get stuff done when you treat people like human beings."

He turned around, his sculpted body so perfect it was ridiculous. "Like the way you treated me? When you stalked me, fucked me, and lied to me? Is that how you define humane?"

I looked away, tired of repeating myself. "I already explained why I did what I did. I wanted to save my father…" The mention of his name made my bottom lip quiver and my eyes water. Regret and pain washed over me. I was losing every family member, one by one. Crying in front of Cato was too humiliating, so I turned my face the opposite way and pretended to admire the landscape again. I cried quietly to myself, waiting for the sound of the closing door.

It never came.

He lowered himself back into the chair beside me. "Is that why you're crying?" His voice was deep and soothing, not aggressive like it'd been a second ago. He sounded like the man I used to know, the lover in my bed. "Because of your father?"

Tears rolled down my cheeks. "Yes…"

He turned silent, but he continued to sit there.

"The last thing I said to him was pretty horrible. I always thought we would have a chance to make amends, to put our family back together. I thought he would see reason, see how money tore everyone apart. But now I'll never get that chance…" I took a deep breath as more hot tears emerged. "I hate to imagine how he died. I hate to imagine what they did to him before they took his life. It keeps haunting me. I know he loved my mother despite what happened, and I hate that he'll never be buried with her, that I won't be able to visit them both. I hate that I can't lay him to rest…to say goodbye." I closed my eyes and wondered why I was telling him all of this. Under this new regime, I felt alone. The only person I talked to was Giovanni, and he was always about business. Cato was my only friend…even though he despised me.

"I'm sorry." It was the most unexpected phrase to come from his mouth. "I wish I could tell you that they made it quick, but I can't. When it comes to these wars, men are never merciful. But he's not in pain anymore… and hopefully that gives you comfort."

I hadn't expected any softness from him, not ever again. "Your father left you?" When I read about him, I only found information about his mother. It didn't seem like a father had ever been in the picture.

"I was five. Bates was three."

"I'm sorry."

"Don't be. My mother did just fine on her own." There was pride in his voice, obvious respect for the woman who raised him. "My hatred stems from my loyalty to my mother. I hate him for abandoning her when she needed him most. That was a pussy thing to do."

"And you don't want to be like that." I wiped my tears away and turned back to him. His arms were on the armrests as he looked out over his property. Handsome as ever, he sat on the chair like it was a throne.

"No," he whispered. "I'm not a coward."

The door opened, and Giovanni appeared with the dinner he'd tried to give me earlier. "I hope your appetite has returned, Miss Siena?"

Cato stared straight ahead.

I had no appetite at all, but Cato had just given me kindness—and I would reciprocate. "It has. Thank you."

Giovanni placed the tray in my lap before he left.

I took small bites of my food to make Cato happy.

He didn't look at me. "Thank you."

"See?" I teased. "You can treat people like human beings."

He shrugged. "Sometimes."

Tears were still hot behind my eyes, but they slowly retreated the longer I sat with him. "I know you don't believe me, but I really did turn around for you, Cato. I wanted to save my father, but in the end, I knew I couldn't do that to you."

"It doesn't change everything prior to that." He brought his hands together again. "It doesn't change the fact that nothing about us was ever real. It was all a setup. You were in the right place at the right time on purpose. Your job was to gain my trust just enough to put me in harm's way. I know nothing about you, Siena." He turned to me, defeat in his eyes. "I knew you were his daughter weeks ago. But I gave you the benefit of the doubt. Maybe you really did just want to start over. Maybe you really were harmless. I don't know what it is about you…but it makes me so soft. I hate it."

"Everything I said about myself was true. The only part that was a lie…was meeting you. Yes, my goal was to make you remember me. My goal was to get into your bed and gain your confidence. But everything in between that…all me. I couldn't make you have a connection with me. I couldn't make you forget about other women…that just happened on its own. That was real—that was us."

He faced forward again, his expression masked by indifference. "It's strange. I don't trust anyone. I trust women least of all…but I trusted you."

"Because I was honest with you. When I said I wanted a simple life, I meant it. My father is dead because all he cared about was money. My mother is dead because of it too. It's only a matter of time before my brother follows suit. I really enjoy artwork. I enjoy wine. And I enjoy you…"

He wouldn't look at me again.

"I miss you."

His jaw started to clench, like I'd said the wrong thing. "I don't miss you. How can I miss something I never had?"

"You did have me. You could still have me."

"Really? Or is that another ploy? Will you fuck me to save your life?" His eyes landed on mine, and they burned me from the inside out.

"I'll fuck you because you're the man I want to fuck. You're the best I've ever had, the only man who's ever really made me feel like a woman. I'll fuck you because your smile makes me melt and your body keeps me warm. You've already made your decision, and I'm sure you'll see it through. Doesn't mean I don't want you in the meantime."

His gaze hardened just like his jaw. "I don't trust you, Siena. I will never trust you again."

"I'm not asking you to trust me."

"And I'll never want you again."

His words shouldn't hurt me since I planned to escape, but they did. They hurt me more than I expected. "Then why are you sitting with me right now? Why are you comforting me?"

He faced forward again and didn't give an answer.

I knew it was because he didn't have an answer. "I turned around, Cato. I turned around because I didn't want to hurt you. Maybe my intentions were wrong in the beginning, but they were right at the end. You can't judge me for wanting to save the only parent I had left. You can't judge me for trying to save my family. It's not right—and you're being stubborn."

"I'm being stubborn?" he asked coldly. "You tried to feed me to my enemies—on a silver fucking platter."

"But then I didn't—"

"You were going to kill me. You took this mission knowing you were going to kill me."

"Yes…but then I got to know you and couldn't go through with it. Stop acting like that means nothing. It means everything."

"Not to me," he hissed. "A loyal person is always loyal."

"And I was loyal to my father. How could I be loyal to a man I didn't even know?"

"I don't judge your actions," he said. "But don't expect me to pardon them. You did what you had to do. I don't take it personally. But don't expect me to ever want to be personal ever again. Whatever we had…is over."

"And yet…you're still sitting with me."

His blue eyes turned sinister as he rubbed his hands together. A deep sigh came from between his lips, full of frustration and violence.

I put the tray on the table then walked to his chair. My knee touched his, and I looked down at him, seeing a man deeply conflicted. When he didn't get up to push me away, I pulled up my dress to my waist then straddled his hips.

He gripped each armrest and released a quiet groan, like he hated my actions but felt powerless to stop them.

When my pussy rested against his lap, I could feel the enormous cock that used to pound me every single night. Fully erect and desperate, it pressed against his sweatpants like it wanted to slide right into my cunt.

My fingers moved into his hair, and I pressed my face close to his, our lips almost touching. I breathed with him, matching the rhythmic rise and fall of his chest. I could feel his desire ooze from his pores, the invisible restraints keeping his passion at bay. But he wanted me…wanted me as much as I wanted him.

I pulled the dress over my head entirely and let it fall to the ground. Then I placed his large hand against my stomach, right where I imagined the baby was.

He closed his eyes and moaned, like that turned him on even more.

"Forgive me." I leaned in and pressed my mouth to his, kissing the man I'd been separated from an entire week. My body craved his after the long drought, and I could honestly say there was no other man I wanted. Only Cato could please me. Only Cato knew how to please a woman.

He didn't kiss me back. His lips were immobile, and then they turned ice-cold. He pulled his mouth away then rose to his feet, taking me with him.

I hoped he would carry me to the bed and take me inside.

Instead, he threw me onto the bed and walked out.

I waited for the sound of his footsteps to return, but I knew they weren't coming.

Because he would never forgive me.

4

Cato

I HATED THAT WOMAN.

I'd thought I was the devil. No. It was her.

She could cast a spell on me like a witch. One moment, I hated her, and then the next, I was under her trance. I listened to her cry with pity in my heart. Instead of walking away and leaving her in solitude, I stayed so she wouldn't feel alone. Then I consoled her…and lingered. Every time she asked why I stayed, I didn't have an answer.

Because I knew I shouldn't be there.

She was a traitor and a liar.

Why did I give a damn about her?

When she crawled on top of me, I had to use all my restraint to pull away. As far as I was concerned, she was just a surrogate. She would give birth to my son or daughter, and then she would be dead. There was no other way.

And I shouldn't fuck her anymore. I could fuck anyone I wanted now—and as many women as I wanted. Monogamy was over. She was the first woman I'd given it to, and it'd all been a waste.

A part of me still wanted her, but if I caved, it would

be a terrible idea. That woman fooled me once, and I couldn't let it happen again. She was a snake that shouldn't be in the garden—or my bed.

But something inside my chest ached when I thought of her father. My sources told me how he died. They hung him from a noose, and as he suffocated, they stabbed him to death. It was the cruelest execution I'd ever heard of.

No matter how much I wanted to hurt her, I would never tell her that.

The truth would die with me.

I didn't know what they did with his body, but I was certain it was in an oil drum somewhere. When my father left us, I always wondered where he went. As I aged, I wondered what he was doing on Christmas as I waited for my mother to come home from work. I wondered what his life was like, if he had another family. It haunted me for a long time. When he showed up and harassed my mother, I was furious, but it also gave me closure. Now I knew he had nothing. He was so pathetic that he returned to the woman he'd abandoned for a payout. Then I never had to wonder again.

Maybe he only regretted his actions because I became a billionaire. I could be taking care of him right now, buying him a yacht so he could sail the Mediterranean with my mother. Or maybe he genuinely regretted his decision, that it haunted him every day until he couldn't take it anymore.

Either way, it was the closure I'd always wanted.

Maybe Siena was entitled to the same thing.

———

THE MEETING HAD BEEN SET.

I walked into their lair with my men in tow. When my

men were asked to drop their weapons, we refused.

I didn't drop my weapons for anyone.

My stubbornness wasn't challenged, and I was led inside. In the center of the room sat Micah. About Giovanni's age, he was several decades older than me, and all the smoking had turned his skin to shit. Damien lingered behind him like the little bitch that he was.

Micah stood up but didn't come closer. There were ten feet separating us. "Nice to see you're in one piece."

"I was hoping you'd be in several." Siena and I had left the shootout before it turned ugly. There were a few causalities and blown-up tanks, but the important players survived—unfortunately. But once a war had been ignited, it never ended.

Micah shrugged. "Not all wishes come true—even when you blow out the candles. So, what can I do for you?"

My eyes moved to Damien, and I remembered what Siena had said several times, that the guy threatened to rape her and kill her. That he wanted her to fail just so he could have her. I wanted to snap his neck then and there. I turned back to Micah. "I'm here for a truce."

Micah cocked an eyebrow instead of keeping a straight face. I wasn't the kind of man to call a truce. I destroyed my enemies until there was nothing left—at all costs. "A truce?" he asked, like he didn't understand the word.

"Yes. We can forget this whole thing."

Micah crossed his arms over his chest, trying to understand my angle. "In exchange for what? Money?"

"We both know I already have all the money."

His nostrils flared.

"Give me Stefano Russo's body. That's it."

Micah cocked his head to the side. "You're calling a truce over a corpse? That's all you want?"

"Yes. Hand it over, or tell me where I can find it."

Damien gave me the same disgusted look I gave him. "Damn, she must be something in bed…"

My eyes flicked back to his, and I silently threatened him.

"That's what this is all about, isn't it?" Damien said. "For that bitch?"

Quicker than Damien could react, I pulled the pistol out of my belt and shot him in the left shoulder.

"Jesus!" Damien staggered back and clutched himself.

All my men drew their weapons.

So did Micah's.

"What the fuck, asshole?" Damien screamed, the blood dripping down his arm to his hand.

I returned the pistol to my belt. "An eye for an eye. Or better yet, a shoulder for a shoulder." I looked at Micah. "We have a deal or what?"

Damien gripped his shoulder as he walked away, probably to attend to his gaping wound.

Micah nodded. "Yes. We have a deal."

———

BATES WAS STANDING outside when I pulled up to the house. It was ten in the evening, so he'd obviously heard about my deal with Micah. It was the only reason he would stand like a gargoyle outside my house.

I walked up the stairs and met him face-to-face.

His eyes looked like bullets. "What the fuck, Cato?"

"Let it go, alright?"

"Let it go?" he hissed. "Are you fucking with me right now? Since when do we call truces with assholes who try to assassinate you?"

"They were never a threat to us."

"Doesn't matter. That's not how we treat our enemies."

"It wasn't worth our time." I stepped around him and headed into the house.

He grabbed me by the arm and yanked me back. "We make these decisions together, asshole. Not only did you not tell me, but you did it behind my back."

"I knew you would never agree. And what I do to the people who try to kill me is my business. This had nothing to do with work or a deal, so no, I didn't need your approval. It's done now, so drop it."

"Maybe in another situation, I could drop it, but you did this entirely for her. The woman who stabbed you in the back as she fucked you. But here you are, laying down your coat on a puddle so her feet don't get wet."

I didn't bend over backward for this woman, despite what he thought. "She deserves closure."

"That bitch doesn't deserve anything."

"They gave her a mission she never would have accomplished. Either way, she lost and her father died. It was a lose-lose for her. Everyone deserves closure. Her father was slaughtered, and she just wants to bury him. It's not that much to ask."

"It is when you have to call a truce to make it happen." Spit flew from his mouth as the cord in his neck throbbed.

"Let it go, Bates."

"I can't let it go. This whore is poisoning your mind."

"I'm not fucking her. I will kill her. You need to calm down."

He threw his hands down as he stepped away. "I still don't like this, Cato. I promise you, if you don't pull the trigger, I will. She's fucked with your brain since the day you met her, and even now that we know she's a traitor, she still gets under your skin. The day she's gone, I'll get my brother back—and that day can't come soon enough."

5

Siena

Cato and I didn't speak for another four days.

I spent my time in my room because I had my own TV. When I needed exercise, I walked around his property. He had a winding path that had to be at least a mile long. I usually did my walks in the morning before it got too hot and then again late at night.

Now I sat on my bed without the slightest idea what to do. Without a job or freedom, I was bored. The only thing I looked forward to was eating because Giovanni was the best cook in the entire world.

Cato walked inside my room abruptly, dressed all in black. It looked like the same outfit he wore the day we were supposed to visit my mother.

I held his gaze but didn't know what to say. The last time we were in the same space together, he rejected my advance. He tossed me on the bed then stormed out.

"Come with me."

"Where are we going?"

His eyes narrowed. "Does it matter?"

"Yes. How do I know what to wear?"

"Your outfit is fine."

I was in black jeans and an olive blouse. My flats were on the floor by the door, even though I hardly wore shoes because I never went anywhere. "This place is way too boring for me. It's not like I can take off, so how about you let me get my job back? It'll give me something to do during the day."

Cato acted like I hadn't said anything at all. "Let's go." He walked out without waiting for me.

I slipped on my shoes and followed him downstairs. We moved outside, got into the car, and then left the house. I still had no idea where we were going, and I suspected we were headed to a doctor's visit or something related to the baby.

Fifteen minutes later, we approached the cemetery where my mother was buried.

I turned to him. "Cato?"

He looked out the window and ignored me.

"Are you taking me to see my mother?" I asked, shocked that he would do something nice for me. He'd pushed me away the last time we were together, and it didn't seem like he could ever forgive me. Now he was giving me a wonderful surprise a few days later.

"Yes." He opened the door when the car stopped at the curb. "And your father."

The blood drained from my face.

Cato opened my side of the car and helped me to my feet.

"What are you talking about…?"

He guided me to the grass and past the other tombstones until we reached my mother's headstone. The stone slab had my mother's birth and death carved into the surface, and there had always been a blank spot underneath where my father's name would appear.

And it was filled out. His birthdate and death were marked.

The ground covering where my mother's coffin lay had been dug up, and a second coffin had been placed on top. Too speechless to say anything, I stared at the sleek black coffin and knew my father was lying in there, joined with my mother for all eternity. The surface of the coffin was shiny, with the exception of the few drops of dirt sprinkled on the black paint. I felt too many emotions to feel anything at all, so I just stood there.

Then I started to cry. "Father…" I moved to my knees and stared at the grave where both my parents now lay. Joined together in death, they would lie there forever. Only Landon and I survived, and I suspected we would both be in the ground soon enough.

I forgot Cato was there entirely as I continued to cry, staring at the coffin in agony. I'd done my best to save him, but I knew in my heart I never had a chance. The men I was up against were far too formidable—and I was just one person.

Cato stood over me then handed me a few tissues.

I didn't look at him as I took them. "Thank you…" I wiped the tears away and blew my nose before I started to sob again. They said the most pain you could ever feel was losing a child. I think losing a parent was just as hard.

Cato stepped back and left me to mourn in peace.

Minutes later, another car pulled up to the curb, and a man stepped out. Dressed in a black suit, he was prepared to mourn. His features were difficult to make out through my tears, but when he came closer, I knew who he was.

"Landon?" I moved to my feet and stared at my brother in shock. Everything seemed surreal. Cato arranged all of this, and that was the most surprising part of all. I didn't have to mourn alone. I could mourn with the only family I had left. It was the greatest gift anyone had given me.

Landon was grief-stricken the way I was. He expressed fewer emotions than I did, or at least he hid them better. While his expression was hard, there were no tears in his eyes. It just seemed like he was having a bad day—a really bad day.

"Siena." He wrapped his arms around me and held me next to the grave.

I clutched him hard and buried my face in his chest. The tears kicked up again, and I heaved with the sobs. It was a blessing having him there, but it also reminded me how alone we were. Now we were the last survivors of our family.

"I'm so glad you're here…" His cologne was exactly the same as I remembered. It reminded me of all the holidays we spent together. When we met in the back of bars, we were hiding from the world. But now I could actually hold him—and treasure it.

"Cato tracked me down somehow."

"You aren't as smart as you think you are."

He pulled away and gave me that amused smile. "You're the one who got captured."

"Looks like we're both dumb."

"Yeah." He turned to the grave and looked down at Father's coffin as he wrapped his arm around my shoulders. "At least they're together now. They'll never have to suffer again."

"Yeah…"

We stood together in silence for a long time, staring into the grave with our bodies held close. Landon breathed quietly while he stared at our father's coffin. Tears didn't emerge, just a distinct look of regret. "You were right about Cato. You should have asked for his help."

"I don't know…he probably would have killed me."

He turned to me, an incredulous look in his eyes. "He retrieved Father's body and contacted me for this moment. He gave both of us closure, brought peace to our family. The last thing he wants to do is kill you."

I looked past his profile and saw Cato standing near the car. He slowly paced back and forth as he spoke on the phone.

My eyes turned back to Landon's. "I don't know why he did this. But his intentions aren't as good as you think they are."

"Why do you say that? You're still together after the shit hit the fan."

"It's not how it seems…" I focused on the casket in the ground. "He was going to execute me until I told him I was pregnant."

His arm tightened around my shoulders. "What?" He lowered his arm and pivoted his body to face me. "You're pregnant?" His eyes moved down to my stomach even though there were no visible signs of pregnancy.

"Yes…and that's the only reason I'm alive."

"Well, that's damn lucky."

I didn't want to tell my brother the truth. It would only break his heart. But I didn't want him to wonder what happened to me once I was gone. "He says he'll kill me after the baby is born."

Our father's grave seemed unimportant now that the truth was on the table. "So he'll keep the baby and get rid of you."

"Yes."

He glanced at Cato over his shoulder before he looked at me again. "If that were the case, why would he do this for you? Why would he bring me here so we can bury our father? For a man intent on killing you, he sure seems to care about you."

"I…I don't know." I couldn't explain his actions logically. "There's still chemistry between us. I can feel this tension anytime we're alone together. I know he still wants me, but he despises me for what I did."

"Any man would understand you were just trying to survive."

"He sees the world differently."

"I still think he's full of shit. He would never do this for you unless you meant something to him. He's not gonna kill you."

"I hope you're right…but I'm gonna try to run anyway."

He shook his head. "I don't think that's a good idea. If he catches you, then he might actually kill you."

"I can't let him raise my child. They'll be born into the nightmare I've spent the last five years running from. They'll be exposed to greed and corruption. Violence will seem normal to them. That's not the kind of upbringing I want my child exposed to."

"They'll also inherit billions of dollars, Siena."

"When will you learn that money ruins lives? Look at us right now. Look at our parents."

He kept his eyes on me and didn't look at the grave. "There are worse situations to be born into."

"I disagree." A simple life was the key to happiness. My family was always on the run, or someone else was on the run from us. It never stopped. It was one business venture after the next, a new deal that didn't go down the way it should. There was never a calm before the storm. It was a constant storm.

"I think you should focus on getting Cato back on your side. He's pretty much there anyway."

"Easier said than done."

Disapproval was in his eyes. "You should reconsider."

"Even if he didn't kill me, what then? What kind of life would I ever have? He would boss me around forever."

"And he would also protect you. Cato Marino can make anything happen. He can even get Father's body back. As long as Cato is on your side, there's nowhere safer for you to be—and the little one."

I wanted a life where I had all my rights, but I suspected that would never happen. Cato would always treat me like everyone else did—like he owned me. But he would never own me the way I wanted him to.

Landon kept watching me. "I know you're stubborn, so you're probably going to try to run anyway. If you do… make sure you don't get caught. The consequences will be catastrophic, pregnant or not." He looked at my face and didn't ask about the bruises that were still visible. He probably figured out exactly where they came from, but he didn't show me any pity. "Well, looks like I'm going to be an uncle…"

"Yes." My hand moved over my stomach. "Yes, you are."

"And you're going to be a mother." He gave me a slight smile. "It's what you've always wanted."

"I just hope I live long enough to enjoy it."

6

Cato

I GAVE THEM PRIVACY TO MOURN THEIR LOSS, BUT I WAS certain Siena had notified her brother of everything that had happened.

That I would kill her once she had my baby.

He wouldn't retaliate, not unless it was a suicide mission.

When they were finished, they walked away from the open grave. Close together, they returned to the cars parked at the curb. The caretakers on standby immediately moved to the grave and began to shovel the dirt on top.

Landon walked up to me, his hand extended while his eyes were locked on to mine with respect, not hostility. "Thank you for burying our father. It means a lot to both of us."

I shook his hand then looked at Siena. Her eyes were puffy from crying, and the whites of her eyes were now red. It was amazing how beautiful she looked even when she sobbed. Nothing could taint her allure, not the puffiness or smeared mascara. I'd been with many women, but none of them could pull that off.

"Siena told me you're having a baby. Congratulations."

"Thank you." It was surprising that he said that, considering I would kill her shortly afterward.

He held my gaze like a man, like he was an equal rather than her brother. "She wanted to tell you everything and ask for your help. She said it multiple times, and I always talked her out of it. Siena was in a bad situation and—"

"Landon." Siena shook her head, silencing her brother.

Landon ignored her. "She didn't have a lot of options, Cato. No one can judge her for her actions, not when she was in such a difficult situation. Anyone else would have done the same thing in her shoes."

"Of course they would have," I said quietly. "That was never the problem."

"Then give her another chance," Landon said. "She's a good person."

It broke my heart to listen to my brother fight for me.

"We're both men of the underworld," I said. "So you understand exactly how loyalty works. She didn't show it. She lied to me—every day. I appreciate what you're trying to do, but my decision is final." I stepped away and dismissed the conversation. "Let's go, Siena." I opened the back door for her and waited for her to get in.

She turned to her brother and hugged him hard, her face buried in his neck.

He hugged her with the same affection.

"I love you," she whispered to him.

"I love you too." As he released her, he kissed her on the forehead. As if lingering would just make everything harder, he abruptly turned around and walked off.

Siena watched him get into his car before she finally obeyed me.

I got into the car with her, and we drove away.

She stared out the window with pain in her eyes, but she didn't shed another tear.

I expected gratitude, and I would say nothing until I got it. She had no idea what I'd sacrificed to get her father's corpse back. It was a few weeks old, so identifying him was no picnic either.

After a few minutes, she finally addressed me. "I don't know what to say…"

"Thank you is a good start."

"Of course…thank you." She turned to me, her cheeks pale as snow. "Knowing he's with my mother comforts me. Landon and I got to mourn him properly and say our goodbyes. Not knowing where his body was…would have haunted me forever."

I gave a slight nod.

"How did you do it?"

"I made a deal with Micah. He gave me your father in exchange for something."

"What?" she whispered.

"A truce. I won't come after them unless they provoke me."

"Oh…" Her eyes tilted down as the words soaked in. "You're sure it's him?"

"I identified him myself. Don't worry about that." He'd just begun to rot, and the smell was disgusting. But thankfully, his face had been mostly intact so I could verify his identity. The rest of his body was pretty much destroyed. He had a death so cruel I would never speak of it to her.

Thank god she didn't ask. "Thank you, Cato. Again, I don't know what to say. I don't know how to show my gratitude."

"Your words are enough." My brother's accusations were right. I did bend over backward to do this for her. For a man who didn't care about anything, I sure cared about her. My respect for her still burned bright like a fire in the hearth. Despite what she did to me, she deserved a certain amount of dignity.

"And you brought Landon too…"

"I didn't want you to be alone."

"You're a good man, Cato. Even if you still kill me, my opinion won't change."

That would only make killing her more difficult. Listening to her hate me would make it a lot easier to shut her up.

"That was a sweet thing to do. I still can't believe it happened."

"You did everything to save your father. You failed, but you still deserved to bury him. It'll give you closure."

"Yes…it will." She faced forward again.

I stared at the side of her face, examining the subtle beauty of her high cheekbones. Her freckles gave her a hint of girlish charm against the rest of her distinctly womanly appearance. Her lips were plump like pillows, and her slender neck was as long as her legs. If she gave me a daughter, I knew I would have a serious problem on my hands. "I shot Damien for you."

She turned back to me, her eyebrows furrowed. "You shot him?"

"In the left shoulder. But he'll live."

The sadness left her eyes for a moment, replaced with heated vengeance. "Thank you. I just wish you'd aimed for his head."

I smiled, liking the fire that roared out of her mouth. "Next time."

———

TWO WEEKS HAD COME and gone.

I hadn't gotten laid.

For a man who got sex on a regular basis, two weeks was equivalent to two months.

I considered going out and picking up pussy. But my mind always wandered back to the mother of my child, the woman I'd fucked more than anyone else. She was already pregnant, so I never had to worry about knocking her up again. I didn't need a condom, but I would need to wear one with someone else.

But I was still pissed at her.

I could do whatever I wanted with her. I could force her even if she said no. I could chain her up and turn it into a punishment. The idea was arousing.

But I was too stubborn to do it.

After what she did, I should never want her again.

I was sitting on the couch in the private living room of my master bedroom when there was a knock on the door. Giovanni had already served me dinner, so I knew it wasn't him. He wouldn't bother me at this hour unless it was important. I could see the bedroom door from the living room, so I called out, "Come in."

Siena walked inside, dressed in pajama shorts and a white tank top without a bra.

My eyes immediately went to her nipples.

Her hair was pulled back in a slick ponytail and her face was clean of makeup, but I started to realize I actually preferred her that way.

"Can I talk to you?" She stayed by the door, her long legs tanned and toned.

All I could focus on was those legs in those shorts, those tits in that shirt, and that gorgeous neck I used to grab. "Yes."

She shut the door then joined me in the living room.

She moved to the couch beside me and watched the soccer game on the screen. "Sports fan?"

"Yes."

She looked at my glass of scotch on the table like she wanted to take a drink. Of course she couldn't, so she sat back and turned her gaze on me.

I tried not to stare at her legs in those little shorts. I tried not to look at her tits in that thin cotton shirt. Even though she genuinely looked ready for bed, she'd never looked sexier. She could have walked in here in lingerie, and my reaction would have been the same. Maybe she was intentionally antagonizing me under the false pretense of going to sleep. "Something you need?"

She looked at my shirtless chest, not bothering to hide her need for affection. Maybe she'd tried to fuck me last week to screw with my head. Or maybe she just missed sex as much as I did. "I wanted to ask you something."

"I'm listening."

"I do nothing all day while you're out and about—"

"You aren't going to work." Being a prisoner meant she had no freedom. Working was a freedom that she didn't deserve. "You will stay here constantly unless you accompany me somewhere." Not even her sexy legs could change my mind about that.

Disappointment was in her eyes, but she pushed on for another request. "Then can Landon come to the house and visit me? He'll want to spend time talking to the baby. And I could use the company…"

"You think I'm gonna let your brother, who tried to talk me out of killing you, come into my house?"

"Even if he wanted to, there's no possibility of him doing anything. You don't need to worry about that. He's not happy about the situation, but he does admire you for what you did for our father."

Only certain people were permitted on my property. It didn't matter if Landon was outnumbered a hundred to one. "No."

"Then can I meet him for—"

"No."

"Can I talk to him on the phone, then? Can I have a phone?"

Denying that request would be extreme. There was no harm in it. "I guess."

She sighed, appreciation in her gaze. "Thank you. But I hope you reconsider letting him come to the house. This is his niece or nephew, and he has the right to spend time with them."

"Has the right?" I asked. "That implies you have rights —which you don't."

Her eyes narrowed at the insult. "Even when I'm gone, Landon will still be family. One day when our child grows older, they're going to be curious about me. They're going to ask questions. And it won't be that hard to find out exactly what happened to me. What will you do then?"

"Tell them what you did."

"I think anyone other than you understands how difficult the situation was."

"Don't care."

"You don't care that your child may hate you?"

I looked at the TV. "No."

"You say that now. But when you hold that baby in your arms, that's all you'll care about."

I still couldn't believe I would be a father. Even with all the help I could hire, my life would be completely different. Bates and my mother wouldn't be the only family I had. Soon, it would grow.

"I hope you reconsider."

"You forget that I don't owe you anything."

"But I don't forget that you have a heart." She stared me down like a predator that had just cornered its prey. "I understand you're still mad at me right now, but you do still care about me the way I care about you. You're also just as stubborn as I am, so you'll come around on your own time. I'm patient enough to wait."

I grabbed the remote and turned off the TV. My peaceful evening had been interrupted by this obnoxious woman. "I don't care about you."

"You say that, but everything you do contradicts it. Why did you return my father? I never asked you to do that, and it wasn't your obligation. But you made it happen anyway."

I would never admit the answer she was looking for. I would keep lying until I couldn't do it anymore. "Everyone should be able to bury the ones they love. It was the humane thing to do."

"To the woman who betrayed you?" she asked. "You called a truce with a group of men you would ordinarily slaughter—for me. You're going to have to give me a better answer than that." She shifted closer to me on the couch then tucked her leg between my knees. She turned into me and rested her face close to mine, her lips dangling just inches away. "I said I was sorry, Cato." Her hand moved to my cheek, and her fingers brushed against the scruff of my beard. "How many times do you want me to say it?" Her perfume washed over me in delicious waves. Her fingertips felt like rose petals against my skin.

I felt the same pull I'd felt last time, the magnetic energy between us. It seemed like I wanted her more now than I had when she was mine. My hand ached to yank down her shorts so I could see the panties she wore. I wanted to yank up her tank top so I could see those beautiful tits. "What do you want from me, Siena?" I pulled her hand off my cheek.

"Just you." Green gems looked into my eyes as she whispered to me.

I wanted to trust this woman, but I couldn't. I could never trust someone who'd lied to me for so long. "You want to fuck the man who'll kill you? Or do you think you'll be able to fuck me so good that I won't kill you? It can't be the first one, so it's gotta be the second one. And I'll save you the trouble of hoping. I will put a bullet in your brain the second your purpose is fulfilled. So, tell me, do you really want to sleep with a murderer?"

Her hand slowly glided down my chest while her eyes stayed locked on mine. "I guess I don't believe you'll do it either way, whether we're together or not."

"Trust me, I would have shot you already if you weren't pregnant."

"But you would have regretted it—and you know it."

My eyes shifted away.

"And if you really are going do it, I would rather enjoy all the nights I have left with the only man I want to be with."

I refused to look at her as my body hummed to life. My sweatpants did a terrible job concealing my hard-on. Within seconds, I was thick and hard, the outline so visible, it couldn't be ignored.

Her hand grazed over it, starting at my balls and moving to my head through the material. "You want me. I want you. Stop fighting it."

I kept my lips away from hers, fighting her seduction.

"Cato." She dug her fingers into my hair and pressed her lips to the corner of my mouth.

My eyes closed involuntarily.

Her hand slipped into my sweatpants until I was hot in her hands. Then she kissed me again.

This woman seduced me. She was smarter than I gave her credit for, and she was using my desires against me. She knew I cared about her, saw through my lies and noticed my actions. When she got me between her legs, I would be lost. I pushed her off. "Suck my dick and leave. Or just leave now." I pushed my boxers and sweatpants down and let my cock rest along my stomach. I wouldn't fuck her, but she could suck me off like a whore. That was the best she would get out of me.

That seemed to be a compromise she liked. "I'd love to." She moved to her knees on the floor and pulled her top over her head. Her perky tits came into view, with their hard nipples and firm size. She pulled her hair out of her ponytail and let it fall around her shoulders. "I want to thank you for what you did…and I can't think of a better way." She wrapped her hand around my length, stared at it lovingly while licking her lips, and then deep-throated me instantly.

My head immediately rested back against the couch. I'd forgotten how much I enjoyed getting my dick sucked until now. Her flattened tongue rubbed against me perfectly, and she practically unhinged her jaw to accommodate my girth. The best part was the way she stared at me as she sucked my dick, like getting me off was more than enough pleasure for her.

Her hand played with my sac while she kept moving up and down, keeping those plump lips wide apart.

"Harder."

She moved deep and hard, slobbering her saliva all over my length. She pushed me deeper like I asked, slightly gasping every time my crown penetrated her as deep as it could go.

I hadn't had any action for two weeks, so this became the greatest sexual experience of my life. My hand moved behind her neck, and I pulled her at the pace I liked, making her work hard to take that big dick.

I didn't give a damn about pleasing her, so I had no inhibitions. I yanked her mouth far over my dick and came in her throat, groaning and thrusting my hips upward. I dumped a mound inside her, but she didn't gag. She swallowed it as I gave it to her, taking my come like a pro.

When I finished, she licked all the drops from the head of my cock, getting every single ounce of my seed before she licked her lips. She pulled her shirt over her beautiful tits then walked out without trying to stay.

I stayed on the couch with my pants around my ankles. All the muscles in my body relaxed as the chemicals in my brain kicked in. That was a damn good blow job. It made me wonder how good the sex would have been. But that was all she was getting from me. If she wanted me that bad, she would have to settle for sucking my dick.

7

Siena

I DIDN'T MIND GETTING ON MY KNEES FOR CATO.

It was a treat for me.

When a dick was that beautiful, it deserved to be sucked.

The interaction was more than enough for me to return to my room and please myself. With the taste of his come still on my tongue, I could picture his focused expression as he came deep inside me.

I would rather have the real thing, but this would work for now.

Until he decided he would finally put out.

A few days later, Cato walked into my room unannounced. He was in a navy blue suit, like he'd just finished a meeting. The house was so big that I never really knew when Cato was home or not. Sometimes he was in Florence, and sometimes he had meetings in his parlor downstairs. I was told not to bother him during work hours.

He held up a cell phone. "This is for you." He tossed it onto the bed.

Black and sleek, it probably had games and access to the internet. I didn't have a laptop or a device, so it would be a nice change to have access to the outside world. "Thanks."

"Your text messages and conversations will be tracked —just so you know."

"I expected nothing less."

He slid his hands into his pockets as he stared at me, towering over me by an extra foot. Whether he was clothed or not, he was gorgeous. That suit looked fantastic on him and made me picture what was underneath. His muscles stretched the arms of his suit, and even his thighs filled out his slacks.

We used to have sex constantly, and now that it was gone, it drove me wild. It was the best sex of my life, and it had vanished. I wondered if it was the abstinence that drove me crazy or if it was the hormones or if it was because of the generous thing he did for my family. Either way, I wanted him badly—especially when he looked that good in his suit.

I moved to him as my fingers reached for his belt. "Can you fuck my mouth?" I loosened the leather then unfastened the button on his pants.

His eyes narrowed on my face, clearly surprised by the abrupt question. He'd barely been in there for five minutes before I made an advance on his package. He wasn't ready to have sex with me, but getting his dick sucked was enough distance that allowed him to enjoy it.

Little did he know, I enjoyed it more than he did.

All he did was provide a slight nod.

I unzipped his slacks and pulled his bottoms to the floor as I moved to my knees.

"Top off."

I pulled my shirt and bra off and sat in my jeans. I

pointed his big dick toward my mouth then slowly sheathed him, pushing him to the back of my throat slowly so I could stretch. If I fucked him too quickly, my gag reflex would be ignited. I flattened my tongue and adjusted my pace to the way he liked.

His hand dug into my hair, and he watched me with concentrated pleasure. He didn't thrust his hips inside me, and instead, watched me do all the work. Whenever I pulled my lips away from his dick, a string of spit formed. I broke it with a swipe of my tongue then jerked him off with my hand.

His fingertips dug into my skull.

I put him back in my mouth and forced him into the back of my throat. I tried to hit his balls, but his length was just too long. No matter how hard I pushed, I couldn't make it happen anatomically. I gripped his powerful thighs, and I made love to his dick with my mouth, the dick that put a baby inside me.

When he was about to come, I pulled him out of my mouth and aimed him at my chest. "Come on my tits." I jerked him forcefully, working his shaft as firmly as I could so he could come hard.

He exploded with a groan, coating my tits everywhere. "Fuck." He dumped so much on me I wasn't sure I would have been able to swallow it.

I stayed on my knees while I felt the come slowly slide down my chest.

Like his purpose was complete, he pulled up his pants and put his suit back together. Then he walked out without conversation.

That was exactly what I wanted.

I dropped my clothes then lay on the bed and opened my legs. I smeared his come all over my pussy before I rubbed my clit. My eyes closed, and I pictured him on top of me, thrusting into me just the way he used to. The smell of his come was potent and only heightened the sensation. It felt like he was really there, even if his fat cock wasn't inside me. It took me less than a minute to hit my climax.

Cato walked back inside and halted when he saw what I was doing. Men like Cato weren't easy to catch off guard, but he was glued to the spot. Immobile, he watched me rub my pussy with his come. With wide eyes and shaking shoulders, he didn't know what to do.

The climax hit, so I finished it, not stopping even for him. My head rolled back, and I rubbed myself harder, my thighs shaking because it felt so good. Cato's presence made it even better, made it seem like we were really together.

"Jesus Fucking Christ."

I lay on the bed and caught my breath, my fingers still between my legs. I didn't feel any shame for what I'd just done. He didn't want to please me, so that was fine. I could handle my own needs.

Like he couldn't handle it, Cato stormed back out—making sure to slam the door this time.

8

Cato

BATES AND I HAD JUST FINISHED A MEETING, AND NOW we rode in the back seat of my car.

My brother rolled down the divider to speak to the driver. "Take us to that club you took me to last week." He hit the button again and closed the divider. "After dealing with assholes all afternoon, I say we get drunk—on pussy."

"I'll have a drink or two. But I need to get back."

"Why?"

I glared at my brother. "You think I'm actually going to answer you?"

"I'm your brother. You should answer me."

I looked out the window and ignored him.

"This better have nothing to do with that bitch."

Hearing him call her that all the time got old, but I didn't have the right to correct him. She did betray us.

"It doesn't."

"Then you'd better take two women home with you tonight—to Tuscany."

The blow jobs were good enough for me, but when I caught her touching herself with my come dripping between her fingers, I lost my shit. It enraged me for so many reasons, but the biggest reason of all was because I wondered if she did it on purpose—to torture me. She wanted me to fuck her the way I used to, and I refused. I wanted all the power, but she was trying to take it away.

I'd never seen anything sexier in my life, and even though I'd just fucked her mouth, I was desperate to fuck her again.

I'd never wanted a woman more.

The image of her on her bed with her legs spread was ingrained in my mind forever.

I would picture it when I fucked other women.

I would picture it when I was alone.

I wanted to retaliate in a harsh way, to prove to her that she meant nothing to me. Bringing two women home was the perfect way to do that—to show her I wasn't hers. "Fine."

Bates clapped me on the shoulder and smiled. "That's my brother."

———

FINDING TWO WOMEN WAS EASY.

I wasn't picky.

They were all over me, sitting in my lap and sucking my neck. Their dresses rode up to their hips and exposed their brightly colored thongs, but security didn't dare enforce the dress code.

I got hard, but not like I did with Siena.

Truth be told, she was all I thought about.

Bates came to my side. "I'm taking off with Roberta."

"Isn't her name Carlotta?"

He shrugged. "I'm so rich I can call her whatever I want. See you later."

"Bye."

"Happy fucking." Bates took his woman and walked off.

Joanna squeezed into my side, clearly buzzed. "When are we going home?"

"Yeah?" Catherine was on my other side, pouting her lips and drumming her fingers against my chest.

"How about now?"

Joanna smiled. "Yes. Let's do it on a bed of money."

"Yeah," Catherine said in agreement. "We can stick the bills in our panties."

Lines like that would have turned me on six weeks ago. But now I thought about Siena, the one woman who genuinely seemed to dislike me because of my money. She was the only woman in the world who felt that way. "Then let's go."

9

Siena

"WHERE DO YOU LIVE?" I SAT AT THE KITCHEN COUNTER while Giovanni washed the dishes. He'd made me a Cobb salad with a side of fresh baked bread. It was delicious, like everything else he made.

"Here, of course."

"Really? So even when you aren't working, you're still here?"

"Oh, I'm always working." He rinsed the dishes and set them on the counter to be placed in the dishwasher.

"Always?" I asked, finishing my last bite of food. "You can't be serious."

"Seven days a week. Unless I'm ill."

"But that's not right." For a man so rich, I didn't understand why Cato would do that to such a sweet man.

"Don't get too upset," he said with a chuckle. "I love working here. The pay is great, the accommodations are world-class, it's safe, and Mr. Marino is a pleasure to serve."

"You would say that even if he weren't."

He chuckled and finished the last dish. "That's what

makes me a good butler." He grabbed my plate from the counter. "Finished, Miss Siena?"

"Yes, but I can take care of it, Giovanni."

"Absolutely not." He turned back to the sink and rinsed it. "This is my joy."

I found that hard to believe, but everyone was different. "Can I ask you something?"

"Of course." He stacked the dishes in the dishwasher.

"Why do you enjoy working for Cato so much? I know you told me why, but why are you so loyal to him?"

"The nature of any butler is to be loyal. When a master takes on a servant, he's actually adding a member of the family. At least, that's how I feel." He shut the dishwasher door and started the dishes. "Mr. Marino has always been good to me and the rest of the staff. It's easy to serve someone you respect."

"And why do you respect him so much?" I leaned against the counter and crossed my arms over my chest.

"Mr. Marino is a strong leader. He understands he needs to be tough to keep his power. He makes hard decisions others wouldn't be able to make. But he's also fair and generous. He can be any man you want him to be—depending on how you treat him."

"If you work all the time, what do you do with your money?" I realized how rude the question was. "If you don't mind me asking."

"Not at all." He washed his hands then patted them dry with the towel. "Everything goes to my kids."

"Oh, that's sweet."

"Yes. I've been divorced for about twenty years now. My kids are grown—both in college. One goes to school in America, and education isn't free there."

"I hear it's pricey."

"Yes." He shrugged. "But it's worth it. And I certainly don't mind how I earn it."

I smiled at him. "You know, you're my favorite person here."

His cheeks tinted, and he looked down at the floor. "My favorite person is Mr. Marino…but then again I have to say that."

I chuckled. "We both know it's me."

He shrugged again, a guilty look on his face.

The sound of laughing came from the entryway. Two high-pitched sounds that were distinctly feminine echoed off the vaulted ceilings. "Oh my god, this place is huge."

"Ooh," another woman said. "We should do it on the stairs."

Cato's voice emerged a second later. "Wait until you see my room."

"Ooh…" the first woman said.

I couldn't believe what I'd just heard.

Giovanni looked awkward, like he wished he hadn't heard it at all.

I marched into the entryway and found Cato heading up the stairs with a woman under each arm. After watching me touch myself with his come, he was supposed to come running to me, not find some skanks at a club.

I wanted to slap him so hard. "Cato."

When he reached the top of the stairs, he turned around to look down at me from the third floor. He didn't look apologetic whatsoever, as if my distress was exactly what he was looking for. It was a sick power play—because he had to be the one in charge. "Goodnight, Siena." He guided his two dates down the hall to his bedroom.

I stood at the foot of the stairs and watched him disappear. When he was gone, I didn't know what to do. I knew what would happen in that bedroom for the night. With two women to juggle, I would be the last thing on his mind.

He was trying to hurt me.

I walked to the third floor and entered my bedroom, my mind racing as I tried to figure out what to do. Asking him to stop wouldn't be enough. He wouldn't listen to my protests at all. And I had no right to interfere anyway.

But I still didn't want it to happen.

An idea came to mind, a desperate attempt to prevent this nightmare. I stripped off all my clothes and marched down the hall buck naked. Giovanni or one of the other staff members might see, but that didn't matter right now.

I marched to Cato's door and was relieved to hear talking. I opened the door and invited myself inside.

Both women were naked and on the bed, while Cato stood in his boxers near the dresser. He'd just finished taking a sip of scotch from his glass. The blonde turned to me, her eyebrow rising and her bitchiness coming out full force. "Is she the maid or something?"

"If she is, she should put some clothes on," the other said. "Because she's dirty."

Cato had to force the drink down his throat even though it seemed like he wanted to spit it out. He looked me up and down, admiring my nakedness. I was nervous, so my nipples were as hard as diamonds.

I placed both hands on my hips and marched toward him. "I want in."

Cato gave me a blank look, all the muscles of his body tensing.

"Get rid of the blonde. I'll take her place."

"Excuse me?" the blonde hissed. "Who the hell—"

Cato interrupted her. "Catherine, leave."

I hoped he wouldn't be able to resist my offer. This was his ultimate fantasy, and watching me bend to his will turned him on. Not only was it sexy, but it gave him more power. He got off on it more than money.

Catherine looked appalled, but she pulled on her clothes and left without argument.

God, I was really gonna do this.

Be with another woman.

The other woman gave Cato a seductive look, playing nice now that she knew she could get kicked out too.

"Alright." Cato pulled down his boxers and revealed his rock-hard cock. "Let's do this."

My heart was beating so fast.

"With pleasure." The woman left the bed and walked up to him. Then she pressed her hands against his chest and kissed him.

I had to look away because it made me sick to my stomach. I'd never been the jealous type, and Cato and I had a relationship based on lust and friendship, not love. But I was jealous anyway. Like, the heartbroken kind of jealous.

Cato kissed her back then turned to his dresser to pull on a condom. Then he dimmed the lights.

No way in hell was I gonna let him fuck her.

All three of us got onto the bed, and Cato kissed the other woman again. He moved on top of her and ran his hands through her hair.

I had to stop myself from kicking her.

Finally, it was my turn. He moved on top of me and pressed his face close to mine. Instead of kissing me right away, he hesitated, like a kiss was too much for him.

I opened my legs and circled them around his waist. My hands glided up his back until I reached the soft hair I used to fist all the time. I cradled his face to mine and forced the kiss to happen.

It was exactly as I remembered.

His lips hesitated once our mouths came together, not because he didn't like it, he'd just forgotten how wonderful it could be. He breathed into my mouth before he kissed me again, kissing me in a different way than he kissed the other woman.

I pointed his cock at my entrance then grabbed his hips and forced him inside me.

I moaned into his mouth when I felt how big he was. My mouth remembered, but my pussy didn't.

He moaned too, even though latex separated us.

My fingers fisted his hair again, and we moved together slowly, like every single sensation was too good to speed up. My heels dug into his ass, and I breathed into his mouth. It felt so right, even better than it had before.

He rocked into me a little harder, his mouth still cherishing mine.

Then he was pulled away from me. The woman lay on her back beside me then guided his mouth to hers. She tugged him harder, forcing him out of me.

Not gonna happen, bitch.

I yanked Cato back to me then kicked her.

"Ouch, bitch."

I forced his mouth to mine and pulled the condom off his length. Then I forced him inside me, making him feel just how good it was when it was just the two of us.

He moaned louder this time, his mouth halting because the sensation was so wonderful. He pressed his forehead to mine and closed his eyes, his cock twitching inside me.

I did the rocking, pushing my hips forward and backward to take his length. I was wet, and my cream already coated his shaft. As if our bodies were perfect for one another, they fit like two pieces of a puzzle, like they were made to be together. I knew he didn't want those other women in the first place, and now I gave him a strong reminder of that truth.

He breathed against my mouth as he brought his thrusts to a stop. His arms shook as he held himself on top of me, not from the exertion, but from the sensation.

The dumb bitch beside him tried to get his attention again. She grabbed him by the arm and dragged him toward her.

He threw her arm down without even looking at her. "Leave us." He scooped his arms behind my knees and stretched me wide apart, putting me at the angle he liked the most. He wanted to give it to me good and hard—just like old times.

"Are you kidding me?" she hissed.

"Then watch." He rested his face close to mine and observed my eyes react.

My fingers moved into his hair, and I moaned against his lips, my body so happy to be reunited with his. I didn't want to share him with anyone, especially women who only cared about the size of his wallet and his package. At least I really knew him, really understood him.

The woman dressed with a loud sigh and finally left.

Now it was just the two of us.

Exactly how it should be.

His thrusts picked up, and he rocked into me at a regular pace, giving me long and even strokes that hit me in the right spot every time. His headboard tapped lightly against the wall, and his eyes remained focused on mine, like having me was the greatest sexual experience he'd ever had.

"This is the only pussy you want." I gripped his lower back and forced him deep inside me, pulling my body back into his in response.

He moaned as he fucked me harder.

"Say it." I kissed him hard, my tongue circling his. "Say it."

He sucked my bottom lip as he fucked me harder. His cock thickened inside me further.

I felt the climax hit me unexpectedly. Like a freight train slamming into a brick wall, the sensation nearly knocked me to the ground. My toes curled until both of my feet cramped, but that didn't stop me from enjoying the greatest orgasm I'd ever had. I clawed at his back and moaned in his face.

He watched my performance with a focused gaze, his cock raging inside me.

"Say it."

His eyes narrowed, and he slowed his thrusts down to a gentle rock.

"Say it, then come inside me."

His jaw clenched like he didn't appreciate being bossed around, but it clearly turned him on at the same time. "This is the only pussy I want to fuck." He shoved himself completely inside me and released. His moans were louder than usual, coming out as masculine grunts.

I closed my eyes as I cherished the way he filled me. I fantasized about this every night when I touched myself, tried to imagine the weight of his seed. Having a man like him come inside me made me feel like a woman, more than I ever had before. "That feels so good…"

He stopped his thrusts and sat idly inside me, his big dick slowly softening. His lips found mine, and he gave me a soft kiss as he enjoyed the last of his high, the remaining aftershocks of pleasure.

I wanted to do this every single night. I wanted to sleep beside him every night. I didn't want to stay in that room on the other side of the house anymore. This bed was where I belonged, even though it was at least five feet too wide.

He slowly pulled out of me, and the come seeped out from between my thighs.

I missed that feeling so much.

He rolled over onto his back and faced the ceiling, his powerful chest still rising and falling as he struggled to regain his breath. Sweat glistened on his beautiful skin. His eyes closed, and he seemed to drift off immediately.

I moved into his side and rested my face on his shoulder as I wrapped my arm around his waist. My leg tucked between his, and I closed my eyes, finding the place where I belonged. Those tramps were gone, and I'd reclaimed my territory. This man was mine again. Actually, he'd always been mine.

He suddenly moved away from me and got out of bed. "I'm going to shower. You'd better be gone by the time I'm finished."

"What?" I heard his words perfectly in the silence of his bedroom, but I didn't understand any of them.

He rose to his feet and stared down at me, pissed off like he'd been the last time I'd seen him. Fucking me hadn't subdued his resentment and rage. As if nothing had happened at all, he resumed his animosity. Letting his guard down and giving in to me had probably aggravated him even more. He'd thought he had the power—but I took it away. "Just because I fuck you doesn't mean I sleep with you. Get out."

10

Cato

MY PLAN COMPLETELY BACKFIRED.

I was supposed to hurt Siena, make her feel as shitty as she made me feel. I wanted her to know how insignificant she was, that my generous gestures didn't mean a damn thing. But she caught me by surprise and gave me an offer I could refuse.

I thought she'd kneeled to me, caved to my desires. She never wanted a threeway but was willing to make an exception—for me. That gave me all the power. And it gave me a rush of arousal I'd never known before. Watching a woman like Siena submit was the sexiest thing I'd ever seen.

But then she played me.

She got me right where she wanted me.

And I didn't want to leave.

Once my cock was inside that bare pussy and she spread wide open for me, I didn't want to go anywhere else. She had the best kiss I'd ever tasted, much better than the ones I'd exchanged with the two girls. The idea of going back to them wasn't remotely appealing. All night I'd been thinking about Siena, and once I was inside her, I couldn't go back.

I only wanted her.

It made no sense. This woman lied to me from the beginning and betrayed me. She couldn't be trusted, and I had to fulfill the promise I made to execute her. If I didn't, Bates would just do it anyway.

But I found myself slipping further and further into a black hole.

First, I buried her father and reunited her with her brother. Then I kicked out two beautiful women so I could just be with Siena. Those were actions I would never take with anyone else—and she knew that.

What the fuck was happening to me?

Refusing to let her sleep with me was my pathetic attempt to get some dignity back. Also to avoid the questions she might launch at me.

I knew I didn't love her.

But I'd never felt this way about a woman.

It seemed like I would always want her, regardless of what she did to me.

In other words, I was a goddamn pussy.

I hated myself.

I worked out early in the morning and headed to work so I wouldn't have to see her. I didn't have a meeting until after lunch, so I sat in my office and looked through emails to entertain myself.

My mother called me, so I answered. "Hey, Mother."

"Hey, honey. How are you?" She spoke with a deep and refined voice, like an old-fashioned movie star. Even at her lowest point, she was still classy. She would come home from the cannery and mask her pain with a smile so my brother and I wouldn't pity her.

"Well. You?"

"I haven't heard from you in a long time. Been busy?"

I hadn't spoken to her since I'd met Siena. That was more than six weeks ago. Keeping in touch with my mother had fallen off my list of priorities once I had a serious woman in my life. "You know how it is. It's one thing after another."

"That's too bad. I was hoping you were busy with a woman—or a man. Just someone."

My mother never asked me about my personal life. She respected my privacy. But apparently something had changed her mind about that. "No. Just work."

"Well, you shouldn't work too much. Life will pass you by so quickly, and you'll have nothing to show for it."

"I don't think a twelve-billion-dollar company is considered nothing." I didn't appreciate being challenged, not even by my mother. If she were somebody else, they'd receive a much harsher response.

"Of course not. But you can't line your coffin with cash and take it with you."

This argument was going nowhere. "Let's get dinner this week. We'll go to your favorite place." If the purpose of this phone call was to make me feel guilty for not calling, it worked. "I'll let Bates know."

"Oh, that sounds nice," she said cheerfully. "Let me know the place and time."

"And, Mother? That asshole hasn't bothered you, right?" My men reported no signs of him, but I wanted to make sure.

"No, honey. Not at all."

I got off the phone with her, and Bates walked in fifteen minutes later.

"You're at work early." He fell into the leather armchair facing my desk.

"Since I'm always working, I'm neither early nor late."

"I figured you would need to sleep longer after the night you had." He grinned wide. "My night was pretty fantastic. Maybe tonight I'll do a replay."

I changed the subject before Bates could ask me the details. I couldn't lie to him, and the truth would just piss him off. That would start a whole argument, and I was tired of talking about Siena. "Mother just called me. We're having dinner with her this week."

"I haven't talked to her in a while, not that she cares. You're her favorite. I'm sure she was pissed when she didn't hear from you over the past six weeks."

I raised an eyebrow. "How do you know I haven't talked to her in six weeks?"

His smile slowly faded. "She mentioned it."

"You just said you haven't talked to her in a while."

"Yeah, two weeks. That's a while." He rubbed his palm across his chin and touched his beard. "She mentioned you hadn't called her. Bitched about it. We all know you're her favorite, but it would be nice if she tried to hide it a little bit." He rolled his eyes and brushed it off like he didn't care, but we both knew he did.

I didn't deny it because it was true. I'd always been Mother's favorite, ever since we were young. As we aged, that became more apparent. Now that we were adults, she had a distinctly different relationship with each of us. I wasn't sure if it was because I was the oldest or I was the quietest, but she bonded with me better. "She asked me if I was busy with a woman."

Bates said nothing in response.

"Did you tell her about Siena?"

My brother wouldn't lie, so he squirmed in silence until he spat out the truth. "I may have mentioned you'd been spending time with someone…"

"And why would you do that?"

"Because you'd been seeing her for a while. I just said it in passing. I didn't tell her anything serious was going on."

"You never mention my private life to her in passing. You know she'll hold on to that."

He shrugged. "She asked if you were busy, and I told her the truth, alright? Chill."

I'd shut down the discussion with my mother, so I guess it didn't matter anymore.

"Besides, you'll have to tell her you're having a baby. So it's gonna come up either way."

I hadn't even thought of that. I'd never planned on telling her. When the tabloids found out about it, I guess that's how I expected her to learn the news—even though that was cold. "Fuck…"

"You are going to tell her, right?"

I rubbed my temple with my fingers as I silently cursed Siena. This pregnancy ruined my life. If this baby weren't on the way, I would have eliminated Siena from my life, and I wouldn't have to tell my mother I was having a kid… and then explain to her that I knocked someone up. It wouldn't be a fun conversation. She would want to meet Siena, and that would be a nightmare in itself.

Bates cocked his head to the side. "You're gonna wait until the kid is born or what? Then have the baby tell her on its own?"

"Shut up, Bates."

"You want this kid so bad, why are you pussyfooting around?"

"I don't want this so bad," I snapped. "But it's my child, and I take responsibility for that. Doesn't mean I'm happy about it."

"You could make it all go away. There's still time. No one knows besides the three of us."

I could never do it. "No."

"You're the cruelest man I know. You can't blow her brains out?"

"No." I couldn't hurt someone with Marino blood. I couldn't be the same piece of shit my father was. "And stop asking."

"Fine. Then you need to tell Mother."

"I'd rather not."

He cocked an eyebrow. "You're just not gonna tell her?"

"I'll wait until we hit the second trimester. No point in telling her until I know there're no complications with the baby."

"Well, how long has she been pregnant?"

"No idea."

"Maybe you should find out."

I'd been meaning to take her to the doctor anyway. We needed to start her vitamins and whatever other bullshit came along with it. "I will. So how about dinner on Thursday? Are you free?"

He shrugged. "Doesn't matter to her whether I'm there or not."

"I may be her favorite, but it's not like she hates you, Bates."

"Still gets old. She could at least show some class and hide it."

"You're a grown man," I countered. "You shouldn't care."

"You would care."

"I really wouldn't, Bates."

He wore a black suit with a matching tie, and his ankle rested on the opposite knee. His dress shoes were shiny like they were brand-new. "So what happened last night? Did Siena see you?"

"Yes," I said truthfully. "She did."

He grinned. "Must have pissed her off."

"Yes."

"Good. That dumb cunt needed to know you aren't wrapped around her finger."

No, I was just deep in her pussy.

"So, how were they?"

I rose from my desk and brushed off the question. "Let's get to the conference room and start the meeting early. I have somewhere to be afterward."

Thankfully, he rose to his feet and didn't argue with me. "I'm always in the mood to make money."

———

I WALKED to her bedroom and let myself inside, half expecting to see her touching herself again.

Unfortunately, she was on the couch in her living room, fully clothed.

We hadn't spoken in days, not since that threesome in my bedroom. I avoided her, and she wasn't stupid enough to knock on my bedroom door late at night.

Today, her hair was curled and pulled over one shoulder. Her makeup was done, and she wore a blue sundress that showed off her cleavage and her long legs. Summer was over, and we only had a few weeks left until the real chill of fall arrived. She was enjoying every moment of warmth we had left.

I approached the couch with my hands in the pockets of my jeans. "I'm taking you to a doctor's appointment." When I locked eyes with her, it was impossible not to think about the last time we were together. The second my cock was inside her unbelievable pussy, I was lost. I hadn't wanted to pull on a rubber and fuck someone else, not when she had the best cunt in the entire world. Coupled with her kisses and sexy moans, I knew there was nothing I could do to resist. I ordered the other woman out of my bedroom because I didn't want to share myself. All I wanted was the woman underneath me.

She seemed to be thinking about it too, judging by the desire in her eyes. It was the same look she gave me before she kissed me, before she ran her fingers through my short hair. "Right now?"

"Yes. Let's go."

She rose to her feet, wearing the blue dress with sandals.

She looked phenomenal.

Before I did something stupid like drop my pants, I left the bedroom and headed to the car outside.

She followed me and got into the back seat beside me.

Now there was nowhere to run. We had twenty minutes until we arrived at the doctor. A lot could happen in twenty minutes.

We headed to the main road and approached Florence, the center divider up in the car so my driver couldn't see me or make small talk.

I hated small talk.

"What are we going to do today?" she asked as she looked out the window.

"Routine checkup. He's the best obstetrician in the area."

"I'm sure he's fine. I wonder if we'll get a sonogram."

"No idea." I didn't know what to expect. We could be in and out of there in fifteen minutes.

She rested her hand on her stomach, which didn't look any different. She showed no signs of pregnancy, other than her bouts of morning sickness. "I don't feel any different. Not yet at least."

Maybe she wouldn't talk about what happened the

other night. That would be ideal. My feelings toward her were still pretty clear. I wouldn't be sleeping with anyone else, but that didn't make me hers. I would never be hers.

She turned her gaze from the window and looked at me.

I met her look, staring into those green eyes just the way I did when I fucked her. Something about their color drew me in. Everything about her features captured my fascination. She was undeniably the most beautiful woman I'd ever been with. When she stormed into my bedroom naked and fought for me…I nearly exploded. She claimed me in the middle of a threesome and turned it into a twosome. Only a truly confident woman could pull that off.

"I want to suck you off before we get there." She said it without missing a beat, like sucking my dick in the back seat of the car would give her no greater pleasure.

My cock immediately swelled to full size and pressed against the front of my jeans. I'd expected her to say a million other things, but not that. This woman was obsessed with sucking my cock. She'd been that way since the first night she looked at my package. Maybe that was just a technique to get under my skin, but if it was, it was definitely working.

I gave her my answer by pushing down my jeans and boxers. "Get to work."

———

AFTER THE DOCTOR gave his examination, he conducted an ultrasound of her belly. It didn't take him long to find the baby inside her, and within minutes, he displayed the picture on the screen—along with the heartbeat.

Siena lay on the table with her belly exposed. Absolutely still, she stared at the black-and-white image of the baby growing inside her. The heartbeat was strong and regular, but the other features couldn't be determined. The baby was just too small.

I stood beside her and stared at the monitor, my heart beating much faster than my child's.

Fuck. I was going to be a father.

The doctor excused himself to give us privacy.

We both kept staring at the image of the little person growing inside her, the tiny person we'd made together.

Siena's eyes watered, and then tears streaked down her cheeks like two small waterfalls.

I still couldn't believe this was real. My son or daughter was inside her, alive and well.

She cried quietly to herself, her pristine makeup turning into muddy rivers. "So beautiful…"

I wondered if she cried from happiness or sadness. She would never know this child, not a single day after it was born. She would give birth like an animal then be slaughtered. The only time she would ever really spend with her child was when she was pregnant. So perhaps that was why she was so emotional, because these were the only moments she would ever have.

She pulled the screen closer to her so she could get a better look. "I can't believe what I'm seeing…"

I couldn't either. That was my baby in there. I would raise someone entirely on my own.

"It's a girl."

My eyes moved to her face. "How do you know?"

"I just do," she whispered. "I can't explain it."

I watched Siena with the same fascination as I'd just looked at my child. Her wet eyes reflected the fluorescent lights overhead, and even when she was in tears, her beauty couldn't be diluted. "We'll know in a few months."

SIENA HAD a copy of the sonogram, so she looked at it on the drive back to the house. Sometimes she brought it closer to her face so she could see the details better. Other times, she held it at a distance or turned it.

I watched her stare at our baby.

"Do you want a boy or a girl?"

"A boy," I said immediately.

"Why?"

"Because a boy will grow into a man. And a man can take over my legacy when I'm dead."

It was the first time she stopped looking at the picture in her hand and turned to me. "You're joking, right?"

"A woman couldn't do what I do. It's not just about running a business, but keeping the underworld under strict control."

Her eyebrows rose high on her face. "That's the most sexist thing I've ever heard."

"I'm not sexist. A woman could run an ordinary bank. But she couldn't intimidate the Skull Kings, the mob, and all the other assholes out there. They would walk all over her. They would mislead her, and raping her would be their ultimate achievement. That's the last thing I would want for my daughter. I would never let the business fall into her hands."

"I don't want our son or daughter to have anything to do with your line of business, but I still think that was an asshole thing to say."

"After your mother and father were killed, I'm surprised you would have the stupidity to disagree with me. You've always detested your family business and craved a simple life. It's the exact thing you don't want."

"For a son or a daughter," she hissed. "It has nothing to do with the gender."

I looked out the window and ignored her, knowing she was being argumentative just for the sake of it. On the ride to the doctor, I got a great blow job, but now we argued like an old married couple. "Just look at the picture and shut up."

She moved across the seat and slapped me across the face. "Don't tell me to shut up."

I snatched her wrist and yanked it down, showing her that I outmatched her strength fifty times over. "You think I won't punch you in the face as hard as my brother did?" I squeezed her wrist hard, watching her slowly fight the discomfort until she started to cringe. "I will, Siena. I'll give you another black eye." I released her arm.

She didn't massage it or whimper. "No. I don't think you'll do that."

"You really want to try me and find out?" With wide eyes, I challenged her, tested how stupid she was.

"Alright." She slapped me again.

I turned with the hit and felt my cheek immediately become inflamed. No woman in my life had slapped me as much as this one. It had to have been at least a dozen times. Sometimes I liked it, and sometimes it pissed me off.

I turned back to her, my eyes burning with fire.

She challenged me with her stern look. "You won't do it."

My hand shot out, and I gripped her by the neck. Then I squeezed.

She didn't fight it. "You won't hurt me."

"I can hurt you without hurting the baby." I squeezed her hard until she could barely breathe.

"That's not why—and you know it." Her words came out weak because her lungs didn't have enough air for her to speak. Her hand gripped my wrist, but she didn't try to fight for her freedom. She just held my gaze, keeping her pride despite her vulnerability.

I squeezed her until she couldn't breathe.

Instead of pushing me off, she grabbed my shoulder and pulled me toward her, her lips aimed for mine. Then she kissed me, kissed me the best she could while suffocating.

My anger vanished when our lips touched, so my hand slackened against her throat. I made up for the savage way I had gripped her earlier by sliding my hand into her soft mane of hair. I fingered her strands as I brought her closer to me and kissed her harder.

She shifted onto my lap with her dress pulled up. Her hand slipped into the back of my hair, and she kissed me softly, taking her time like there was no reason to rush it. She kissed the corner of my mouth then trailed her lips to my neck. She kissed me everywhere, her hand moving under my shirt to feel my abs. Her lips pressed against my ear. "You would never hurt me."

I hated myself in that moment. Absolutely loathed myself. But her kisses and touches thrust me into a sea of desire, so I didn't think about that anger. This woman pissed me off but also stole my obsession. I hated her but needed her at the same time.

She moved her lips to mine and kissed me again, her soft lips giving me a purposeful embrace. She grabbed my hand and placed it over her stomach, right where our baby's heartbeat would be.

My fingers spanned her entire stomach, and I moaned into her mouth. I had no idea why this turned me on so much. A pregnant woman wasn't sexy to me. Getting her pregnant had only made my life chaotic. But during moments like this, when we were just a man and a woman, it turned me on more than anything else ever did. I was the one who put that baby inside her, the one who made that little heartbeat. Now she was carrying it, carrying a piece of me. It was so arousing.

She unzipped my jeans and popped open the bottom. She'd just swallowed my come on the drive there, but that must have been an appetizer for her. Now she wanted the entrée. She pulled my boxers down so my cock could be free. Then she yanked her thong to the side and slowly sheathed my length.

Fuck, how did I keep forgetting how good her pussy was?

Jesus fucking Christ.

She straddled me and started riding me.

My hand stayed on her stomach because I didn't want to pull it away. I could barely think straight because her pussy felt so damn good. Fucking another woman sounded disgusting. Going to a bar and picking up two women sounded like the dumbest idea I'd ever had. Why would I want that when I could have this?

Even if she betrayed me.

She was manipulating me, doing whatever she could to save her life.

I didn't judge her for it. Anyone else would do the same.

I just had to remember none of this was real. The passion, the lust, the connection—all of it was fake. When the moment came, I would have to forget all those feelings and pull the trigger.

But for now, I couldn't resist. "Fuck me, baby."

———

WHEN WE RETURNED to the house, I turned my back to

her and went straight to my bedroom. I'd just fucked her in the car and finished a minute before entering the driveway, but now I turned cold and distant again.

She followed me until she reached her bedroom door. "Are we going to keep playing this game?"

"No game," I said without turning around. "I just don't want you." I got inside and hopped in the shower. The afternoon took longer than I expected, so I hurried in the shower and put on a pair of slacks and a blazer for dinner.

When I was dressed and ready to go, I headed downstairs and stopped by the kitchen to see Giovanni.

Siena was there with a pan of freshly baked cookies on the counter. She held up the image of the sonogram so Giovanni could see it. "Isn't it amazing? This little person is inside me right now…with a little heartbeat."

Giovanni examined the picture with his black apron tied around his hips. He never made cookies because I didn't eat anything like that, so he and Siena were obviously spending the day together. "It's wonderful, Miss Siena. Honestly, I'm excited to have another Marino around the house. Mr. Marino is so predictable, he's easy to take care of. It'll be nice to have a challenge."

"I can always step it up," I said coldly.

Giovanni nearly jumped out of his skin when he heard my voice. "Sir, I didn't mean anything—"

"Don't apologize to him," Siena said. "You did nothing wrong." She took the sonogram from his hands. "I was just showing Giovanni the baby we made together. He decided to share his family recipe for the best chocolate chip cookies in the world—that way I can make them for the baby someday."

My eyes narrowed in annoyance. "You'll be dead the day they're born. And I'm pretty sure a one-day-old baby can't eat cookies."

She set the sonogram down and crossed her arms over her chest, looking fiery.

Giovanni walked out of the kitchen without waiting to be dismissed.

"Knock it off, Cato. Every time we get closer together, you pull this stunt. Just stop fighting it."

"We aren't getting closer together. Nothing has changed."

"It changes every passing day." She stepped closer to me and held up the picture. "And it should change every day."

I pushed the picture down and gave her a glare. "Regardless of what happens between now and then, when the time comes, I will kill you. So don't mistake my lust for anything else. I'm a man who keeps my promises, who carries out his executions. You're no different. You just have more time than the average person."

She let the picture stay on the floor as she put her hands on her hips. Like those words meant nothing to her, she ignored them. "Where are you going?"

"Out."

"Out where? I know it's not to pick up some skanks."

I wished I could tell her she was wrong. "I'm having dinner with my mother."

"Oh…are you going to tell her about us?"

Every time she referred to the baby as a real person, it made the situation feel more real. "Not right now."

"She's going to be a grandmother. You should tell her sooner rather than later. I'm sure she'll be happy."

Or disappointed that I was stupid enough to knock up a traitor. "Good night, Siena." I turned around and walked to the kitchen door.

"I'll be waiting on your bed buck naked when you get home."

I stopped at the door and begged myself not to turn around. I didn't want to be provoked by her comment, but the image of her naked body in my bed made me lose my breath for a moment. I turned back around and faced her. "I wouldn't do that if I were you—unless you want to be fucked in the ass."

———

THE THREE OF us had a private room in Mother's favorite restaurant. She talked about her garden, what happened on her favorite TV show, and how she was considering giving her downstairs bathroom a makeover.

I kept picturing Siena naked on my bed.

Would she be there when I got home?

Or would she take my warning seriously?

Because that was a serious threat. I would hold her down and drill her in the ass even if she told me not to. She'd been warned, so I didn't feel bad for doing it. She shouldn't test me. Maybe I wouldn't punch her in the face, but that didn't mean I wouldn't force anal.

"Cato?" Mother's voice came into my ears. "Are you alright?"

"Yes." I grabbed my glass of wine and took a drink. "Just a lot on my mind."

Bates gave me a knowing look from across the table.

"You work too much," she said. "And it'll take years off your life. Doing manual labor for so many years really wore down my body. Even now, I'm still tired." She held her glass and took a drink. "I really wish you would enjoy everything you have more often. Travel more. You've always talked about yachting around the Caribbean."

That was to fuck a bunch of women on a boat and drink all day. Now I was fucking just one woman. Didn't work as well. "Maybe next spring." The baby would arrive at that time of year, so I probably wouldn't be traveling for a while.

Mother wore a disappointed look, but she didn't press me on it. "Anything else new with you?"

"Giovanni made cookies before I left. That's something you don't see every day." The most interesting parts of my life pertained to work, but I couldn't tell her about all the threats I made that day, how much money I earned in investments, or that I was still waiting to find out if Connor Beck had struck oil or not. If he didn't, I had to execute his whole family and put them in oil drums. But no mother wanted to hear that.

"Cookies?" Bates asked. "You don't eat cookies."

"I guess he was in the mood," I said with a shrug.

"Or he made them for someone else…" Bates grinned before he drank his wine.

Mother knew our behaviors well because she raised both of us. She could read between the lines better than anyone else. "Is there someone else living with you, Cato?"

It was a direct question, and my natural impulse was to tell the truth. I didn't like to lie, not because I was noble, but because lying was cowardly. It meant you were too afraid of the other person's opinion to be honest. And in that instance, they had more power over you.

"Yeah?" Bates pressed. "Is there?"

I would punch my brother right in the face the first chance I got. He loved every moment of this. When I told my mom I'd knocked up a woman I wouldn't marry, she would be disappointed in my foolishness. That would make Bates look pretty damn good.

Mother set her glass down and watched me, knowing I wouldn't lie to her.

"Yes, there is someone else living with me."

Bates grinned.

"Who?" Mother asked. "Who's living with you?"

"A woman. Her name is Siena." I skipped the pregnant part.

"I thought you said you weren't seeing anyone?" she asked.

"Because I'm not," I said calmly.

"Then who is this woman?" She began to grow frustrated the longer this didn't make sense.

"This is going to come as a big shock, Mother." I held her gaze before I told her news that would change her life. "Siena and I are having a baby. She's living with me in the meantime so I can be there for her throughout the process."

When she brought her hands to her face to cover her mouth, she knocked over her glass of wine, but she was so overwhelmed by the news she didn't even notice.

Bates righted the glass. "Yep. Cato knocked up some lady."

"Honey." She lowered her hands from her mouth, her eyes watering. "You're having a baby?"

"Yes." Now I waited for her to give me that look of disapproval, that disappointed expression every man feared from his mother.

"I'm going to be a grandmother?" she whispered. "Honey…that's the best thing I've ever heard."

Bates couldn't hide his shock.

She grabbed my hand on the table. "When is the baby due?"

"In the spring," I answered.

"Aw, that's wonderful." Mother rose out of her seat to hug me. "You have no idea how happy that makes me."

I'd never expected my mother to react this way, to be so supportive over a mistake. "I'm glad you feel that way."

"You're going to have your own family." She patted my back before she sat down again, still teary-eyed. "That's so wonderful. I have to meet Siena. I bet she's lovely and will give you a lovely baby."

That was a situation I hadn't foreseen. "Uh, maybe in a few months."

"In a few months?" she asked. "She's barely a few months along. It's not like she can't get around."

Having them interact was a terrible idea. Siena could easily tell my mother what my plan was, and my mother would be so appalled that she wouldn't let me go through with it. Only one woman in the world had the power to affect my decisions—and that was my mother. "We're still reeling from her pregnancy, so maybe when everything dies down, you two can meet then."

Now my mother looked livid. "Cato, this is the mother of your child. The mother of my grandchildren. You bet your ass I want to meet her."

Bates smiled again.

I gave in just to make her happy. "Alright."

"Good," she said. "Are you going to marry her?"

"No." I would never marry anyone, whether there was a baby involved or not. "She and I aren't together, like I said."

"But you're living together?" she asked incredulously.

"She doesn't have the resources to take care of the baby on her own. Living with me just makes it simpler." I hated explaining my personal life to my mother like it was any of her business. "I want to be involved to keep them both safe. I'm afraid if she's alone, someone might try to hurt her because of me."

Mother grabbed her glass again and took a drink. "What's she like?"

"Beautiful," I blurted, choosing that single word to

describe her completely. "Absolutely stunning. I'm afraid if we have a daughter, she'll inherit Siena's looks…and make my life a nightmare."

Mother smiled. "I knew she would be beautiful. My son has very particular tastes. What else can you tell me about her?"

"She's an art collector. She decorated my home, and that was how we got to know each other."

"And her family?" she asked.

"Her parents are both gone," I answered. "She has one brother."

"Oh…that's too bad. Is there any chance the two of you could work it out?" She tilted her head as she looked at me, unable to keep the hope out of her eyes. "Call me old-fashioned, but I think a mother and father should stick together if it's possible. You're a family now, Cato."

"No. There's no possibility." My tone turned stern, subtly warning my mother I didn't want to discuss this anymore. "We're having this baby together, and that's it. We have a good relationship, so that should be easy."

She took a long drink of her wine and dismissed the conversation, knowing I'd had enough. "Well, let me know when the time is right. I really want to meet the woman carrying my grandbaby."

———

I WALKED up the stairs and down the hallway. My anger was still rampant because Bates threw me under the bus. Then my mother pressured me about meeting Siena, which was the last thing I wanted to happen.

Now I really hoped Siena was on my bed—beautiful and naked.

Because I wanted to fuck her in the ass until she cried.

I stepped into my room, and my eyes immediately darted to the bed, expecting to see that beautiful white skin against my dark comforter.

She was there, buck naked like she promised. She lay on her back with her body propped up by her arms. Her long legs stretched out across the bed, beautiful and sculpted. Her brown hair was across her shoulders, and her makeup was darker than usual.

I was hard in three seconds.

With my heated gaze locked on to hers, I stripped off my blazer and dropped it on the floor. My shirt came next and then my belt. I stopped thinking about why I was angry in the first place and just felt the anger instead. Siena called my bluff in the kitchen, and I would make her regret it.

I stripped down until I was naked and approached the bed. "I warned you."

She sat up on her knees so our eyes could be level. "And I know you've been thinking about this moment all night. The second you walked in the door, you looked at the bed like you'd be livid if I weren't there."

"Because I want to punish you." My knees sank onto the mattress. "Because I wanted you to call my bluff." I inched closer to her then grabbed her by the neck. "Because I want to fuck you in the ass so hard you cry. And when you beg me to stop, I won't. I won't feel bad about it because I warned you. I warned you not to come here tonight."

She ignored the hand around her neck and leaned in to kiss me.

I turned my mouth away and rejected her. Then I pushed her onto the bed, making her stomach hit the sheets.

That's when I saw the jewel in her asshole.

Jesus Christ.

She looked at me over her shoulder. "Do your worst, Cato."

My cock twitched so hard it actually hurt.

"You know there's no one else you'd rather have in this bed. You know you couldn't stop thinking about me tonight. You know you don't stop thinking about me every single day when you're at work. You know your finger won't squeeze that trigger when the time comes. You know you want me too much. And when you fuck me in the ass, you're only going to want me more."

Fuck.

I tried to hide the desire in my eyes, but it was impossible. I'd never been this hard up for a woman in my life. I hated her so damn much, but that didn't stop me from wanting her so damn much.

I opened my nightstand and pulled out a bottle of lube. I squirted it onto my length and rubbed it to my balls, getting myself as slick as possible. That was a small asshole, and this was a big dick. I moved on top of her and stared at the beautiful jewel looking back at me. "Been fucked in the ass before?"

"No."

I was just about to pull out the jewel, but I stopped to take a breath. "You have no idea how much this is going to hurt."

"I can handle it."

A shiver ran up my spine, the pleasure radiating to every extremity. I pulled out the jewel and stared at the small asshole left behind.

It was perfect.

I crawled farther up her body until my chin was above her head. Then I pointed my cock at her opening and pushed gently, watching my thick crown press against her without slipping inside. Her asshole tightened the second she felt me. "Relax." I pushed again and slipped through her muscles, the lube making it possible. When a few inches of my length were inside, it felt so damn good. Her ass was a million times tighter than her cunt. I pushed again, feeling her tense up the farther I went. I watched her grip the sheets and breathe harder as I shoved my big dick in her ass. We hadn't even started yet, and she was beginning to understand just how much it hurt.

I moved my lips to her ear. "I told you." I kept sliding in until my length couldn't go any farther, at least her body wouldn't allow me to. I still had several inches hanging out, but most of my shaft was inside. I closed my eyes as I treasured it, felt how warm and tight she was. I usually had to pay money to fuck a woman in the ass, at least if I wanted to fuck her hard.

The second I started to thrust, I knew I wouldn't last long.

Fuck, it was too good.

She clawed at the sheets and suppressed her moans of pain as she kept taking my big dick in the ass.

"You can say stop, but I won't stop. You can cry, but I won't stop. And just so you know, I hope you do cry." I rocked into her harder and worked my hips back and forth as I took her. She had the nicest ass and the most beautiful back. With that long brown hair trailing down her spine, she was such an erotic sight.

Her gasps became louder when she couldn't tolerate the pain as well. Perhaps if she'd known how painful her first time would be, she would have listened to me and did as I asked. She yanked on the sheet and cursed. "Fuck."

I enjoyed hurting her, punishing her. I didn't have the balls to hit her in the face. I didn't have the balls to ignore her dead father. But I had the balls to do this, to sink so deep that my balls tapped against her ass. "Now you wish you had listened to me?"

Her moans of pain got louder.

I fucked her harder, my dick enjoying it so much that I wouldn't last much longer. "Do you?"

"Yes…" The sound of tears was in her voice.

I rested my forehead against the back of her head as I moaned, getting off on the sound of her pain. She'd hurt me so much, made a fool out of me, and now I was finally getting some revenge. The best revenge I'd ever gotten.

I grabbed her chin and directed her head back so I could look into her face. I saw the rivers on both of her cheeks, the puffiness under her eyes. She didn't sob the way she had at her father's funeral, but her eyes were wet enough that drops of liquid were stuck in her eyelashes. She bit her lips during the moments of pain, but that was just sexy. "Ask me to stop." No way in hell was I stopping. But I wanted to deny her.

"No." Even in her pain, she was stubborn. Tears streamed down her face, but she refused to cave.

I couldn't take it any longer. Even though I wanted to keep hurting her, it just felt too good. This moment was an overload. I increased my pumps then dumped inside her with a moan so loud my hands went numb. "Jesus…" My cock throbbed as I dumped all my come inside her ass. It went in deep, where it would sit for a long time. I shoved my entire length in so she could take it all as deep as possible.

I stayed on top of her until the effects of the climax completely wore off. My evening had been a nightmare, but fucking her like that more than made up for it. I was glad she'd defied me, glad she thought my dick in her ass would be easy to take.

I slowly pulled out of her and headed to the bathroom

to shower. I rinsed off and soaped my body before I got out and dried my hair with the towel. I didn't bother styling it because I would just be going to bed.

When I walked back into the bedroom, she was gone.

The door had been left open.

I'd expected her to try to sleep with me until I told her to leave. But this time, she left the second my back was turned.

———

I LAY in bed for over an hour but couldn't fall asleep. I usually dozed off almost instantly, probably because I worked out so hard in the morning then stayed on my feet all day. But now I lay there thinking about the woman I'd just ass-fucked.

I'd enjoyed every second of it, but now the guilt reached me.

Did I really hurt her?

Did she not enjoy it at all?

Why did I care?

I shouldn't care.

I closed my eyes and tried to sleep again.

All I did was lie there for another thirty minutes. My mind wandered to work, my mother, and then it came back to Siena again—along with the nagging guilt.

I finally gave up and got out of bed.

I pulled on my sweatpants and walked to her bedroom down the hall. It was late so she might be asleep. If she was, I would just leave. I opened the door quietly then poked my head inside.

She wasn't in bed.

I stepped inside and spotted her sitting on the couch while the glow of the TV hit her. She was staring at the phone I'd given her, reading something on the screen. She seemed fine on the outside, but she must not be if she was still awake.

I walked into the room and announced my presence so she wouldn't be scared. "It's me."

She didn't jolt upright at my unexpected entrance. She set her phone on her lap then looked up at me, indifference in her gaze. "Can I help you? It's almost midnight."

I sat on the couch beside her and saw the news on the screen. It was on mute. She was probably watching something else until the show ended and the news came on next. She didn't seem like someone who cared much about events around the globe. "Why are you still awake?"

"Couldn't sleep. You?"

"Me neither."

Her makeup was gone, and she was in her little shorts and her tank top. Even when she was tired, she was stunning. The woman didn't have to do anything to be beautiful. She was all natural. Whether she gave me a son or daughter, they would be gorgeous. She looked at me for a few seconds before she looked at the TV again.

"Are you alright?"

Her eyes darted back to me. "Do I not look alright?"

"You left before I got out of the shower."

"Weren't you going to kick me out like last time?"

I didn't give her an answer.

"You're just here because you feel guilty. You feel guilty for hurting me. Like I said, Cato, you aren't the bad man you pretend to be. At least not with me. And that's not a bad thing…if you would just admit it."

Never. "Did I hurt you?"

"At the time. It took a few hours for the pain to subside."

The high I felt earlier didn't return when I heard that admission. "Did you enjoy it at all?"

"No," she said honestly. "Would you enjoy something that big in your ass?"

I tried not to smile at her sarcasm. "I warned you."

"Well, I guess I didn't understand what it would be like."

"It was your first time. It always hurts your first time."

"Well, there won't be a second." She pulled her knees to her chest then looked at the TV again.

"It takes practice. Don't swear it off completely."

She turned back to me, her eyebrow raised. "You really think I'm gonna let you fuck me in the ass again?"

"I don't think you're in a position to *let* me do anything."

She rolled her eyes. "I'm not afraid of you."

I wanted to tell her she should be, but I couldn't. I was sitting on the couch beside her because I cared about her. Somehow, I always wound up in this position. I always wound up checking on her. "I want to ask you something. And for once, I want the honest truth."

Siena pivoted her body and faced me, ignoring the TV altogether. She wore a serious expression as she held my gaze. "Alright."

"What do you want from me?"

"I don't understand the question."

"It's not complicated." I leaned back against the couch and stared at her, the light from the TV giving her a gorgeous glow. "If you could have it your way, what would you want? If you could leave and go home, would you still want me? Would you keep the baby? What would happen?"

Her eyes shifted back and forth slightly as she looked at me, considering the question. The silence passed and filled the space between us. Her eyes flicked down for a second as she tightened her ponytail. "Even after everything that's happened, I would still want to see you, Cato. I'm not just throwing myself at you in the hope you don't kill me. I'm doing it because I genuinely want you. You think I would touch myself with your come if I weren't insanely attracted to you?"

My neck felt hot just thinking about that moment. "And the baby?"

"Of course, I would keep the baby. I didn't get pregnant on purpose, Cato. It was just a rare…miracle."

"Miracle? That's how you describe it?" It was a nuisance to me.

"In a heartbeat," she said seriously. "I've always wanted a family. I didn't want a family like this, but I wanted a man who wanted to be a father…and that's you."

"That's inaccurate. I don't *want* to be a father. I will be a father because it's my obligation."

She shook her head slightly. "Doesn't matter. At the end of the day, you're here—with me. That makes you a good man. It would be easy for you to kill me or have your brother do it. But you don't. You're protecting your child without even knowing them. That's what a father does."

She gave me more credit than I deserved. "Do you think I'll be a good father, then?"

She turned quiet, like her next answer wasn't as good as the previous one. "Given your situation, I think that answer is obvious."

"Not to me." I tried not to be disappointed by her answer, but what else did I expect?

"You're a crime lord, Cato. Our child will always be a target for kidnapping and ransom. They'll be exposed to the kind of lifestyle I don't want them to see. And if they follow in your footsteps, they'll have the same empty existence that you do. I know the money inflates your ego, but we both know you aren't content with your life. No, I don't think you're the ideal man to be the father of my child."

The answer wasn't surprising, so I shouldn't care about her opinion.

"So if you had it your way, you would raise our son on your own?"

She opened her mouth to answer but then shut it abruptly again. "I…I want to say yes, but I can't. Because I don't think I would ever deprive my child of the right to know who his father is. I would never keep you two away from each other…because it would be wrong."

I immediately thought of the pledge I made, that I would kill her once the baby was born. That was exactly what I would be doing to our child. I would take away their mother, depriving them of the right to know her. Maybe Siena gave the answer she did because of that reason…or maybe she didn't think about it at all.

I watched her for a long time as I gathered my thoughts. This conversation hadn't been planned, and I didn't know why I was asking her all these questions.

She stared at me, her beautiful eyes reflecting the light from the TV screen. "My turn. What do you want from me?"

I held her gaze without blinking, unsure what my answer was. "You know I want you." There was no point denying it. Every action I took showed that truth. The second her lips were on mine, I caved. "And only you." Bringing those women back to the house was a mistake. I wasted their time and my own.

"Then let's be together. I'll move back home, and we'll start seeing each other again."

"You know we can't do that."

"Then I'll live here, and we can start seeing each other

again. No more pushing me away. No more pretending there isn't something here."

That sounded good in theory, but it wouldn't work in reality. "I know you don't believe me, but when the day comes, I will kill you."

Her pupils dilated slightly, the threat clearly affecting her.

"It doesn't matter if I don't want to. It doesn't matter what we have. I'm Cato Marino, and I don't let traitors go. If I let you walk away, the world will see me as weak. If I kill you, then my reputation will be amplified tenfold."

Her eyes filled with disappointment. "And that's why you're so miserable, Cato. Because you care more about power than what really matters. You're just like my father...and you will die like my father. But first, you will watch all the people you care about disappear...one by one."

No other words had resonated with me like those did. She painted a picture in my head, an image of my ending. I did my best to stay ten steps ahead of my enemies and my allies, but it would be arrogant to think they would never catch up with me. One day, someone might be smart enough to take me down. When that happened, what would I lose? Only my wealth because I had nothing else I was afraid to lose.

"If you do it, you'll regret it. You'll regret it every single day for the rest of your life."

"Maybe. But you didn't give me another option."

"Forgiveness. That's your other option."

I shook my head. "That's something I can't give you. Everything we had was a lie."

"And look at us now. We still want each other as much as we did before. In fact, we want each other more. You're telling me you want to spend the rest of your life with dumb bimbos who want to do it on the staircase? Who only care about your money?"

"You said I wasn't your type—and you meant it."

"You weren't," she said. "Not at all. But things change…"

"You don't think I'll be a good father, so why would you want to be with me? Being together would put you in the exact position you don't want to be in. You would be living the life you ran away from."

She didn't have a response to that. Her eyes shifted back and forth before she sighed. "I don't know what I would want in the future. But for right now, in this moment, you're the man I want. Maybe in a few years that will change. Maybe I'll want someone else. Maybe you'll want someone else. That's fine. But if you kill me, we'll never know. More importantly, taking me away is going to hurt our child the most. I would never take you away from them, but you would do it to me?"

My right hand massaged the knuckles on my left hand as I was unable to come up with a response. "You betrayed me. You plotted to kill me, Siena. Let's not pretend it was nothing."

"And let's not pretend I didn't turn that damn car around."

I turned my head and looked at the TV, not wanting to see the emotion in her eyes. "You're right, I wouldn't hurt you. Even when I'm pissed, I don't want to hurt you. I make threats I wish I could follow through with. But when I kill you, it won't be painful. I'll make it as painless as possible. It'll be over and done with in less than a second."

"How sweet…"

I turned back to look at her. "I just want you to know this is real. It's not a bluff. So if you're just fucking me in

100

the hope I'll change my mind, you're wasting your time. If anything, you should want nothing to do with me."

"I know…" She dropped her gaze, her voice turning quiet. "I know I should want nothing to do with you. Even when we were seeing each other, I wasn't supposed to like you, but I did. Now I shouldn't like you at all. I despise your business, and I despise your choices. I despise your lifestyle. I despise your stubbornness. But for some reason…I just can't stop feeling this way. I see past your flaws and see your qualities like bright beacons. I excuse all your mistakes because I love your successes. I don't seem to care about the bad because all I see is the good. I'll never forget all the things you've done for me, things you weren't required to do. And even though you're a monster, I just don't see you that way…no matter how hard I try." She kept her gaze down and wouldn't look me in the eye. "When I saw you come home with those two women…I felt terrible. I was jealous, heartbroken, livid. And I just had to do something, anything to make it stop. Watching you kiss her…made me sick to my stomach. Then I did something I never thought I would do. I agreed to a three-some just to fight for you. For any other guy in the world, that never would have happened. But with you, I didn't think twice. My feelings for you don't make any sense. Maybe it was because I knew you didn't really want them anyway…or maybe not." She stared at the edge of the couch with a blank look on her face. She didn't seem to be thinking about anything anymore, just sitting there in silence.

Now my feelings for this woman were even more confusing. I felt so many things for her but refused to share them out loud. Even though I didn't trust her, I still believed her. I believed every word she said.

At least, I wanted to.

She lifted her gaze and met my look again. "I know you meant everything you said. But I still don't believe you'll do it. I know you better than you think, and I know you're better than that. And even if I'm wrong…I would rather enjoy every day with you like I'm right. I would rather die not expecting it."

11

Siena

"I KNOW HOW TO COOK A FEW THINGS, BUT I CAN'T cook like this." I sat on the stool at the counter and ate my lunch. Eating nutritious meals for the baby wasn't difficult when I had a gourmet chef who could whip up any healthy meal. "The salmon is so tender but so delicious. How do you do it?"

He shrugged, but the delight was written all over his face. He loved taking care of Cato's home, but the place he shone the most was in the kitchen. "Many years of practice. It's not just about the preparation, but the source of the ingredients. I go to the store every morning and fetch new ingredients to cook with every day."

"Every day?" I asked incredulously.

"Every day," he said with a proud nod.

"Unbelievable."

The kitchen door opened, and Bates stepped inside, wearing a full suit like he had a meeting with Cato. "Thought I heard voices in here." He stepped farther inside with his hands in his pockets, and when he looked at me, there was obvious threat in his eyes. He hated me as much as he did the last time he saw me—when he punched me in the face.

Giovanni stood at the counter across from me and chopped up the ingredients he was preparing for tonight's dinner. "How are you, sir?"

"Great." He stopped at the counter close to me and addressed Giovanni without looking at him. "Cato was supposed to meet me here fifteen minutes ago."

"Must be running late," Giovanni said. "He's always so busy."

Bates leaned against the counter right beside me, invading my personal space, and he watched me eat each bite. He was so close, his cologne burned my nostrils. He was a handsome man like his brother, but he'd definitely inherited the evil gene. "Enjoying your luxurious lifestyle? Quite an upgrade for you."

"Yes, having my freedom taken away is a dream come true…" I should probably play nice with Bates, but I couldn't stand him. He was a temperamental son-of-a-bitch. Even if he was just being loyal to his brother, he was over the top in his intensity.

"I think you should be grateful. You're safe in a mansion while you grow that baby."

"Until I'm shot in the head."

Bates grinned. "I can't wait until that moment comes."

I turned back to my food and ignored him.

But he continued to stand there.

"Can I help you with something?"

He tilted his head as he examined me. "I think you're a pain in the ass, but you're still a beautiful pain in the ass. Maybe I should bend you over this counter and fuck you."

Cato wasn't there, but I still felt protected by him. "Cato would kill you."

"He doesn't give a damn about you."

"He's not a monster like you. Of course he cares."

Without telegraphing his intentions, he grabbed the blade from the cutting board and pointed the tip right at my neck.

I stilled when the point of the blade pressed hard against my skin. I could feel how cold the knife was. I could even feel the lime juice on it burn my skin when he slightly pierced through. "It's very difficult to eat lunch when a knife is held at your throat."

"It must be more difficult with a slit throat." He gripped the back of my head and held me still. Like an asshole, he played with his prey before he actually made the kill.

"I'm still pregnant, asshole."

"Yes. It makes you think you're invincible. Well, bitch. You aren't." He poked the knife harder until I started to drip blood.

Giovanni held his position, still at the counter, and watched in horror as Bates tortured me. "Mr. Marino, I really don't think Mr. Marino would like this."

Bates pressed his lips to my ear, the smile in his voice. "I don't think he'd mind."

Giovanni looked at the door then eyed his supplies on the counter, obviously wanting to interfere, but he didn't know how. Hopefully, an idea came to mind because he walked out of the kitchen in a hurry.

And left me alone with the asshole. "Cato will hurt you for hurting me."

"He doesn't care about you enough. You overestimate your value."

"And I think you're blind to what's right in front of you." Even though it was dangerous, I threw my elbow into his gut and made him hunch forward. The knife cut me across the neck in the process, but at least I was free. I hopped off the stool and kicked him in the knee.

This time, he was ready for me. The knife was still in his hand so he turned on me with it raised. "I was just playing games. But now, I think I will bend you over the table and fuck you—while this cold steel presses against your neck."

"You really don't want to do that." I held both hands up, ready to get my fingers chopped off as I protected my stomach.

"No. I think I do." He charged at me with the knife aimed at my throat.

At that moment, Cato ran through the door with Giovanni close behind him.

"Oh, thank god." I dodged to the side and fell to the ground, knowing Cato would handle his brother.

"What the hell are you doing?" Cato threw himself at his brother, punched him so hard in the face, Bates flew back against the other wall. The knife came loose, and Giovanni snatched it from the floor before he rushed to me.

Bates chuckled from his position on the floor. "That little bitch was talking back to me. Decided to punish her."

"Liar!" I let Giovanni help me up. "I was eating lunch, and he held a knife to my throat and threatened to rape me."

Cato suddenly turned rigid, his ferocity palpable. His presence took up the entire room, along with his rage. He slowly inched toward his brother, his broad shoulders thickening as the muscles tightened. "Get to your feet so I can push you back down."

Bates chuckled again, like this was a game. "Come on, who cares? I was just having some fun." He moved to his feet. "It's not like she actually means something—"

Cato slammed his fist hard into his brother's face, making blood explode from his nose.

"Fuck." Bates stumbled back against the wall. "Fine, I deserved that. But I couldn't help it—"

Cato hit him again. "Don't touch her again. I mean it."

Bates's face dripped with so much blood, he was hardly recognizable.

Cato walked to Giovanni and snatched the knife out of his hand. "You did that to her?"

He must have seen the blood dripping down my neck. He'd examined the situation so quickly it was almost impossible to believe he could be that fast.

Bates squeezed his forefinger and thumb together. "It's just a little tiny slice—"

Cato snatched his arm and sliced him down the forearm, cutting through his expensive suit and making him bleed.

"Shit!" He yanked his arm back and gripped the wound. "Come on, that was my favorite suit." He made a joke like this was funny, but he gritted his teeth with pain.

"Touch her again, and I'll kill you. Do you understand me?"

"Until she has your baby. Got it."

"Not even then." Cato didn't raise his voice, but it seemed like he was yelling. "I mean it, Bates. I understand you don't like her or respect her, but if you like or respect me, then you'll listen to me. That woman is carrying my child, and I will do everything necessary to protect her. So fuck with me, and I'll put you in the ground. Alright?"

Blood dripped from Bates's arm and onto the ground. It got all over his hand as he kept pressure on the wound. "Yeah, whatever." He moved to get around Cato.

Cato got in his way. "That's not good enough. Do you understand me?"

Bates rolled his eyes. "Yes…I understand you. Now if you'll excuse me, I gotta take care of this."

This time, Cato let him pass.

Bates walked out.

Cato watched his brother go before he walked over to me. "Fuck, this looks bad. You've got blood all over your neck."

"It's not as bad as it looks," I said honestly. "It feels like a paper cut."

"I should take you to the doctor." He grabbed a towel and wiped away the red blood that had smeared all over my neck. When he'd cleaned most of it away, he held the towel over the small incision.

"Really, I'm fine. It doesn't even hurt." I didn't just say that to be brave. It was a small injury, nothing I wouldn't recover from. It wouldn't even leave a scar. "And I'm sure the baby is fine. The whole thing lasted less than five minutes."

Cato pulled the towel away to see if it was still bleeding. "Looks like it's stopped."

"See?" I said in relief.

Giovanni grabbed a bandage from the first aid kit and handed it to Cato. "Sir, I have to tell you that Miss Siena was provoked. The two of us were just talking when Mr. Marino came inside and turned hostile."

Cato placed the bandage across my neck. "Don't worry, Giovanni. I know my brother better than you do."

"And he threatened to rape me—twice." I could deal with being knocked around a bit, but being threatened like that bothered me the most. It was barbaric and made me think of Damien—the man I hated the most.

Cato met my gaze, the rage entering his expression. "He did?"

"Yes," Giovanni said. "Said he would bend her over the counter."

Cato's nostrils flared like an enraged bull. "I'll handle him. Don't worry about it."

"I'm not." There was no doubt in my mind that Cato would take care of me. He would never let his brother hurt me—and not just because I carried his child.

"You're sure you're alright?" he asked. "I know you like to act tough, but you don't need to do that with me."

"I'm fine, Cato. I got some good hits in." When I looked down at my shirt, I saw the bloodstains had ruined my blouse. Even though my injury was small, I really looked like something worse had happened. "I should probably take a shower and get rid of these clothes." I walked away from the two men and exited the kitchen.

Cato started speaking once I was gone. "I don't know what to do about him…"

"You better do something," Giovanni said. "Because Miss Siena deserves better."

"Didn't know you were so fond of her."

Giovanni was quiet for a while. "She's the best thing that's walked into this house in a long time."

———

I STOOD under the warm water in the shower and tried to forget what had happened. If I'd had a gun, I would have hit him right between the eyes because I was an amazing shot. I could lock on to my targets within two seconds and hit the mark. My father and brother always told me I had a knack for it, regardless of the distance to the target or how quickly it moved. If I'd been armed, I wouldn't have missed.

I'd survived worse, but I knew Bates was a real problem. Maybe Cato could forgive me in time, but Bates never would. He saw me as a traitor and a nuisance, and the second my baby was born, he'd want to get rid of me. If Cato couldn't pull the trigger, Bates would make it happen. I believed Cato wouldn't hurt me, even though he'd pledged he would.

But Bates was a whole other story.

If Cato hadn't stopped him, Bates might have beaten me to death.

The sound of the running water cleared my thoughts. The steam kept my skin warm, and it was easy to forget about the nightmare that had just taken place. But remembering what Giovanni had said about me made me smile.

Such a sweet man.

I rubbed soap over my stomach and thought I felt a subtle change in my belly. It'd only been a few months since I'd gotten pregnant, but my fingers detected a slight curve to my stomach. I looked forward to the moment when I really started to show, when I could really feel my baby inside me. I would finally get to know them, to share every moment with them.

The door opened and Cato stepped inside, tall, buck naked, and sexy. His blue eyes took in my figure and the way I lathered soap against my stomach. He joined me and shut the door behind him.

His fair skin had a slight tan, like he ran shirtless outside in the morning. I'd never witnessed him work out, but he obviously did if he looked like that—like the sexiest man in the world. Just his arms alone were enough to get me off. So muscular and ripped at the same time. His lats were perfect, like two walls that hugged his spine. Only a man committed to physical perfection could look like that.

My hands slicked my wet hair out of my face as I moved over to share the hot water with him.

He stepped under the steam and let the drops lick his body. His narrow hips had a dramatic V in the front because the tightness of his abs was remarkable. Farther down, his limp cock led to a well-groomed sac. He kept his package manicured, which made it easy for me to suck him off often. He tilted his head and let the water soak his short hair.

My nipples started to harden the longer I stayed out of the water. The humid air was warm but not as comfortable as that hot water.

Cato looked at me as the water hit his shoulder, his blue eyes staring at my hard nipples. I'd just been assaulted, but his mind always went to sex.

"You're hogging the water."

"There's room for both of us." He positioned me tight against his body so we could feel the water dribble over our skin. His hands rested around my hips, but they slowly made their way down to my ass cheeks. He squeezed them both in his big hands.

"It's the middle of the day. I'm surprised you don't have work."

He shook his head slightly. "I work when I feel like it. And right now, I don't feel like it."

"Because you're worried about me." I couldn't picture this man ever hurting me, not after the protective things he'd done. He always seemed to be my savior rather than my tormentor. As much as he wanted to make me disappear, he knew he would be miserable without me.

He didn't confirm it or deny it.

"I'm fine, Cato. Really. I've been through worse."

His eyes moved to the wound at my shoulder, the scar I would carry for the rest of my life. "Bates is complicated. He comes off as a violent psychopath, but he's just—"

"Trying to protect you. I understand."

"He doesn't go around raping and beating women."

"I figured. When you're handsome and rich, you don't really need to rape anyone…"

"He sees you as a threat to me, someone who hurt me and disrespected me. I brush things off better than he does. With him, he just can't let things go." Cato was definitely the pragmatic one of the two. He described his brother with astute observation, speaking about him without rage in his tone. "I'm not justifying his behavior. But that's how he feels."

"I get it. But when the day comes you're supposed to execute me, watch him. If you don't pull the trigger, he will. If you don't want that to happen…I suggest you be prepared." I turned my head into the water so I could rinse out my conditioner. Bates was definitely the adversary I needed to be wary of, not Cato.

Cato didn't respond to that.

"How does your mother feel about all of this?" He hadn't mentioned her in a long time. "Have you told her?"

"I told her a few nights ago. Actually, Bates told her. I still owe him another punch for that."

"And what did she say?"

"She was happy. Excited to be a grandmother." He obviously had no intention of washing his hair or soaping his body. He just stood under the water with me, enjoying the comfort that surrounded us both.

"Really?" I asked in surprise. "What does she know about us, exactly?"

"Mostly the truth. We're having a baby together, but we aren't together."

"And that didn't make her angry?"

"She would prefer we were a family. But no, she's not angry about it. I'm a thirty-year-old man, so it would be ridiculous if she threw a fit. I think she's just excited that

I'm starting a family. She wants me to settle down. She says I work too much and thinks I let life pass me by."

"You do work too much."

The corner of his mouth rose in a smile. "I think she's going to like you."

"I would hope so. I'm carrying her grandchild."

"She wants to meet you. I tried stalling for some time, but my mother can be aggressive."

"Well…now we know where Bates gets it from," I teased.

Just like he did before everything went to shit, he smiled slightly. It was a charming look on him, a hint of happiness that he never showed outside the two of us. To the rest of the world, he was always deadly serious. "Strong men come from strong women. And she's one of the strongest women I've ever known."

"And who are the others?" I asked, genuinely curious to know what other women he admired. It seemed like he only liked to screw dumb bimbos who wanted to suck his dick for money.

His hands glided up my body, past my stomach and to the area right below my rib cage. His thumbs pressed against the center of my stomach while his remaining fingers dug into my back. "Just one woman. You."

My lungs immediately sucked in a breath, making the area below my ribs rise against his fingertips in response. His thumbs pressed harder into me, hitting me in the sternum. This man said the most unexpected things, sweet things that contradicted his cold nature. That made everything he said much more potent because it was sincere. He spoke the truth no matter how hurtful it was, so when he gave a compliment, it was that much more meaningful. I moved into his chest and kissed his skin at the top of his sternum, the place where my lips naturally landed, given his height.

His arms wrapped around my waist, and he rested his chin on my head, holding me under the warm water.

This was what I missed most of all, those nights when he held me. Having a strong man in my bed became the best part of my life. The sheets always smelled like him, and he radiated such heat that I never got cold. I never worried about someone stepping inside the house because he chased everyone else away. Maybe he might kill me someday, but being by his side was also the safest place in the world.

His hand moved up the back of my neck and underneath my wet hair. "I promise I won't let anything happen to either one of you. I let my guard down when I shouldn't have, but it won't happen again."

Never in my life had I felt so safe. The second my mother was gone, I slept with one eye open. I used to think my father was powerful enough to protect our family, but then I realized he was the problem. I went on my own path, but I slept with a gun under my mattress. I constantly looked over my shoulder to see who was following me. But with Cato, I stopped worrying about that. If there was any man in the world who could keep me safe, it was him. "I know."

———

WE HADN'T HAD sex in a week.

The last time we did was when he fucked me in the ass. It hurt for three days before it returned to normal. I didn't think it would be that big of a deal, but since Cato had such a huge dick, it was definitely a big deal.

I still had a scratch on my neck from the knife. With

every passing day, it became less visible, but the scar was still fresh enough to be seen with the naked eye. Bates hadn't returned to the house since that horrid afternoon.

And Cato didn't touch me.

It was the last week of summer before fall officially started. I didn't mind the fall because the temperature was mild and the colors became brilliantly beautiful, but I hated winter. It was so damn cold, my bones ached. Good thing this place had much better heating than my old house.

I was looking up different cribs on my phone when Cato entered my bedroom. I sat on the couch with my back to him, but since no one else ever stepped inside without knocking, I knew it was him. "I'm looking up stuff for the baby."

He came up behind me and looked at the screen. "That's a girly crib."

"Which is fine because we're having a girl."

"What makes you so sure?" He took the seat beside me. I had my back against the armrest with my feet stretched out over the cushions, so he lifted my legs and placed them on his lap. He was in his sweatpants without a shirt, the signature outfit he wore late in the evening before bed.

"A mother's instinct."

"You're barely pregnant."

"Doesn't matter. I just know."

He rested one hand around my ankle while his other arm lay over the back of the couch. "Even if it's a girl, that crib is way too girly. I'm not raising a spoiled princess."

"She's gonna be spoiled no matter what you do, unfortunately." If she grew up in this mansion and watched her father run the biggest bank in the world, she would be a bit entitled. It wasn't the life I wanted for her, but there was nothing I could do about it.

"Well, she's not gonna be an annoying princess."

I liked that—a lot. "Alright. Forget the pink crib." I looked through the other selections. "Where will the baby's room be?"

"Next to mine. There're a few vacant rooms on this floor."

If it was on this floor, it would be easy access from my room.

Cato watched the TV while I continued with my online shopping. Like a couple unwinding after a long day of work, we sat together in comfortable silence. His hand moved to my foot, and he started massaging it.

My head immediately rolled back, and I closed my eyes. "Oh…"

He chuckled. "You don't even make that noise during sex."

"Because sex has never felt this good."

He used his other hand and got into the soles of my feet, rubbing the small muscles and even the pads of my toes. His big hands were perfect for the job, perfect for eliminating the tension. "You have cute feet."

"I know."

He chuckled. "You know?"

I shrugged. "You aren't the first person to tell me that."

"Really? Who else has given you that compliment?"

"Well, the first person was my mother. And I've had a few lovers tell me the same."

His hands stopped working.

I opened my eyes and looked at Cato, seeing him stare at my feet with a distinct look of irritation. "What?"

His fingers started working again. "Nothing." He still wore that agitated expression.

"Cato Marino, are you jealous?"

"I just think it's inappropriate to mention old lovers when we're having a baby."

"Inappropriate?" I laughed sarcastically as I sat up and pulled my feet away. "You brought two skanks here just a few weeks ago—while my room was down the hall. You want to talk about inappropriate? I had to get naked and agree to a threesome to get it to stop. So if I want to tell you that my other lovers thought my feet were cute, I will."

He turned my way slightly but didn't continue the argument.

"But I'll admit it's sexy watching you get jealous."

"Not jealous."

"You get pissed when I mention other men. That's the definition of jealous."

He faced the TV again, his jaw clenched. "It was just unexpected."

"What? Did you think I was a virgin?"

"Fucking you for the first time would have been a lot more difficult if you were."

"I think it's obvious I'm experienced. The sex wouldn't be so good if I weren't."

His jaw clenched again. "Are you trying to piss me off?"

I raised an eyebrow. "Wow…you're really jealous." I couldn't wipe off the smile that formed on my face. "I can't even imagine how many women you've been with, and you don't see me getting jealous."

"It's not the same."

"Why? Because I'm a woman and you're a man?"

"No." He kept his eyes on the TV even though he clearly wasn't watching it.

"Then what's the difference?" I crossed my arms over my chest.

He slowly turned back to me, his eyes narrowed.

"Those women meant nothing to me. You had relationships with those men, real feelings. You had connections and secrets. You had enough conversations that they had the opportunity to compliment your feet. That's the difference. So, no, I don't want to hear about the men you used to love."

"Love?" I asked incredulously. "I admit the relationships were longer than one-night stands, but I've never been in love before. I've never told a man I loved him."

The rage reduced from an inferno to a simmer. "I'm surprised. You're so perfect, you could have the man of your dreams in a heartbeat. You could settle down and have the family you've always wanted."

I smiled as I listened to him. "You think I'm perfect?"

"I've never been monogamous before. I think that testifies to my opinion of you."

"I thought that was just your obsession with my cunt."

His eyes darkened as he looked at me. "It's the whole package, baby."

It was hard to believe this was the same man I'd observed in the bar. The one making out with two women in a row even though he'd barely said hello. He was the same man who confronted me outside that coffee shop and subtly threatened me. He was an arrogant and standoffish asshole. But now he was kind, affectionate, and romantic. I dropped my phone on the cushion then crawled onto his lap. I straddled his hips and sat on his dick. It wasn't big yet, but within seconds, it would be. My arms wrapped around his neck and I kissed him.

As I predicted, within seconds, he was hard underneath me, his cock stretching until the head popped out of his sweatpants. His hands dug underneath my tank top and felt my soft skin, his fingers exploring me as they glided up to my tits. I wasn't wearing a bra, so he could palm both of them easily. "And you have the nicest rack I've ever seen. Nicest pussy. Best lips." He kissed me slowly as he breathed into my mouth, his eyes open as he looked into mine.

I cupped his face and slowly ground against him. "You're the sexiest man I've ever laid eyes on." My hands flattened against his stomach and slowly glided up his hard chest. "Beautiful eyes. Sexy shoulders." I rested my hand over the left side of his chest. "And big heart."

His lips faltered against mine, his eyes widening at my words. It took him a second to recover from the compliment before he kissed me once more. He pulled my shirt over my head so he could bury his face between my tits. He kissed the area and smothered it with his tongue as he pushed my shorts over my ass.

I yanked his sweatpants down so his cock could be free.

My shorts couldn't come off completely when I sat like this, so I got to my feet, turned around, and pulled them down to my ankles with my ass toward the sky.

"Fuck."

I gave him a few extra seconds to look at my ass before I turned around and straddled his hips. I pressed his cock past my lower lips and slowly sank down, reunited with the cock that made all my fantasies come true.

He grabbed my hips and yanked me down all the way, like he couldn't wait long enough for my body to acclimate to him. He forced me to stretch apart so he could have me, could have all my wetness and tightness.

I sat on his balls and felt every inch of him inside me. Since he was bigger than any other man I'd taken, I did feel like a virgin when I fucked him. Every time felt like the first time. Not only did he hit me deep, but he stretched me wide. I gripped his shoulders as I enjoyed this man in a way no other woman ever had. "No other man compares to you...not for me." I held his gaze as he throbbed inside me. It was ridiculous for him to be jealous of my old lovers, not when he'd put this baby inside me, not when he fucked me without a condom.

He gripped my hips and guided me up and down his length, his eyes locked with mine. "Baby…you know how to fuck this dick." He thrust his hips back into me, moving with me.

My fingers dug into his hair, and I kissed him as I ground my hips back and forth. I could feel the cream sheathe his length, covering most of his shaft and forming a pool on his balls. I kissed him hard and dragged my nipples against his chest. His dick wasn't the best part. It was this closeness, this affection. I loved feeling his hands all over me, deep in my hair and on my tits. I loved feeling those lips smother me. I loved having an intense and passionate relationship with a strong man. "Because I love your dick."

HE STAYED inside me when he finished, and after a few minutes, he was ready to go again. When we were finished a second time, he stayed inside me on the couch and kissed my neck and shoulders. Then he swelled inside me once more.

"You're gonna get me pregnant again." I tilted my head back so he could kiss the hollow in my throat.

"I do have super sperm." He lifted me from the couch and carried me to the bed with his thick dick big inside me. He moved me onto the bed and got deep between my legs as my head hit the pillow. Then he fucked me hard and deep, his face resting in my neck as he panted and grew slick with more sweat.

I'd never been fucked like this. No other man had the stamina to pull it off.

No other man could make me come for a third time. "Oh, right there." I widened my legs farther and felt the climax burn me like a fire. I grabbed his hips and dragged him into me as I came around his big dick, sheathing his shaft with more of my come and his.

He moaned as he came at the same time, giving me another load of his come as I gave him mine. His cock twitched inside me as he finished.

I had so much come sitting inside me that it would destroy my sheets by morning.

He lifted his body above mine and looked me in the eye. "Fuck. So much come."

"I can probably handle more."

He gave me a heated expression before he kissed me. "Maybe in another hole." He slowly pulled out of me, and the second he was gone, everything seeped out between my legs. He stared at the insides of my thighs with approval. "It's no surprise I knocked you up. No amount of birth control can stop that." He got off me then retrieved his boxers and sweatpants.

I turned on my side and prepared to go to sleep.

Cato came back into the room, but he headed for the door.

"What are you doing?"

He opened the door but kept one hand on the knob. "Going to bed."

"You aren't going to stay?" I asked in disappointment.

He turned quiet, like he was considering it. He used to sleep with me all the time, but now it seemed like he never wanted to do it again. "Good night, baby." He walked out and shut the door behind him.

I WOKE up from a nightmare at five and couldn't go back to sleep. I lay there with my eyes closed, but my heart rate wouldn't slow down. Images of what I'd seen kept flashing across my eyes.

I finally gave up and made my way to the kitchen. I didn't know if anyone was awake this early, but I could probably find some leftovers in the kitchen. I walked into the room as I rubbed the sleep from my eyes and spotted Giovanni in the kitchen, scrubbing a pan in the sink. Cato was at the kitchen table, wearing a workout shirt and shorts. He sipped his morning coffee and read the newspaper. "You guys are awake this early?"

Giovanni turned off the faucet and turned to look at me. "Miss Siena, you're an early riser this morning."

"I woke up and couldn't go back to sleep." I walked to the counter close to Giovanni. "Thought I would get my day started."

"How about some coffee and breakfast?"

"That would be great."

He made me an Americano then turned back to the stove. "I'll make something good. Give me a few minutes."

I carried my coffee to the table and sat across from Cato.

He was still reading the newspaper, his plate untouched. There were white cubes on the dish, along with sautéed vegetables.

I squinted as I tried to make it out. "What the hell is that?"

He lowered his paper and glanced at his plate. "Tofu."

I made a face. "That's not breakfast."

"It has no sugar, no carbs, and no fat."

"So, it's garbage," I said with a straight face.

He smiled slightly before he folded up his newspaper and set it down. "You just think that because it doesn't have cheese on it."

"Even cheese wouldn't make that good." I sipped my coffee, wishing it had caffeine in it. Two things I loved most had been taken away from me—alcohol and coffee. "And why are you awake so early?"

"I'm always awake this early. I work out in the morning."

"You work out at five in the morning?" I asked incredulously. "Five? The sun isn't even up."

"I use my private gym, so it doesn't matter. And if I don't work out in the morning, then when?"

I shrugged. "Don't work out at all."

"Trust me, you wouldn't want me to stop working out." He grabbed his fork and ate a few bites.

Giovanni brought me my plate. "Belgian waffle, egg whites with cheese, sautéed kale and mushrooms, and sourdough toast." He set it in front of me.

"Now that's what breakfast is supposed to look like." I pointed at my plate. "Delicious. Thank you, Giovanni."

"My pleasure, Miss Siena." Giovanni walked back to the kitchen.

Cato watched me as he ate breakfast. "He likes you more than he likes me."

"So do most people."

He smiled as he kept chewing.

I dumped the syrup on my waffle and ate that first.

Cato sipped his coffee and kept watching me.

"Why won't you sleep with me?" I blurted.

His mouth halted for a second as he took in my question.

I'd been living with him for a long time, and not once had it happened. He purposely avoided it.

He took another bite and stalled as long as possible. "I don't want to."

"I figured that part out. But why?"

His eyes dropped as he stabbed a piece of tofu with his fork. "Too intimate."

"More intimate than fucking?" I asked incredulously.

"I just don't want to, alright?" He turned stern, treating me the way he treated Bates when he stepped out of line. He raised his voice as well as his anger, and that made the air in the room feel formidable.

Despite the tender moments we'd shared, he still had his guard up. He always kept me at a distance, even when we looked into each other's eyes and rocked together. He would never give me all of himself, not like he did before. The wound of my betrayal was still fresh.

Minutes of tense silence passed, and we ate our breakfast and ignored the obvious discomfort we both felt.

"I wanted to ask you something."

"Alright." He had been staring at his phone, so he set it on the table.

"I know you already said no—"

"Then that means no."

How could he be so sweet at night and then turn into an asshole in the morning? It was like he was two different people. "This asshole thing is getting old."

"I'm always an asshole—so get used to it."

"No, you aren't," I snapped. "Why are you in such a bad mood?"

"Because you're provoking me. First, you asked me why I won't sleep with you—like I have to give you a reason. And now this? I already gave you my answer, and that's not gonna change."

I wanted to smack him upside the head. Just the other night, he held me in the shower and promised to protect me. He told me I was perfect, got jealous of the men who came before him. Now he acted like that never happened. "I'm gonna eat my breakfast upstairs before your bitchiness erases my appetite."

His eyes widened like that insult wouldn't fly. "I may be your lover at night, but as long as the sun is up, I'm the master of this house. You don't question me like you have rights. Our situation hasn't changed despite what we do in the bedroom. You're my prisoner—and prisoners do as they're told."

It was a really stupid thing to do, but I did it anyway. I threw all the food off my plate and hit him right in the face with it. Syrup stuck to his skin, and the mushrooms and bread crumbs got stuck in the brown goo. "Fuck off, Cato." I marched out of the kitchen without looking back.

———

I KNEW I would have to pay for my outburst eventually.

But Cato didn't make his move right away.

I stayed in my room all day, waiting for the sound of his heavy footsteps outside the door. I disobeyed him right in front of his staff, so there was no way he would let that slide. He would come for me with a vengeance.

But he also told me he would never hurt me.

So what would he do?

I found out later that night.

He barged into my room in his suit. The second he was inside, he slammed the door hard behind him and made all the walls shake.

I jumped off the couch and prepared for a fight.

He marched into the room with an aggressive look in his eyes. His body was revved like a burning-hot engine, and he squeezed both of his hands like he wished he were grabbing a fistful of hair.

"You can't be two different people," I snapped. "You can't be my lover at night then an asshole in the morning. Pick one."

He undid his belt and pulled it loose. "That's easy. Then I'll be an asshole." He folded the belt in half then smacked it against his open palm. The sound of the smack reverberated against the wall, the crack loud and sharp. "Bend over. Or I'll make you bend over."

Now I knew what he was going to do. He was going to whip me with that belt—and he was going to whip me hard. "I'm not letting you whip me."

"You don't have to let me do anything." He struck the belt against his palm again. "I want to hunt you down. Makes it more fun that way." He made his move and walked toward me.

I ran around the couch and dashed into the other room.

He sprinted after me, his heavy footfalls like drums.

I ran past the bed and headed to the door.

"I can whip your ass in here or out there for everyone to see. You decide."

I ran into the hallway then stopped, knowing he would make good on his threat. He would whip me in front of all the staff and make them watch.

Cato caught me by the arm and dragged me back inside the bedroom. He kicked the door shut with his foot then bent me over the bed. My dress was hiked up, and my panties were pulled down.

"Don't you dare—"

He struck me hard, so hard the words died in my mouth.

He hit me again, putting all his momentum into the

hit. It stung so bad, I actually screamed. My ass was reddening right away, the inflammation kicking in. The pain was overwhelming. "Three more."

"Stop."

He smacked me. "Nothing you say is going to make me stop."

"You said you were never going to hurt me."

"Baby, you're tougher than this." He slapped the belt across my ass, the bite terrible.

He kept me pinned down by the neck. "Last one. I'm gonna make it hurt more than all the others. You want to know why?"

I didn't answer.

"Pull a stunt like that again, and I'll do something worse than whip you. Don't question me in front of my staff. Don't disrespect me in my home. I have every right to be an asshole to you, but you have no right to be a bitch to me." He brought the belt down harder than all the other strikes.

And I screamed again.

12

Cato

Siena didn't step out of her room for four days.

She was still pissed at me.

I didn't feel bad for punishing her. Even if I was being an asshole, she had no right to speak to me that way. She thought she could ask me whatever she wanted like she had the right. She seemed to forget she didn't have any rights.

I treated her too well. That was the problem.

She could shut me out as long as she wanted, and I wouldn't cave. She deserved that punishment, and I wouldn't apologize for it.

It was the first time Bates returned to my estate after he cut Siena with that knife. He greeted me like nothing happened, and we stepped inside the conference room.

"Can I still not smoke in here?" He pulled a cigar out of his pocket.

I slugged him so hard in the face, he dropped the cigar and fell to the ground. "What the fuck? Don't tell me you're still mad."

"I'm furious." I grabbed him by the collar and dragged

him to his feet. "Even look at Siena the wrong way, and I'll slit your throat."

He pushed me off him then grabbed the fallen cigar. "Fine."

"No, not *fine*," I hissed. "You threatened to rape her."

"Did I do it?" He threw his arms in the air. "No. It was just a threat."

"Whatever, Bates. It's still wrong, either way. Don't treat my woman like that, or I'll fucking—"

"What. Did. You. Just. Say?" His eyes narrowed, and he slowly lowered his arms to his sides. "Your woman? Did you just call her your damn woman?" He stepped closer to me, getting in my face.

I never meant to say that. The words just flew out.

His eyes shifted back and forth as he looked into mine. Rage was billowing in his gaze like an approaching storm. Slowly, it grew near, spots of lightning scattering in random places. "You're fucking her again?"

"It's none of your business what I'm doing with her."

"Yes, it is, asshole. When you call her your woman, it is my damn business. That bitch lied to you and betrayed you. She can't be trusted. How stupid are you?"

"I never said I trusted her."

"Your cock did."

I pushed him back. "Touch her, speak to her, or look at her the wrong way, and I'll rip your head off. That's the point I'm trying to make. Whether she means something to me or not, she's carrying my baby."

"I didn't touch your baby, Cato."

"But you put her in distress, and that affects the baby. You could have accidentally hurt her."

He rolled his eyes. "I wish she'd never come into our lives…"

"I wish you would stop being a whiny bitch."

"What is it with you and this woman? I don't fucking get it. You can see straight when it comes to everyone else, but with her, it's like you're clueless. If you knocked up some other girl, I know you would have put that bullet in her brain. You can say it's because of the baby, but I think it's because of the woman."

"It's because of the baby, Bates. I'm not our father."

"It's not the same situation, and you know it."

"I'm done with this conversation." I slammed my fist down onto the table. "Leave her alone, Bates. I mean it."

He nodded slightly, his eyes incredulous after what I'd just asked him. He sighed with flared nostrils then turned back to me. "Fine. But I want you to promise that you'll kill her when the time comes."

The room turned silent. I could hear my own heartbeat in my ears. I never made promises I couldn't keep, and being pressured to do it now made my head spin. I always intended to do it, but now I felt like the gun was in my hand—fully loaded. "My word is good enough, Bates."

He cocked an eyebrow. "You won't make the promise."

I wouldn't make a promise I couldn't keep. "I'll do it."

"Then promise me, Cato." He stepped toward me.

"No."

His nostrils flared again. "Don't let that bitch manipulate you. She will make an idiot out of you all over again. When you're deep inside that pussy, don't forget how you got there. Don't forget the lies and the deceit."

"She turned around."

Bates cocked his head, unable to follow my thoughts. "What?"

"When she drove me to the cemetery, she changed her mind at the last minute and turned around."

"So?" He raised his hands again. "She could have turned around for any reason."

"I think she did it to save me. I think she knew it was wrong and tried to get me out of there."

"That's what you want to believe."

"That's what I saw, Bates."

He rolled his eyes. "I'm trying to protect you. You piss me off most of the time, but I always have your back. I'm telling you that my instinct deep in my gut…" He slammed his fist into his stomach. "Says this woman will betray you again. Don't fall for it."

"Trust me, I won't."

"Then promise me."

"I can't. Just because I can't doesn't mean I won't kill her. And just because I can't doesn't mean I trust her. She burned that bridge, and it can never be rebuilt."

He bowed his head and sighed. "Whatever. I did my best. I could argue about this forever, but we've got more important shit to do. I just got word from our security team that someone is gonna hit us tonight."

Siena quickly moved to the back burner. "Which facility?"

"Our main headquarters. The Beck brothers are delivering half our cash tonight, and I guess these guys found out about it. They're gonna hit us hard, too. They've got a militia under their belts."

"Who the fuck are these guys?"

"I don't know much. I hear they're from Siberia."

"And they're just gonna drive tanks and shit into another country without notice?"

"I'm sure they have allies here. They probably cut a deal."

Well, there would be no deal when they were all dead. "We need all our men on the ground."

"I agree—for the first time in this conversation."

Those idiots thought they were gonna take two

hundred and sixty million dollars from me—like it would be a walk in the park. "Everyone dies. No exceptions. But I want whoever is in charge brought here. I want to kill those motherfuckers myself."

"Me too."

"When is this happening?"

"When the money arrives. Midnight."

"Then we have no time to lose."

———

MY OFFICE WAS RIGHT next door to Siena's bedroom, but I wasn't concerned about her bothering me.

I stared at the monitors on my desk, which all had different feeds from the cameras my men were carrying.

Bates smoked a cigar beside me, taking deep breaths and letting the rings rise to the ceiling.

I drank scotch right out of the bottle.

Our men were hidden throughout the alleyways of the city, a hundred strong and all heavily armed. We had tanks, ammunition, and even rockets if it became necessary. If they managed to escape with my money, I would rather blow it up than watch them drive away with it.

Connor's men pulled up to the bank in a completely invulnerable car. Security stood around as they made the transfer.

That's when the Siberians made their move.

Then it turned into a war.

Shots were fired, men were killed, explosions rang into the night, and the sound of police sirens filled the distant streets. It was too chaotic to understand what was happening, but it seemed to be going in our favor.

It went on for thirty minutes. One of the cameras belonging to my men fell to the ground, obviously because he'd been hit. The other cameras continued to operate, and we watched the bloodbath.

I would have made an appearance myself, but a true leader didn't fight in battle—he controlled it.

Bates didn't say a word as he studied the monitors, smoking his cigar like it was a casual night.

There were screams. There were explosions. And there was death.

Finally, the war died down.

My phone rang, and I answered it immediately. "Cato."

"The money is secure, and we got the main players. What are your instructions?"

"Transfer the money as planned. Then bring those assholes to me. How many are there?"

"Five. Four men and one woman."

I raised an eyebrow. "A woman?"

"Yes," he answered. "She waited in the rear with a few other men. They weren't part of the fight. I think they're reporting directly to the head honcho. I've questioned them, but they aren't talking. I think they were supposed to follow the money back out of the city."

Man or woman, I didn't care. If they were responsible, they would be executed. "Dispose of the bodies and bring me those five. I want to kill them myself."

"Of course, sir." The line went dead.

"Depending on what she looks like, maybe we'll have some fun." Bates waggled his eyebrows.

"I'm a murderer, not a rapist."

"Speak for yourself."

"And neither are you," I said coldly. "We'll question them, then shoot them."

Bates took a long puff of his cigar. "You're no fun."

"That's why we're still in business."

The door opened, and Siena stepped inside, dressed in her shorts and tank top. She quickly crossed her arms over her chest and hid her tits from Bates's view. "What's going on in here? I heard shooting."

"We're playing a video game." Bates tilted his head back and released smoke rings toward the ceiling.

Siena turned her gaze on me and ignored my brother. She didn't trust anything he said. "Cato?"

"Bates and I are taking care of business." I rose from my chair then straightened out my jacket. "Stay in your room until morning. And shut your windows—you may hear loud sounds pretty soon."

Siena grew more uncomfortable by the second. "Should I be worried? Is something going to happen?"

"Everything is fine. We'll talk about it later. Now, go."

Siena opened her mouth to defy me but abruptly changed her mind. She shut her mouth and walked out.

Bates kept enjoying his cigar. "She's got beautiful legs."

I turned around and gave him a deathly stare. "You want to be the sixth person I execute tonight?"

He grinned before he blew smoke out of his mouth. "Sorry. I won't disrespect *your* woman again."

13

Siena

I DIDN'T KNOW WHAT WAS HAPPENING, BUT I KNEW SOME serious shit was going on.

Lots of guns. Lots of explosions. Lots of death.

And it was coming to our doorstep.

I listened to Cato and Bates pass my bedroom on their way to the entryway before I changed my clothes and poked my head out the door. The double front doors were wide open, and a ton of his men were stationed outside.

I moved to the center of the balcony so I had a clear view of the roundabout and the fountain. Both men stood there in their suits, their hands in their pockets as they waited for something.

Or someone.

All the men stationed on the property carried assault rifles and wore bulletproof vests. I knew Cato would never allow anyone on the property unless they were under his control, but seeing that many men carrying weapons made me uneasy. It reminded me of the afternoon I was yanked from the car and thrown on the ground. The men prepared for my execution in the same way.

Someone was about to die.

Then a caravan of black SUVs made its way through the gate. One by one, they pulled up to the roundabout and the door was opened. They yanked one man out of each back seat and put him on his knees in front of Cato and Bates.

When the fifth car arrived, they yanked a young woman from the back, about my age, and she was placed on her knees like the rest.

I watched in horror as Cato wordlessly stuck out his hand to one of the men and a pistol was placed in his palm.

He was going to execute each one of them.

I didn't know if I could watch.

Cato went to the first man and kneeled in front of him. It was impossible to hear what was being said because they were too far away. He was probably questioning them, looking for answers about whatever pissed him off. When he didn't get what he wanted, he stepped back and pointed the gun at the man's skull.

Then he pulled the trigger.

The sound of the bullet was so loud it echoed off the walls in the house. It was loud enough to make me jump and scream because it seemed like it happened right beside my ear.

Cato moved on to each one, kneeling in front of them for the conversation, and then rising before he shot them in the head.

I didn't know why Cato thought they would talk—if they were just going to die anyway.

He moved to the young woman at the end, and she got the exact same treatment. He spoke to her for a few minutes before he stood upright and pointed the gun at her head.

She sobbed. Her words couldn't be discerned, but it was obvious she was pleading for her life. Tears fell down her cheeks, and she lowered her head because she couldn't look at the barrel of the gun.

I knew I shouldn't sympathize with her more just because she was a woman, but I couldn't help it. She wept and begged, and I couldn't imagine she did something so horrible to deserve that fate. I didn't want Cato to do it.

But he did.

He pulled the trigger, the gun went off, and then she was dead on the ground.

The blood from all five corpses ran back to the fountain, streaks of bright red that were visible even in the darkness.

I should have stayed in my room like Cato ordered. It was the only time I wished I'd actually listened to him. Now those images would forever be burned into my brain. I would think about that woman constantly, how she hadn't been spared of her crime. She could have been a mother. She could have been a daughter. But Cato pulled the trigger anyway.

It made me wonder if he would pull the trigger on me.

———

I DIDN'T SLEEP all night, not after what I witnessed. I was too scared. If I closed my eyes, my dreams would bring me images of torture. I would see that woman in my mind, blood spraying from her skull.

When the sun rose the next morning, I skipped breakfast and stayed on the couch, contemplating what I should do. I'd never been seriously afraid of Cato, but I obviously didn't understand what he was capable of.

I was pissed at him for whipping me, but I'd gotten off easy.

It was better than being shot in the head.

Sometimes, my nights with him made me want to stay there forever. It made me think raising a family with him would be a wonderful experience. But when I was exposed to his world, I was given a painful reminder of my true situation.

We would never be safe here.

Even if he let me live.

This wasn't a life I wanted to be a part of. I didn't want people executed in my driveway. I didn't want to put head-phones over my child's ears so they wouldn't have to hear the gunshots. Staying here would only force me back into the life I ran away from.

I couldn't stay here.

I hadn't expected Cato to visit after what happened last night. I assumed he was too busy dealing with what-ever problems he was having in his business to think about me. But he walked inside and joined me on the couch. He was in his suit and tie, so he probably had been to the office that morning. It wasn't the suit he'd been wearing last night, so he hadn't stayed up all night like I had.

He rested against the back of the couch and watched me, his blue eyes somber. He didn't seem angry, sad, or anything else. He seemed indifferent. His hands rested together on his lap, his corded veins webbed from his knuckles to his wrist. "I warned you to stay in your room."

"What makes you think I didn't?"

"Your face is the color of snow."

I rested my arms across my stomach, still feeling the remnants of the nausea I had in the morning. I thought it was morning sickness, but maybe it was just disgust in this case. "What happened?" I didn't think he would answer, but I wanted to ask anyway.

He faced forward. "There's a group in Siberia that found out about a transfer happening last night."

"A transfer?"

"One of my clients paid back his debt. The truck delivered the cash to my main bank. Somehow, the Siberians found out about it and tried to intercept it. I knew about the heist before it happened, so I was able to catch them."

"Why didn't you just call the transfer off?"

"Because I needed to exterminate them. The only way to make sure a cockroach doesn't survive is to cut off its head."

My arms tightened over my stomach.

"So my men took out theirs. The transfer went through. And they located the people in charge and brought them here for their execution. I like to do my own dirty work. People know I mean business."

"So those five people…were in charge?"

"They were working directly for their boss. I asked for information, but they wouldn't give it."

"Even the woman?" I whispered.

He shook his head. "Said she didn't know anything."

"How do you know she was lying?"

He shrugged. "I don't. But I can't take any chances."

My heart fell into my stomach. "Won't the people in charge come after you in retaliation?"

"With what men?" He rubbed his palms together. "I killed them all, including the accomplices they trusted. They know I'm onto them, and it's only a matter of time before I track them down. If they're smart, they'll disappear. Everyone knows you only have one chance to take me out. If you fail, I won't stop hunting I've killed you and your entire family."

"What about Micah and Damien?"

"That was an exception, one I'll never make again."

The nights we spent alone together made me think Cato was a regular guy. We had deep conversations, tender embraces, and he said the sweetest things to me. He was soft and gentle, kissing me like he loved me and fucking me like I was the only woman he wanted for the rest of his life. But that couldn't mask the truth—he was a crime lord.

He turned back to me, reading the distress on my face. "What is it?"

My answer came out as a whisper. "Nothing."

He reached his hand out and touched me on the ankle. "Baby?"

"What do you want me to say?" I pulled my ankle away so he would let go. "That I'm terrified of you?"

It was the first time he'd shown me that look of sadness, like he was genuinely disappointed by the way I felt. "You don't need to be terrified of me."

"You whipped me with a belt for talking back to you. Then you executed a bunch of people."

"Not a bunch," he said. "Just a few."

"Oh, so that makes me feel better?" I asked sarcastically.

"And I only whipped you because you threw a plate of food in my face—in my own house in front of my butler. You thought I wouldn't punish you for that?"

"You were being a huge bitch."

He cocked his eyebrow. "A huge bitch?"

"There's no reason to talk to me that way."

"There's no reason to question me. You had no right to do that."

"No right?" I asked. "I'm carrying your baby. I can ask you whatever the hell I want. Is it really that terrible that the woman you're sleeping with actually wants to sleep with you? Because it's one of the things she misses the most? Is it really that terrible that I wanted to ask if my brother could visit me because I feel alone?" I got off the couch because I was finished with this conversation. "Just get out, Cato. I was already upset with you, but now I really want nothing to do with you." I stepped into the bathroom and shut the door because that was the only room in my bedroom with a door—unless I wanted to walk into the closet.

I listened for movement outside but didn't pick up on anything. He must still be on the couch, thinking about his next move.

A few minutes later, his footsteps sounded. But instead of heading for the door to leave, he stopped in front of the bathroom. He didn't try to come inside. "Baby?"

"Don't call me that."

He tapped his knuckles against the door. "Please."

Cato Marino knew that word? "Just leave me alone, Cato."

"Open the door. Or I will open the door. I'm giving you the chance to do it on your terms."

"Is it really on my terms?" I leaned against the counter with my arms crossed over my body.

"It's as close as you're going to get."

I stared at the door and noticed the shadow of his feet under the crack. My stubbornness forced me to wait, to stick to my guns as long as possible.

It was only a matter of time before Cato made good on his word.

I unlocked the door and stepped back.

He opened it so we could stand face-to-face.

I gave him a look full of hatred. One moment, he was my savior. And the next moment, he was a murderer.

He walked up to me until his hands gripped the sink on

either side of me. He stood with his face just inches from mine, his eyes shifting back and forth.

"You told me you would never hurt me."

"Whipping doesn't count."

"It does to me. I still have the welts on my ass. I'm carrying your baby, and you disrespect me like that?"

"You disrespected me first," he whispered.

"Your hostility was unnecessary. I'm just as temperamental as you are. If you provoke me, I will respond. That's how I am, and I won't apologize for it. If you don't want food in your face, you'll be nicer to me."

His eyes continued to shift back and forth as his hands clutched the counter tighter, restraining his rage.

"You owe me an apology."

"You're wasting your time," he whispered. "I'll never give you that."

"Then you need to promise you'll never hurt me again—that includes whipping."

"Why should I do that? I'll have no way to keep you in line."

"if you treat me with respect, you'll never need to keep me in line."

He breathed a quiet sigh, like he couldn't believe he was negotiating with me when he'd just executed people last night. "Alright. I promise. But that doesn't include the day I kill you."

He said he intended to do it, but I still didn't quite believe it. But now I wasn't as certain as I was before, not after watching him shoot a crying woman. Maybe I was wrong about Cato. Maybe I was still right. "Alright."

The second he thought our fight was over, he pressed his lips to mine and kissed me.

I didn't kiss him back, keeping my lips pressed tightly together in protest.

He pulled away, irritation in his gaze.

"I'm still mad at you."

"I made amends."

"Doesn't chase my anger away. Doesn't erase what I saw last night."

"I did what I had to do last night. People tried to steal from me—and I can't show mercy. I need to make an example of my enemies. Don't expect me to feel bad for what I did. Don't expect me to lose sleep over it. This is the real world—this is reality."

I still didn't agree with it. I didn't see the point in living this way, in killing over money. All I wanted was a little house with enough money for food, to have just enough to be happy. Constantly fighting over the wealth I had seemed like too much work.

"I'll make it up to you."

"How?"

He rested his forehead against mine. "As a gesture of good faith…I'll let your brother visit you."

I inhaled a deep breath, relieved I was getting the one thing I wanted.

"But only when I'm in the house. He's not allowed on my property unless I'm present. That's the best compromise you'll get from me."

"And it's more than enough. I just want to talk to him, have lunch with him…stuff like that. You can join us if you want."

"We'll see." He grabbed my dress and slowly lifted it to my waist to reveal my black thong underneath. "I miss you." His eyes flicked down to my panties, and he stared at my long legs.

I hadn't missed him all week. I'd been too pissed to feel anything but anger. So I said nothing.

"I'll make you miss me, then."

"I want to know why you won't sleep with me."

He grabbed my panties and pulled them down over my hips. "I told you."

"I want a better reason."

"We're just fucking, and I want to keep it that way." He moved to the floor as he pulled my panties down to my ankles.

"But I want more."

He stood upright and lifted me onto the counter. He pulled my knees apart before he stripped off his jacket then dropped his slacks. He unbuttoned his shirt and loosened his tie as he held my gaze. "There will never be more. You had me, but you betrayed me. You don't get to sleep with me anymore."

"I'm not asking you to love me, Cato. I'm not asking you for something unreasonable. I just want you on some nights."

"Why?" He scooted me to the edge of the counter then placed one leg over his shoulder.

I slid my arm behind me to support myself while my other hand gripped his shoulder. I felt him push inside me, feeling my wetness even though I had just been angry with him. I felt his thick inches slide deep inside me, exactly where it belonged. "Because you make me feel safe."

14

Cato

She'd asked me for a sacrifice I couldn't make.

Even if I wanted to.

It was the distance I needed not to get wrapped around her finger—more than I already was. It was the only protection I had, the only way to keep her from getting under my skin. The second we started sleeping together, everything would change. There would be no reason for her to have her own room at all.

And then everything would get complicated.

Not that it wasn't already complicated.

I knew I was in trouble when Bates asked me to promise to kill her—and I couldn't make that promise.

Deep trouble.

I'd just stepped out of the conference room when Giovanni walked up to me. "What is it?"

"This may be redundant, but your mother is here to see you, sir." He stepped out of the way and presented my mother, who wore white slacks and a blue blouse. Her short hair was curled, and her diamond necklace sparkled around her neck.

Having my mother drop by was the last thing I needed. "Mother, nice to see you." I tried to cover my surprise as I kissed her on the cheek.

"Since you haven't called, I thought I would drop by." She smiled at Giovanni. "Thanks so much for hunting down my son." She smiled and watched him walk away. "Giovanni is so wonderful. I always look forward to seeing him."

"Yeah, he's great," I said quickly. "You know, today isn't really the best day for me—"

"You can't even have a quick lunch?" she asked incredulously. "You have to eat sometime."

I skipped lunch most of the time, actually. "It would be easier if we just rescheduled."

"Well, I'll just eat with Siena. She's the reason I'm here anyway."

Of course she was. I didn't want my mother and Siena to spend any time together, but since Bates had sold me out, it couldn't be avoided. I wanted to threaten Siena to keep her mouth shut, but I had no way to enforce it. I'd promised I wouldn't hurt her, so there was nothing I could do.

"It's a nice day today," she said. "A little cool, but there's still just a bit of summer left. I'll ask Giovanni to prepare our lunch on the patio." She walked into my kitchen and helped herself to my staff like she owned the place. My mother had never crossed the line like this before, and I knew she was being pushy because I was being secretive. If she didn't take control, she wouldn't get what she wanted. She wasn't wrong about that.

I called Bates as I headed upstairs. "You're going to have to make do without me today."

"Why?" he demanded.

"Mother stopped by, and she wants to have lunch with Siena. I can't let them be alone together."

"Oh…that's rough. You know what would fix your problem?" he asked sarcastically. "If you killed her." He hung up.

I shoved the phone into my pocket and walked into her room. She sat on the couch with a stack of baby books in front of her. Covering diapers to adolescents, she was reading everything she could about raising a child—like she would live long enough to do it.

She was wasting her time. "My mother is here."

She shut the book and looked up at me. "Right now?"

"Stopped and invited herself to lunch—us included."

Siena grinned. "I like her already. It's nice to see a woman walk all over you."

Siena walked all over me too—she just didn't realize it. "Get dressed and let's go."

"Get dressed?" She stood up, wearing jeans and a blouse. "What's wrong with what I'm wearing?"

"I just thought you'd want to dress nicer to meet my mother."

"When she stopped by unannounced?" she asked incredulously. "No, I'm not putting in the effort."

I dropped the argument because I couldn't force Siena to change. I didn't think she looked bad. I just didn't think she looked wealthy, like a mirror image of myself. "Alright."

We left her bedroom then headed to the patio outside to join my mother.

"Anything I should know?" she asked as she walked beside me.

"She knows we aren't seeing each other. You're living with me because you need help with the pregnancy."

"But we are seeing each other."

"We're fucking—not the same thing."

When we stepped outside, my mother pulled off her sunglasses and rose to her feet. She smiled wide, and her blue eyes were bright with excitement. Her gaze was reserved for Siena. "It's so lovely to meet you, Siena." Instead of giving her a polite handshake, my mother wrapped her arms around her. "You have no idea how happy I am. Ever since my son told me the news, it's all I've been thinking about. I've wanted a grandchild for the last decade. I was afraid neither one of my sons would give that to me." She pulled away and cupped Siena's face. "My god, you're gorgeous. I knew you would be, but you exceeded my expectations."

I could tell Siena was a little overwhelmed by my mother's warmth. Even I was surprised. My mother had always been affectionate with me, but she had never been over the top like she was now.

"Thank you so much," Siena said. "You're very sweet."

My mother looked at her stomach. "You don't look pregnant, but it's exciting knowing that you are. These next six or seven months will go by so fast. You'll get more comfortable by the day, but trust me, it's worth it."

Siena placed her hand over her stomach. "Thanks for the advice."

"Excuse me, I haven't introduced myself. I'm Chiara."

"It's lovely to meet you, Chiara."

"The pleasure is mine, dear." Mother sat down and slid her sunglasses back on.

I pulled out the chair for Siena.

She almost rolled her eyes at me before she sat.

I moved to the other chair.

"It's nice to see my son behave like a gentleman," Chiara said.

"I am a gentleman, Mother."

Siena let out a slight laugh. "Yeah, okay."

I narrowed my eyes.

Mother turned to Siena, a smile on her face. "I'm not an idiot. I know my son has an ego that's bigger than a blimp. He thinks the world revolves around him until someone teaches him that it does not."

"Thanks, Mother," I said sarcastically.

"I thought you were too busy to join us." She turned to me, her passive-aggressive tactics kicking in. She was clearly angry with me for not calling her—a second time.

"I cleared my schedule." I kept my eyes on Siena, hoping she would behave herself so I wouldn't have to intervene.

Siena turned to my mother. "You're right. Cato can be very difficult. He's set in his ways and rarely changes his mind."

I felt like she had my balls in her hand.

"But I've also learned that he's honest, protective, and has the biggest heart I've ever seen," Siena added. "You just have to get past that cold exterior to see the warmth underneath. It takes a while to see it…but it's there."

Mother smiled before she turned back to me. "Seems like she knows the good and the bad."

"I know the good and the bad too," I countered.

"There's no bad," Siena said. "Cato even told me I was perfect."

Fuck, I did say that.

"If she's perfect, then why aren't you together?" Mother asked.

I didn't appreciate the personal question. "That's between Siena and me. We're having this baby together, but we're just friends."

Mother turned to Siena. "Tell me the real reason my

son wouldn't want to be with a stunning woman who's not afraid of him?"

This lunch was turning into a nightmare. My mother was the one person who could do whatever she wanted without retaliation. If she were Bates, I would slap her upside the head.

Siena shrugged. "It was an unplanned pregnancy, and he's not looking for a wife."

"A wife is exactly what he needs," Mother said. "I see all those pictures of him online and in the tabloids. Always out with those stupid bimbos that are just waiting to get their hands on his money."

"Mother." I didn't want this to go on any longer. Maybe I was her son, but discussing my personal life so candidly was inappropriate. "You barged in here and demanded to have lunch without being invited. You've been rude enough for the day. So stop insulting me and play nice." I didn't want to be disrespectful to my mother, but I didn't let anyone talk to me like that.

Mother turned to Siena and rolled her eyes.

Siena laughed back.

I grabbed the glass of wine and took a drink. "Fuck."

———

THE TWO OF them talked about wine, art, and their love of the countryside. They seemed to get along well, better than my mother and I ever did. I spent most of the time in silence, looking over the landscape of my backyard and thinking about work.

My mother mentioned my father. "Cato's father left us when he was very young. It was hard on the boys, not just growing up without a father, but knowing they'd been abandoned. I'm proud of my son for not being that way, for standing by you even though this was unplanned."

It was a compliment, but I didn't acknowledge it since it wasn't directly said to me.

"Cato will be a great father," Siena said. "I've never been worried about that. He's very loyal to you and his brother. In fact, one of the reasons I fell for him in the first place is because of the way he talks about you. There's so much pride in his voice, that you raised him on your own and did such a great job."

Mother slowly turned to me, a slight smile on her lips with emotion in her eyes. Her hand reached to mine on the table. "Honey…" She squeezed my hand.

I squeezed it back.

"I love you," she whispered. "You've been my greatest joy."

"I love you too, Mother."

She smiled then released my hand.

Siena gave me a different look than she ever had before. She was full of emotion and affection, and it seemed like that moment meant as much to her as it did to us.

"Excuse me," I said as I rose from the table. "I need to make a phone call." I stepped inside the house but left the door open. I called Bates, but it rang and went to voice mail.

Mother's voice reached my ears. "You love my son. It's written all over your face."

Siena said nothing, letting the silence linger. It seemed to go on forever before she addressed it. "I have a lot of respect for him. He's a good man…even though he tries so hard to hide it. He always makes me feel safe, like everything is going to be okay even when it doesn't seem that way."

Mother waited a few seconds before she responded. "I can tell he loves you too. When a man looks at a woman like that, everyone in the room can see it. I'm not sure what your problems are, but put them aside and work it out—and not just for the baby."

———

MY MOTHER FINALLY LEFT, relieving the stress from my shoulders.

That lunch didn't go well, but it didn't go as badly as I'd thought it would.

Siena and I walked into her bedroom when my mother was gone. "Your mother is lovely. She reminds me of my mom."

"You mean, she runs her mouth and speaks her mind?"

"Yep." She slipped off her shoes then sat on the couch.

"I'm surprised you didn't run your mouth."

"What's that supposed to mean?"

I sat beside her and wondered if it would be stupid to mention it. "You could have told her the truth. No one in the world besides my mother can dictate my actions."

"I thought about it." Her smile died away when the conversation turned serious. "Judging from her personality, she would never allow you to do such a thing. She wouldn't have to raise her hand or her voice. Guilt would be enough. But then I changed my mind."

"Why?" Since I'd compromised with her, was she being more cooperative?

"Because I know you won't do it." She held my gaze with sincerity in her eyes. "I know your heart, Cato. It's too big to do something that terrible. Your need for revenge isn't nearly as important as your need to protect your child's mother. And not even just that…but because you care about me. So why tell her any of it when I believe in you? I want to prove that I believe in you."

It was the first time someone had ever said something that left me speechless. I didn't have a single response to that, any kind of coherent thought. She made me feel like shit and made me feel good at the exact same time.

"You're angry with me because I betrayed you. It would be easy for me to ruin everything by confiding in your mother. I could destroy your pristine reputation and hurt your relationship. But I won't. I could betray you again, but I don't. I hope that makes up for what I did—by not ratting on you. And I'm gambling my life to do it."

I couldn't look at her because it was such a deep wound. It was difficult for me to feel guilty about anything when I didn't have a soul. But I certainly felt guilty about this. "Siena...that makes me feel like shit. And it makes me feel worse because it won't change the outcome."

Her eyes fell in sadness. "I still believe in you, Cato. Even if you don't believe in yourself."

15

Siena

His mother was a breath of fresh air. She was funny, real, and she put Cato in his place just the way I did.

And she really did remind me of my mother.

I considered telling her the danger I was in, but I thought proving my loyalty to Cato would soften his resolve.

It didn't seem to do anything.

Now I didn't know what to do.

Maybe I did need to run away.

Now that I had permission to see my brother, I wanted to take advantage of it. I walked down the hall to Cato's bedroom later that week and let myself inside without knocking. I'd picked the perfect time to barge in because he stepped into the bedroom with just a towel wrapped around his waist.

"I don't have to knock," he barked. "But you do."

"This is a two-way street." I tilted my head as I examined him up and down, his perfect physique impossible to ignore—especially with those little drops of water. "And I really like this street."

The corner of his mouth rose in a smile. "Then you're about to like it even more." He dropped the towel and tossed it over the back of the armchair.

Even when he was limp, he was still beautiful. I whistled under my breath.

He walked up to me and gripped me around the waist. As if the last conversation we had wasn't at all difficult, he kissed me on the corner of the mouth before he stepped away. "I have a phone meeting in ten minutes. Otherwise, your face would be down and your ass would be up."

"Maybe later."

"Definitely later."

I continued to stand there.

He pulled his jeans and t-shirt out of the closet. "Something you needed?"

I hated the way I was about to phrase this, but I had to suck up my pride and just do it. "I was wondering if Landon could come over for lunch? It looks like you're going to be here today."

He pulled on his boxers without giving any distinct reaction. "He can stay for two hours. But that's it. He'll pass through two security checkpoints before getting access to the house. If he has even a pocket knife, I'll shoot him on sight. You got it?"

That didn't surprise me at all. "That's fine."

"Then have a good time."

I felt the gratitude surge inside my stomach and I didn't want let it out, but it was impossible to keep bottled up. "Thank you…" I looked forward to seeing my brother. We hadn't been close, but now that he was all I had, I wanted to deepen our connection. Being with him made me calm, made me feel like everything would be okay.

———

I STOOD in the open doorway and watched Landon go through the second security check. The first one had been thorough, but the second one was excessive. Cato's security removed Landon's shirt and his jeans and made him stand in his boxers and shoes. Then they examined every inch of his clothing and even patted down his bare skin, like he might have sewn a weapon inside his body.

Landon shook his head. "I'm not even that hungry."

They finally handed his clothes back to him, and he got dressed. He walked up the stairs and greeted me. "I hope I don't have to get naked every time I come for a visit."

"That makes two of us." I wrapped my arms around him and squeezed him. "I'm so happy to see you." I pressed my cheek into his chest and sighed happily. It was so nice to see his face in my prison. It made me feel less alone and made the place feel more like home.

He patted me on the back then stepped out of my embrace. "If you weren't my sister, I wouldn't have made the drive out here and put up with all those assholes trying to take my clothes off."

"But you did," I said with a smile. "Because you love me."

He shrugged. "I wouldn't go that far…"

I took Landon into the kitchen where Giovanni had prepared lunch. Landon's eyes wandered as he took in the three-story mansion that Cato occupied alone. It was more of a hotel than a residence.

Giovanni had the dishes set on the counter. "Lunch is ready, Miss Siena."

"Great. It smells delicious." I turned to my brother. "Giovanni, this is my brother Landon. Landon, this is my favorite person in this house. He makes the best food, and he's so cute."

Giovanni's cheeks reddened. "Pleasure to meet you,

sir." Giovanni gave a slight bow. "Your sister has been a breath of fresh air to this house."

"With that gargoyle Cato living here, that doesn't surprise me." Landon shook his hand. "I'm glad my sister has a friend."

Giovanni led us outside to the table on the terrace. The weather was cooling down because fall was knocking on the door, but the weather was still lovely. "Take a seat. I'll return with refreshments and lunch."

Landon sat across from me under the umbrella. He examined the exceptional landscaping and the acres of grass that extended into the distance. "This place is enormous."

"I know."

"And he's got security everywhere."

"I know that too." There was no way in or out of this place unless Cato allowed it.

"I have to say, it's not a bad place to be a prisoner." He leaned back against the wrought-iron chair with his hands held together at his stomach. "Besides, the security trying to get you naked all the time."

"Thankfully, they've never done that to me." Only Cato and Bates had.

"Just the psychopath keeping you here," he said bitterly.

"Yeah…"

Giovanni set the water and iced tea on the table along with the sliced bread, cheese, and grapes. Then he placed our entrees in front of us, salad with grilled salmon and lemon wedges. "The iced tea is decaf, Miss Siena."

"I figured it was."

Giovanni returned inside the house and shut the door.

Landon watched him go before he turned back to me. "I need to get a butler."

"You could never afford someone like Giovanni. Your best bet is a good woman who's willing to put up with you."

"No such thing. I don't let women stick around long enough to see how much of an asshole I am. They see the charming guy I am, and before that runs out, they're gone."

"How romantic…"

"It's for their benefit, trust me."

"Because you're so unlikeable?" I smeared the cheese onto a slice of bread. Then I added a drop of honey.

Landon grabbed his fork and went straight for the salmon. "You know I'm an ass."

"How about you just stop being an ass?"

"You make it sound so easy. Like I can just turn it off."

"Well, you'd better. You aren't rich anymore, so it's not like a woman is gonna put up with you."

"But I'm good-looking." He waggled his eyebrows. "And that's more important than money."

I rolled my eyes.

He wore a black t-shirt that hugged his muscular arms. Black ink was down his left arm, reaching all the way to his wrist. He looked similar to Father, but he'd also inherited Mother's features as well. "How's the kid?"

"Doing well, I assume. Other than the morning sickness, I don't feel pregnant."

"I can kinda tell. You're a little thicker around the middle."

"You never say that to a pregnant woman, Landon."

"What?" he asked innocently. "It doesn't look bad."

"Still not a compliment."

"Coming from me, that's the best compliment you're going to get." He ate more of his food, stuffing his mouth and chewing quickly. "Damn, this is good. That guy knows how to cook."

"Yes, he's the best of the best. Maybe the weight gain you've noticed isn't from the baby at all."

"Judging by how quickly you're stuffing your face, you might be right."

I threw a piece of bread at his face.

He let it bounce off his cheek before he kept eating.

We spent the next few minutes eating in silence as we enjoyed the sunshine. There was a slight breeze in the air that played with my hair. The humidity had died down so it was starting to feel crisp.

Landon ate everything off his plate then wiped his mouth with a napkin. "I haven't had a meal like that in a long time."

"Aren't you crashing with some woman?"

"Yeah, but she doesn't cook. I eat out most of the time."

"And who is she?"

"No one." He drank his iced tea. "She's just giving me a place to crash in exchange for good sex. It's a win-win for both of us. I'll probably be leaving soon. Just need to find the next place to go."

"You have money saved, so what are you waiting for?"

"Trying to lay low. I'm sure Damien is still looking for me."

"I'll ask Cato to tell them to grant you immunity."

He cocked his head. "And why would Cato do that?"

"Because I asked him to." He usually did anything I asked him to do, if it was that important to me.

"And I don't see why Damien and Micah would agree."

"Cato can be very persuasive." Cato could make anything happen because he had all the power. Since annihilating the Siberians after they tried to steal his money, Cato had probably reminded everyone in the underworld that he was at the top of the food chain.

"So what's going on with you two?"

I preferred to speak in person because my cell phone was being screened. I couldn't share any secrets with Landon over the phone—not if I wanted them to stay secrets. Talking in person was the only way to ensure we weren't overheard. But I wondered if Cato could hear me anyway, if there was a cracked window somewhere. My eyes scanned the side of the house, but I didn't detect anything abnormal. "We have a relationship, but he still claims that he'll kill me."

"Do you believe him?"

I found it hard to believe that Cato could kill me after the deep bond that had formed between us. I knew I wasn't the only one who felt that pull, that magnetic energy. We weren't just lovers, but something deeper than that. If he ever lost me, he wouldn't brush it off the way he brushed off his other murders. "No. But…I could be wrong. The other night, this organization tried to steal almost three hundred million dollars from him. His men destroyed the group and then brought the people in charge to the house. He executed each one…including a woman."

"What does it matter that she was a woman?" he asked. "Women are criminals and murderers too."

"She cried as she begged for her life."

"Trust me, men do that too."

"I just…it made me realize that could be me. He killed her, so why wouldn't he kill me? He was barbaric and shot five people to their deaths, letting their blood drain into his fountain. Sometimes I forget who Cato really is…what he's capable of."

"He's a stone-cold killer."

"And he cares about his reputation more than anything else."

"Reputation is important," Landon said. "It precedes you in every room you walk into. It dictates the way people treat you. It keeps the monsters in line. Without a powerful reputation, you have nothing."

"Which is why I think it's possible he might do it…"

Landon gave me a look of pity. "You know I would get you out of here if I could. But there's nothing I can do."

"I know, Landon. I would never ask you to rescue me. Now that I'm under his thumb, there's nothing anyone can do for me. The only person who can get me out of here is Cato himself, but he won't."

His eyes fell in sadness. "Does he treat you well?"

With the exception of a few setbacks, my life had been comfortable. "He's very good to me. There are a couple things I dislike about him, but other than that, I really like Cato. He's gentle, kind, and affectionate. When I'm with him, it's easy to forget he's a crime lord. He seems like a man…like a normal person."

Landon's elbows rested on the armrests, and his hands came together. My brother watched me with sympathetic eyes, like he really wished my situation were different. Landon wasn't affectionate, just the way my father was. He failed to express his emotions even at the most critical moments. He was withdrawn and cold, unable to speak his mind. So he turned quiet now, unsure what to say in response.

"But the more I think about it, the more I think I can't stay here. If he is going to kill me, then I may as well run for it. At least right now, he can't hurt me, not while I'm pregnant. And the longer I wait, the harder it'll be for me to get around."

Landon shook his head slightly. "If the Siberians

couldn't take down Cato, you think you're going to outsmart him by yourself?"

I shrugged. "I have to try."

"You wouldn't make it very far."

"Not unless he doesn't know I'm missing for a few hours. That would give me the head start I need. Even if he doesn't kill me, I don't want my child to grow up like this. I don't want my child to look out the window and watch his father execute people. My child will be the number one target of Cato's enemies, and I don't want that either."

"And you think you can not only get away, but manage to live the rest of your life without him finding you?" he asked incredulously. "This isn't some abusive boyfriend you can run away from. This guy has every resource in the world to hunt you down."

"If I change my name and live off cash, how will he find me?"

My brother shrugged. "There are ways."

"I'll go somewhere really remote, somewhere he won't think of."

"Like?"

"Iceland or something."

"That is pretty remote," he said in agreement. "But even if he doesn't find you right away, he will find you. That's a given."

"I have to try, Landon. I owe it to myself and my baby. You know me. When do I ever give up?"

He gave a slight nod. "You don't."

"And that's not going to change now."

He sat forward and rested his arms on the table, his hands coming together. He looked across the terrace and to the perfectly manicured gardens as he spoke. "This guy fetched Father and buried him for us. He takes cares of you. Cato Marino isn't the kind of guy to go soft like that…not for anyone. I think you're better off staying here and hoping he changes his mind."

"Every time I ask him, he says he's going to do it. That he has to do it."

"But if you run and he catches you…then he'll definitely do it."

Now that I was pregnant, my priorities had changed. I wanted the best for my child, and the best was not staying here. If Cato really did kill me, that would be an even greater disadvantage to my baby. The only parent they would know was a cruel and terrifying man. They needed a mother to balance it out. "Cato makes me feel safe…but he also terrifies me. He's capable of anything. I've made up my mind, Landon. I'm leaving."

He turned his gaze back to mine, a hint of disappointment in his eyes. "Then I'll help you."

"I'm not asking for your help."

"You can't do this alone."

"And if I get caught, he'll kill you."

He shrugged. "I would rather die trying to protect my sister and my niece or nephew than do nothing. The world is a scary place, and I know you're strong, but you shouldn't do this on your own. I can protect you from the evil things that will cross your path. I may not be able to protect you from Cato…but I can handle anything else."

"Landon…" I knew my brother loved me, but I didn't expect such a selfless gesture. "Are you sure?"

He held my gaze. "Absolutely. We'll just have to think of a good plan. Cato will need to be at work for most of the day to make it work. You'll need to get off the property somehow, but there's no coming or going without security checks. There's no way you could just walk out of here and jump the wall."

"No."

"Does anyone come and go without being vetted?"

I stared at my plate of half-eaten food. "No. Even the staff does the same security checks. The only person who actually lives here is Giovanni…" My eyes focused on the pink fillet in front of me, and that's when an idea hit me. "Giovanni goes to the store every day…he says he only uses the freshest ingredients for all his meals."

"Your point?"

"He's the only person who leaves without being checked. He has his own car."

Landon rubbed his hand across his chin. "I think you're onto something. Is his car in the garage?"

"It must be. There are never cars in the roundabout, except the one that picks up Cato and drops him off." My heart started to beat with excitement. This plan just might work. There was a possibility I could fool Cato and get out of there without him noticing for eight hours.

"If you could get into the trunk before he leaves, this could happen. When he puts the groceries in the back, you could kill him. I'll be waiting for you, so you'll hop into my car and we'll take off."

"Whoa, back up." I held up my hand. "I'm not killing Giovanni."

"If he lives here, then Cato trusts him the most. He's the person you need to be most concerned about. If you just knock him out, he'll only be unconscious for a few hours. Then he'll call Cato. We need as much time as possible."

I didn't care how necessary it was. "Landon, let me save you some time. I won't do it."

Landon sighed like a bull, his nostrils flaring.

"I'll tie him up and leave him in the back seat of the car. When Cato gets home, he'll realize Giovanni is missing. When he does, the grocery store is the first place he'll look. Problem solved."

"Unless someone sees you tie up an old man."

"He probably goes to the store in the morning, so there won't be many witnesses."

"This is still a bad idea."

"And you think killing him will be less obvious?" I snapped.

"I don't know, alright? But we have to make sure we do this right. This is the most critical step in the entire plan."

"Giovanni and I have a good relationship. I'm sure he'll understand—"

"You can't trust him, Siena. He's loyal to the man who pays his bills, not you."

"But he's very fond of me."

"Doesn't matter," he said. "You aren't paying his bills. He may not want to rat you out, but he will. Losing his life over you isn't worth it. This is about survival. Do what you have to do. He'll do what he has to do."

I knew I had to escape, and that meant I couldn't let Giovanni ruin my plan. If I had to tie him up in the back seat and cover him with a blanket, I would. If I told him what was going on, he probably wouldn't struggle. And under no circumstances would I kill him. There were some people I would murder in a heartbeat—like Damien. But Giovanni was too good to be the victim of a bad situation. "Alright.

"Do you know Cato's schedule?"

"No. He's all over the place. But even if he is home, he doesn't visit me until after two."

"But if Giovanni doesn't return by lunchtime, he'll know something is wrong."

"Yeah…"

"You'll have to make sure you do it on a day he'll be in Florence."

"I agree."

"Wait until that moment comes. When it does, leave everything behind. It'll be too suspicious if you're walking around the house with a bag. Text me and ask me if I want to come over for lunch the next day. That will be your code to me that the plan is happening. I'll wait for you at the grocery store. I won't text back just in case your phone goes off."

"Okay." God, this was really happening. I was really going to make a run for it. Like a lamb, I was going to run from the big bad wolf and hope he didn't catch me. If this plan worked out smoothly, I might have a real chance.

Or it may be only a matter of time before he caught up with me.

It could be weeks. Months. Or it could be hours.

I was about to find out.

16

Cato

I SAT IN MY LIVING ROOM GOING OVER PAPERWORK ON my lap. Ever since that shit with the Siberians happened, business had picked up. People respected the way I handled my enemies, and they also respected the way I protected my money. If men wanted to keep their money safe, putting it in my hands was the best decision.

Because I was the only one with enough balls to protect it.

The TV was on in the background, but I didn't pay attention to it. The news was on, and of course, the media only reported the boring crimes and homicides they were allowed to cover. The heavy shit never made it on the news —unless they wanted to die.

My bedroom door opened and closed, and I knew exactly who it was. I didn't look up from my paperwork. "Need something?"

She came up behind me and rested her hands on my shoulders. Her nails playfully dug into my skin before her hands slid down my chest and to my stomach. She leaned over and kissed me on the neck, her lips grazing my ear with sexy breaths.

I had shit to do, but once this woman was on me, I stopped caring.

Her hands moved all the way down to my hardening cock and back up again. "Fuck me, Cato." She kissed my neck and pulled her hands from my chest. "I'll be waiting." She walked out of the living room, her footsteps growing fainter as she reached the bed. Clothes hit the floor, and then the mattress shifted under her weight.

I stared at the papers and read the same sentence five times.

All I could think about was that naked woman in my bed—and the sexy words she'd just whispered in my ear. I tossed the papers aside and headed to the bed, unprepared for what I was about to witness.

Her legs were spread, and her fingers worked her clit. Naked in my bed with her hair across my pillow, she'd gotten started without me. Maybe those pregnancy hormones were really kicking in.

I watched her touch herself as I dropped my sweat-pants and boxers, my cock harder than I'd ever been. My fingers wrapped around my length, and I gently stroked myself, watching her rub her clit harder. "Can I join you, baby?"

She opened her eyes and looked at me, her fingers still working her nub. "Please." She spoke in a husky voice, so sultry, like a cloud of smoke.

My knees hit the mattress, and I moved on top of her, our bodies melding together instantly. She widened her legs for my arms to lock into my place, and then she stuck her fingers in my mouth so I could taste her.

I sucked everything off, tasting her delicious pussy.

She drew her fingers away and pulled my face to hers.

She kissed me softly, her lips trembling for a moment before she continued the embrace. Her hand started at my cheek then slid into my hair.

My crown found her entrance like it had a mind of its own, and I slid inside her, pushing through the slickness and tightness until I was balls deep in that pussy. My pussy. Our kiss continued as my dick twitched inside her. "Baby…" I couldn't imagine taking another woman after having this. It wasn't just the skin-on-skin sensation. It was also those kisses she gave me, packed with so much passion that she burned me. It was the soft way she touched me, the way she trembled as she enjoyed me. And she was so wet between her legs there was no doubt she truly wanted me, wanted me more than any other woman had. She pissed me off with her stubbornness, but it also made me want her more. She stood up to me when no one else did, not even my brother. She made me better, made me harder, but also made me softer.

I thrust into her as I kept our kiss going, melting inside her perfect cunt.

She gripped my biceps and breathed into my mouth. "I want it slow tonight."

I slowed my pace and gently moved inside her, savoring the buildup of cream on my shaft. I pushed completely inside her and felt the moisture gather on my balls. She was so wet that it leaked between her cheeks and stained my sheets.

Fucking her was the best.

I didn't even mind taking it slow.

She sucked my bottom lip and moaned when I hit her in the right spot. It wasn't hard to make her come. It usually only took a few minutes before I could make her pussy explode around my dick. Her moans grew louder during our kisses, slowly building up until she hit the crescendo. "Cato…yes." She stopped kissing me altogether because she couldn't focus. All she could do was lie there and feel the goodness between her legs. She clawed at me with the nails of a cat and slathered me in even more moisture.

I watched her come around me, watched her reactions match the explosion between her legs. She was the most beautiful woman I'd ever had in my bed, the best pussy my dick had ever met, and I wanted to stay buried inside her forever. I wanted to make this last longer, but this angle felt so good. I loved being on top of her, her legs spread to me, and watching the fireworks go off in her eyes. Seeing her get off on me made me want to get off too.

And I did. With a few pumps, I exploded inside her, dropping a load that would overflow and leak down her ass. "Baby…fuck." Every orgasm was amazing with this woman. She didn't even need to do anything. I could do all the work and be content with that.

She kissed me again as she felt my dick and come deep inside her. "Again."

———

AN HOUR LATER, our fucking finished.

I lay in bed ready to go to sleep, and she got up. She pulled on the robe she'd been wearing and covered herself up. She picked up her panties and tossed them on my pillow. "A gift for you."

I grinned. "Thank you."

"No, thank you." She leaned over me and kissed me on the mouth. "Good night."

"Night." I was surprised she didn't try to sleep with me anymore. Seemed like she'd given up on it.

When she reached the door, she turned around. "Do you have any plans tomorrow?"

I had a packed schedule, from morning to night. "Why?"

"I was wondering if we could go shopping for the baby."

"I can pay someone to do that."

She shook her head slightly. "I want to do that, Cato. So, are you free?"

"Not tomorrow. I'm going to be in Florence all day."

Like that meant something to her, she nodded slowly. "How about the next day?"

"I think I can take the afternoon off."

"Good." She smiled. "We'll do it then."

"Alright."

She lingered by the door, staring at me for several seconds.

"What?"

She suddenly turned away. "Nothing. Sleep well."

17

Siena

NOW WAS MY BEST CHANCE.

Cato would be in Florence all day.

He would probably be too busy to intervene when his staff told him Giovanni was missing.

The next morning, I woke up early, shoved the kitchen twine I'd found in the pantry into my pocket, and pressed my ear against my door. I listened for all the noises, waiting for an indication Cato had left. Thirty minutes later, I heard him go downstairs and exchange a few words with one of his guys. Then he left.

I knew Giovanni had already made breakfast, so I hoped I wasn't too late. He might have already left for the store.

I tiptoed into the kitchen and saw him standing over the sink, washing all the dishes and pans he'd used to prepare breakfast for Cato that morning. As careful as I could, I silently moved across the tile and grabbed all the car keys hanging by the door. Then I stepped into the garage and saw five cars tucked away.

Four of them were fancy cars, Bugattis and Ferraris.

One was a Volkswagen.

That had to belong to Giovanni.

I clicked the button and opened the trunk. Then I cracked the door and hung up the keys before I snuck back into the garage. The trunk was wide open, so I lay down then took a deep breath. Once I shut that trunk, I would be stuck in there until Giovanni opened it. If he didn't go to the store that morning, I could be in there for a few days. Thankfully, there were a few water bottles in there with me. I steeled my nerves and shut the trunk.

I texted Landon. *We're going shopping for the baby tomorrow. Do you want to come with us?*

Then I waited.

————

AN HOUR LATER, Giovanni started the engine and pulled out of the garage.

This was really happening.

Now there was no turning back. I couldn't change my mind because it was obvious what my intentions were. Giovanni would tell Cato he'd discovered me in his trunk, and there was no excuse I could give that would justify my behavior.

I hoped this plan worked, but a part of me hoped it didn't.

Leaving Cato was harder than I thought.

I said goodbye to him in the best way I could, by going into his room and having a passionate night. It was slow, tender, and so good. I wanted to treasure him one last time before he moved on to someone else, but it just made me want to leave less. It destroyed my resolve and made me weak.

I knew I would miss him.

This was the right thing for the baby and me, but I would still miss that man deeply. A part of me hoped I would have a son who looked just like him, so I could look into his face and see Cato every day. I knew I would never find a man I felt so passionate about, not after being with Cato. Maybe I would fall in love someday, but Cato would always be the man I wondered about.

It was a bumpy ride to the store, and I tried not to move to attract Giovanni's attention. Thirty minutes later, the car slowed and then parked. The engine was turned off, and then everything was still.

I wanted to text Landon, but since my phone was bugged, I couldn't.

I just had to keep waiting.

Thirty minutes later, I heard footsteps approach the trunk. A beep sounded from the pressing a button, and then the trunk opened. Giovanni didn't notice me right away because he'd turned back to the cart to begin unloading.

I jumped out of the trunk as quickly as I could before he could shut it again.

"Siena—"

"We can do this the easy way or the hard way. I don't want to hurt you, so I just need you to lie in the back seat and let me tie rope around your wrists."

Stunned, he just stared at me like he couldn't believe the reality right in front of him. "You're leaving Mr. Marino?"

I nodded. "I have to. He killed those five people right in the driveway. I don't want him to do that to me too. So…get in the back seat." I pulled the twine from my pocket and hoped he would be cooperative.

He sighed quietly before he gave a nod. "I suppose it makes it easier this way. I feel obligated to tell Mr. Marino what happened, even if I do want you to be safe. At least this way, I can keep my ethics and allow you to run at the same time." He grabbed the groceries from the cart and loaded them into the trunk.

"You aren't going to talk me out of it?" I asked in surprise.

"No. Humans will do extraordinary things to survive and protect their child. That's exactly what you're doing, and I can't blame you." He shut the trunk then gave me a weak smile. "I know Mr. Marino is dangerous. In my heart, I know he wouldn't hurt you. But my heart has been wrong before…" He pushed the cart back to the retrieval area then sat in the back seat.

I moved beside him and tied the rope around his wrists.

"But I should warn you, Mr. Marino has more power than you can imagine. I don't think you'll be free very long before he finds you. And when he does…he may not be so forgiving. He'll see it as a betrayal."

I nodded. "I have to try, Giovanni."

"Then good luck to you." He smiled at me. "I hope everything works out."

"Thanks for everything. You were my favorite thing about living there."

Like always, his cheeks reddened. "And you were mine."

His hands were tied, but I hugged him anyway. "I'll miss you." I kissed him on the cheek, and before I could get too emotional, I left the keys beside him and exited the car. The second I started to look for Landon, I found him.

He stood outside his black SUV, dressed in all black.

I crossed the parking lot and moved into his chest for a hug.

"That was the easy part. Now comes the hard part."

18

Cato

BATES AND I HAD A LONG MEETING WITH A GROUP OF investors that shoveled money into our bank. They hid their wealth from their respective governments, and then we, in turn, invested that money into various stocks. We split the profits down the middle. They made money off invisible money, tax-free. And we made money doing almost nothing.

But talking about money seemed to last forever.

Siena's words kept haunting me. I was a very successful man, but I didn't have much to show for it. I only had a few friends, but they were just guys I went out drinking with. There was nothing real there. Bates was my brother, but I wouldn't consider him to be a friend. Instead of building relationships with other people, I just stacked my cash higher and higher. Now it seemed repetitive and boring. I'd been feeling that way for a long time, and the emptiness never wore off.

Siena was right about me.

I had nothing.

My phone rang in my pocket, and I glanced at the

screen to see it was one of my security guys. They were always giving me updates, so I ignored it. I returned my attention to Mr. Howard, who discussed inviting more of his colleagues to participate in this move.

My phone rang again. It was the same person on the other line, so I took it. "Excuse me, I have to take this." I cut off Mr. Howard and pressed the phone to my ear. "What is it? I'm in the middle of a meeting right now."

"I apologize, sir."

"Don't apologize. Justify disturbing me. What's so important?"

"Giovanni, sir. He left hours ago and hasn't returned."

I rose from the chair and let myself out of the conference room.

Bates gave me an irritated look, but he resumed the meeting without me.

The second the door was shut, I screamed into the phone. "You interrupted me to tell me that? That he's been gone for a few hours? Are you fucking kidding me? The man has a life. Maybe he's fucking someone."

He kept a steady voice even though he probably wanted to shit himself. "We've tried calling him many times. He's not answering."

"You tend not to answer the phone when you're fucking someone. Don't bother me with this nonsense again." I hung up and walked back into the conference room.

———

HOURS LATER, the snoozefest finally ended.

We all shook hands, and the suits left the office.

Bates immediately broke out the scotch. "Jesus, that was boring. At least it's going to make us a ton of money."

"Like we don't have enough."

"No such thing as too much money." He poured two glasses and handed me one.

"But there is such thing as enough. We have enough, Bates. It doesn't really matter at this point." I took a long drink then looked out the window. It was getting darker earlier, so I watched the sunset begin.

Bates sat down and looked at me like I was crazy. "What's your deal? Do you have any idea how lucky we are?"

"No, we aren't lucky," I said coldly. "We worked our asses off. Don't say lucky ever again."

"You know what I mean. We have everything. You should be happy."

I'd never been happy my entire life, with the exception of a few instances. Just last night I'd fucked Siena in a way I hadn't before. She'd asked for it to be nice and slow, and normally, I would overrule her and fuck her hard like I wanted. But I gave in this time…and I liked it. So many women had been in that bed before her, but I couldn't imagine any afterward. I would fuck them and think about the one woman I actually wanted…the one that I had killed. She was the single ray of sunshine in my life, the only person I confided my real thoughts and feelings in. Those few happy moments I had in life always happened with her.

"We can buy anything we want. Fuck any pussy we want. We're living the dream, man."

I liked money. It was important to me. But once I knew how happy Siena was with nothing, it made me question myself. I needed things to be happy, but she needed nothing. What did that say about me?

Bates kept watching me. "This has something to do with that bitch, doesn't it?"

"Don't call her that."

He rolled his eyes. "I'll take that as a yes."

"And I felt this way before I met her."

"It's just a rut. It'll pass."

If it hadn't passed by now, it wasn't going to. It felt like there was something missing from my life, something distinct. I couldn't put my thumb on it.

"Who was on the phone earlier?"

The question brought me back to my earlier conversation. "Security told me Giovanni had been missing for a few hours. They tried calling him a couple times, but he didn't answer. But he goes to all those little villages and picks up produce, and he doesn't get reception all the time. Maybe he decided to meet someone for lunch. The guy works all the time, so if he wants to slack off a bit, it's not a big deal."

"Maybe something did happen to him. He would be an easy target."

"For what?" I asked incredulously. "Ransom? I wouldn't pay a dime for him, so that would be a waste of time. No one is stupid enough to pull a stunt like that."

"Maybe," he said with a shrug. "But I know you really would pay a lot of money for him."

"I would not."

He rolled his eyes. "Yes, you would. That guy can cook like Siena can fuck."

My hostile eyes burned into his face.

"Sorry, I just needed a comparison."

"Don't use comparisons that include Siena."

"Whatever." He put his feet on the table and drank from his glass.

My phone rang again, my security team flashing on the screen. "Did you find him?" I expected Giovanni to come home unharmed. And I also expected this guy to give me his resignation for bothering me during a meeting.

"No, sir. He still hasn't returned. When he didn't come back for a few hours, I started to get concerned. So I went into the house and looked for Siena…she's not on the property either. We checked every room in the house, every closet, and every bathroom. She's not here, sir."

My hand shook as it held the phone against my ear. I remembered the way she'd lingered in the doorway and looked at me. There was something peculiar about that stare, like she was saying goodbye to me. And she'd fucked me so slowly, it seemed like it was the last time. "I'm on my way."

———

I STORMED into the house and immediately headed to her bedroom. Everything was left as it had been. She didn't take any of her clothes and shoes. Her makeup was on the bathroom counter along with her hair products.

The only thing that was missing was the picture of the sonogram.

The picture she'd kept on her nightstand.

There was no note. No nothing.

"Siena?" I called for her even though I knew she was gone. I did it anyway, half expecting her to step off the balcony or walk out of the closet. Giovanni never would have helped her escape, so I wasn't sure what happened.

I headed back downstairs.

"You didn't find her?" Bates asked, his hands in his pockets.

I flashed him an angry look. "Let's find Giovanni. He'll have the answers."

The head of my security listened to his earpiece before

he spoke to me. "They found Giovanni in the back seat of his car at the grocery store. His wrists were bound."

I knew Siena wouldn't hurt him, but I had to ask anyway. "Is he alright?"

"Perfectly fine," he reported. "Unharmed."

I breathed a sigh of relief. Giovanni was in my house every day, serving me and making my mansion a home. We didn't have serious conversations, but I did care about him and not just because he was an excellent servant.

"He says Siena hid in the trunk of his car. When he was about to put the groceries in the back, she hopped out and forced him into the back seat."

I shook my head, furious she'd orchestrated this whole thing. She'd fucked me the night before thinking it would be the last time. She waited until I was in Florence before she made her move, thinking an eight-hour head start would be enough to get away from me.

Nothing would be enough to get away from me.

Bates turned to me, his eyes wide.

As irritated as I was, one thing was certain. She definitely had balls. She was smart enough to figure out that Giovanni was the only one who came and went without the scrutiny of security. He was also the only person with their own car. The only car in my garage that wasn't expensive was his piece of shit Volkswagen, so it was easy to figure out which was his. She pulled it off overnight, leaving everything behind except a picture of our baby. "Anything else?"

"Giovanni said she left with her brother. He picked her up in a black SUV then drove away."

Now I knew what they had discussed when he'd come over for lunch. She couldn't talk to him over the phone because I was tapping her phone. As livid as I was, I was also impressed. She pulled all this together right under my nose.

And betrayed me again.

"I have men looking through camera feeds in the general area to figure out where they went and what direction they headed," he reported. "When I have a lead, I'll let you know."

"Don't bother." I pulled my phone out of my pocket and pulled up the tracking app on the screen. "I can find her in two seconds."

"Tracking her phone?" Bates asked.

"No. She's too smart for that." When the screen opened, I saw the little red dot on the main road above Milan. They just reached the border of France. "I put a tracking device in her ankle one of the first nights she was here. Put a pregnancy-safe sedative in her drink, and she was out for a long time. Never noticed."

My brother nodded in approval. "Like that bitch could outsmart you."

I watched the little red dot move away, slowly approaching the border of Italy. She probably thought she'd accomplished her goal, that she would start over somewhere else in Europe. Or maybe she would move even farther away, to America or Canada. But little did she know, there was nowhere she could go where I wouldn't find her.

Bates rubbed his hands together greedily. "Let's hunt her down. Or we could wait until morning. Let her think she's safe a little longer."

I stared at the red dot for another moment before I closed the app. "No."

"Then when are we going to make our move?" Bates asked.

I shrugged. "If she wants to get away from me so bad,

let her. Let her see what life is like without me." Let her see what it's like to be alone, to not have me to protect her anymore. She had her brother, but he was nothing compared to me. With a growing child in her belly, every day would get more difficult. She would miss her luxurious life here, knowing nothing could ever harm her or our baby. She probably ran away because she was afraid of me, but I knew she also needed me. I knew she would miss me, that she would think about me every day as our son grew inside her. Then she would wonder if she'd made a mistake, if the life she'd chosen was really better than the one I could have given her.

Bates stood with a confused expression on his face. "You aren't going to punish her? You aren't going to go after your kid?"

"Living without me is punishment enough. As for the kid, I'll keep my eyes on him. My men will watch out for his well-being. But no, I'll let her live with her decision. And watch her suffer for it."

19

Siena

AFTER WE CROSSED INTO FRANCE, WE HEADED INTO THE countryside. It was the middle of the night, and once we entered the small town of Les Estables, we went farther into the country until we reached a village that seemed so remote no one would ever find us there.

There were houses spread throughout the surrounding area, and the small village had a center for shopping, apartments, and a few restaurants. It wasn't a tourist stop because it was far away from Nice and the French Rivera. It was full of natives, and thankfully, my French was pretty good.

It was three in the morning, so Cato knew I was gone by now.

He knew hours ago.

I hated to picture his reaction when he walked into my bedroom and realized I was gone. That I took nothing except the sonogram. I didn't even let him have the one picture of our unborn child.

It was pretty cold.

The guilt weighed heavily in my stomach, not because of my decision, but the way it must have hurt him.

He probably felt betrayed.

He probably questioned how I really felt about him, if my feelings for him were really genuine.

Of course they were.

But he wouldn't give me what I wanted, so what choice did I have?

I had to run off to the middle of nowhere just to escape.

"This is a good place to settle."

"It's way too close to Italy."

"If he really wants to follow you, he's probably going to look at Ireland, America, or Canada. The middle of France is the last place he'll think of. Sometimes it's best to hide in the backyard—the last place anyone would look."

It really was remote. It didn't seem like they would even get cell service here. I wished I could have sold my house first so I would have some money. I didn't have anything to my name. Thankfully, Landon had cash that could get us by for a long time. I would have to find a job in a bigger city working with art, but for right now, that was too dangerous. Cato would probably check every art gallery in Europe.

Landon pulled over to the side of the road, in front of a small inn on the main street. "I say we sleep here and find a place to live in the morning."

"You think they'll take cash here?"

"I think they'll prefer it."

———

WHEN WE WOKE up the next morning, we went house

hunting. There were a few small houses in the vicinity, some of them close enough to walk to town. Since we only had one car, that was ideal. There were no schools in the area, so eventually, we'd have to move somewhere else when the baby started school.

But that was many years down the road.

Landon and I found a small place that we both liked. It was a two-story house with two bedrooms. It had a small kitchen, a garden, and a garage that could only fit one car. It was cheap, and Landon insisted we buy something meager so it wouldn't draw attention. He bought it in cash then we got the keys.

This was really my life now.

I would live with my brother in a small house. When the baby came, it would be even smaller.

Landon bought furniture from a store a few hours away and returned with a moving truck to get all our stuff inside. After a few weeks of ordering everything, we eventually had everything we needed. The small house turned into a home, and we had a dining table, a refrigerator, a dishwasher, a microwave, and furniture for the bedrooms. The only thing we didn't have was a washer and dryer.

The house didn't have the hookups for it.

Now that several weeks had passed, I was further into my pregnancy.

And I'd started to show. My stomach had swelled until it had a distinct curve down the front. I didn't feel any kicking, but somehow, I knew there was life pulsing inside me. Sometimes, I had the impulse to ask Cato to press his hand against my tummy, but then I realized he wasn't there.

We hadn't spoken in all those weeks.

It seemed Landon's plan had worked—Cato couldn't find me.

That relieved me, but it also pained me.

Because I missed him.

There were times when I woke up the middle of the night from a nightmare, but Cato wasn't there for comfort. There were times when I wanted to talk to him about the pregnancy, but he wasn't a phone call away. I hadn't realized how much I needed him until he was no longer there.

I felt safe in this small town, but not like I did living at his estate. Even when executions happened right outside the front door, I was never afraid of something terrible actually breaching the property. I felt untouchable, like nobody could hurt me except Cato himself. I didn't care for luxurious things, but now that I didn't have Giovanni's cooking or those extra soft sheets in my bed, I realized the finer things in life were actually valuable.

A couple weeks later, I started to feel really lonely.

Landon was always there. We watched TV together, played games together, and not once did he complain about his sudden change in lifestyle. When he needed his own time, he went to Nice for the weekend and hit up the bars for company.

Those were the nights I missed Cato the most.

I could go out and find a lover. I was pregnant, but for a one-night stand, a man might not care. But I didn't want to put myself out there and be with anyone else. There was only one man in my fantasies—the very man who'd vowed to kill me.

I lay in bed and looked at the sonogram on my nightstand, the picture that was taken when Cato and I went to see the doctor for the first time. Ever since I heard that heartbeat, I knew I loved my child. And I knew Cato loved them too.

It'd been five weeks since I left Cato, and now I

wondered if he ever tried to look for me at all. Maybe the betrayal was too painful and he didn't want to hunt down a woman who didn't want to be found. Maybe it was a relief to him, that his fatherly responsibility had been taken away from him—and it wasn't his choice.

Maybe he was fucking someone else by now.

It'd been five weeks…of course he was fucking someone else.

He was fucking a lot of women.

The thought made me so sad that tears burned in my eyes. Our relationship had never been based on love, but I always thought there was something else there, something meaningful under the surface. My heart beat for him like no one else. I'd never been in love before, but sometimes I wondered if what I felt was close to that feeling.

But how could I love someone who threatened to kill me?

That would make me a nutcase.

Maybe he let me go so he wouldn't have to kill me. If I weren't under his roof, then no one would expect him to do anything. He was released from his obligation. Maybe he didn't look for me to save me.

If that was the case, I was still sad.

I got what I wanted, but I wondered if this was actually what I wanted after all.

———

THE NEXT MORNING, I washed our clothes by hand then took them outside to hang up. We had a string of rope that extended between two poles, and that's where I hung our clothes to dry. It was old-fashioned and took forever, but it was calming at the same time.

The clothes flapped in the breeze as they hung from the rope. I stepped to the side and clipped a towel to the rope as I looked at the main street a short distance away. People were walking up and down the sidewalk, and there was a man leaning against his car reading the morning paper. He looked up at me from time to time.

I kept pinning my clothes until I saw a shadow appear on the other side of the towel I'd just hung up. A silhouette of a man was visible through the material, with broad shoulders, long legs, and an impressive height.

I immediately thought of Cato.

Had he come for me?

If it was him, why did I feel this jolt of excitement? Shouldn't I be scared?

I pulled back the towel and came face-to-face with my brother. I couldn't fight the crestfallen feeling in my chest, the disappointment that it wasn't the man I hadn't stopped thinking about.

"Everything alright?" He had a tired look on his face, as if his weekend of hookups left him little time to sleep.

"Yeah…you just scared me."

"You don't need to worry about him. It's been five weeks. If he hasn't found us by now, he probably has no idea where to look."

"Unless he never looked for us in the first place…" I was told Cato would find me if he really wanted to, that he had resources I couldn't even dream of. But it wouldn't have taken him this long if that was the case.

"What do you mean?" He pulled a piece of laundry from the basket and hung it up on the line.

"Maybe he didn't bother. Maybe he thought it was the perfect excuse not to kill me…"

"Because if you aren't around, then he doesn't have to keep his word."

"Yeah…" I grabbed another piece of laundry and hung it up.

"I doubt it. He was probably pissed that you left. He probably wanted revenge. He just couldn't find you."

"Maybe…"

Landon hung up another towel while keeping his eyes on me. "You miss him or something?"

"Would you judge me if I said yes?"

"Absolutely. This is what you wanted, Siena. I tried to persuade you to stay, but you wanted to leave. You got exactly what you wanted, and by some miracle, we actually got away with it. There's no reason to be sad."

"I can't explain it…"

"Well, try," he snapped.

When I reflected on our relationship, I missed that closeness. I'd never had a more passionate relationship with a man, someone who could just look into my eyes and make me melt. It wasn't just the physical intimacy that I missed. I missed our emotional intimacy, the conversations we had. "We were close. We weren't just two people who were sleeping together. We weren't more than that either, but we were…together. He has a big heart and a beautiful soul, something he doesn't show to anyone else but me. I know he could be a good man if he wanted to be. I miss that man. And I'll always feel something for him because he's the father of my child."

"But he's threatened to kill you—many times."

"I don't think he would."

"You still left."

"Because I wanted to give my child a better life. But now, I'm not so sure…"

He picked up the last towel from the basket and hung it up. "It doesn't matter now. You can't go back. You have no idea what his reaction would be. He might shoot you in the head on sight."

My brother was right. I would probably be met with Cato's fury.

"So you need to forget about him. This is your life now —our life."

20

Cato

SIX WEEKS CAME AND WENT.

I sat in my office upstairs and looked at the pictures my guy had snapped for me. They were pictures of her hanging her clothes on the line to dry, pictures of her walking into the shops on the main street. In every image, she wasn't looking at the camera, completely oblivious to the five men who watched her every move.

Even Landon didn't notice.

That was concerning. It was a small town. It should be obvious those five men didn't belong there.

I found myself smoking my cigar as I looked at her picture, seeing the noticeable bump of her stomach. It protruded past her waistline and made her shirts stretch tight against her body. It was another curve to that already curvy body.

I thought she'd never looked more beautiful.

Pregnancy suited her.

I hadn't decided what to do about her. I'd watched from a distance, but I couldn't discern her happiness. Was she glad she was gone? Or had she realized that her life with me was perfect and she'd taken it for granted? She hung up her clothes to dry because she didn't even have a dryer. She lived in a tiny house that she shared with her brother. He was seen picking up women in Nice every weekend, while she stayed home alone.

She'd never been spotted with another man.

As long as she hadn't slept with anyone, I wouldn't either.

After six weeks of no sex, I started to feel angry all the time. I jerked off constantly, but it wasn't the same as the real thing. But the idea of sleeping with a woman other than Siena felt wrong.

I didn't owe her anything, especially not after she betrayed me, but it still felt wrong.

Because I knew I was going to drive down there and pick her up any day.

It was only a matter of time before I cracked.

I wondered if she missed me. I wondered what her reaction would be if I showed up on her doorstep. Would she scream in horror? Or would she step into my arms and kiss me? Would she cry and say she missed me?

Or was there a gun on the table, and she would pick it up and shoot me?

Just as I'd threatened to do to her.

I really had no idea.

But judging by these photographs, she was living a dull life. She didn't have a job, and the only thing she did was walk down the market to gather food to cook meals for her and her brother. She busied herself taking care of the house and the laundry. She was basically a housewife in the 1800s.

No way she could be happy.

At least when she lived with me...she had me. I was there for her every night, and I was the father of her child.

I provided everything she might need. I may slaughter people on the doorstep from time to time, but that wasn't an everyday occurrence. It wasn't the life she'd pictured, but it was the life she'd received nonetheless.

I had everything anyone could ever want—but now I felt like I had nothing at all.

The one thing that mattered to me was gone.

I wasn't happy. In fact, I'd never been so miserable.

I had all the money in the world, but I was miserable.

Ironic.

21

Siena

Now that I was well past my first trimester, I needed a checkup at the doctor.

I used my brother's phone to make a few calls to Nice so I could get in to be seen. It would be another two weeks before I could see an obstetrician. That was a while away, but I took the appointment anyway. Nothing abnormal had happened in my pregnancy, but I thought it was smart to make sure everything was okay.

"Landon?" I'd finished making lunch so we sat at the small table together.

"Yeah?" He was scrolling through his phone while he ate, texting one of the women he'd met recently.

"What are we going to do when the baby comes?"

"I thought they would sleep in your room?"

"No. I meant with the delivery. If I check in to a hospital, I'll have to give my name. If Cato wants to take the baby, he'll be checking for that everywhere."

"I hadn't thought about that…"

Now that I missed him, I didn't care if he wanted to see the baby. But I was afraid he would take the baby away from me and leave me behind. That would be a worse fate than death.

"I guess you could give birth here. Women used to do it all the time."

"And most women died in childbirth," I countered. "That's too risky."

"Then I don't know what the answer is. I could call a guy to prepare fake documents for you. That might be the only way around it."

"Yeah…" I didn't know what to name the baby. But I wanted them to have my last name. Even if I registered under a different name, Cato might scan the birth records. I also felt bad giving the baby my last name when they should have Cato's. It seemed like I was denying my baby their birthright.

"We've got several months before we have to worry about that." He finished his lunch and left the dishes in the sink. "I'm going to take a nap. Got a headache."

"Alright." I finished my lunch then washed the dishes in the sink. Then I washed the laundry before I carried it outside. It was supposed to rain in the next few days, so I knew I needed to do all the laundry now—unless we wanted our clothes to smell like rainwater.

I hung up Landon's shirts and jeans then moved on to my clothing. I also had all our towels to get through. One by one, I hung them up, clipping them into place so the sunlight and breeze could dry them out.

Just when I was about to step back from the last towel, I saw the silhouette of a large man through it. With muscular shoulders, a foot of extra height on top of mine, and long legs, his outlined reminded me of Cato's. I'd thought the same thing before when I saw Landon, but then I remembered my brother was inside the house.

I stood motionless as I stared at the towel, stared at how still the man was. He didn't make a move or a sound.

My heart started to race, both with fear and painful relief. If Cato was on the other side, it would probably be bad news for me. But I couldn't help but be excited that I was about to step into his arms and feel at home again. My eyes watered slightly, but I didn't let any tears fall. Then the baby started to kick for the very first time.

My hand moved over my stomach and I felt it, the powerful kicks that my baby made. It was the first time I'd felt so much life in my stomach, so much excitement from the little child growing in me. Maybe my spiked heartrate excited them. Or maybe they knew their father was just inches away from me.

He pulled back the towel and stepped forward.

It was him.

In dark jeans, boots, and a long-sleeved shirt, he was the same powerful man I remembered. Muscular, strong, and brutish, he was threatening in every way—except the softness in his eyes.

The softness I used to see every single day.

His eyes shifted back and forth slightly as he looked at me, like he was memorizing the way I looked. His gaze slowly drifted to my stomach and where my hand rested, looking at how much my stomach had grown. He stared for a long time before he lifted his gaze again.

Silenced by his look, I didn't speak. After all this time apart, I didn't know what to say. His presence didn't seem to be hostile, but without an introduction, I really didn't know. "This is the first time I've ever felt the baby kick." I grabbed his hand, feeling the hot thrill down my spine, and placed it over my stomach.

His eyes focused on my tummy, and when a soft smile spread across his lips, I knew he could feel it. He closed his eyes to focus on the movement even more. Then he placed his other hand against my belly and enjoyed it. "Beautiful." His eyes lifted to mine, and he sighed quietly under his breath. He must have noticed the thin film of moisture in my eyes because his expression softened even more. "Baby, come home." His hands moved over my belly to my waist as he stepped closer to me. "This isn't where you two belong."

I didn't want to put up a fight at all. I didn't want to fight for my rights or explain why I left in the first place. All I wanted was this man. I didn't understand just how deeply I'd missed him until I felt him again. "I have one condition."

He pressed his forehead to mine and closed his eyes. "Alright."

"You have to sleep with me every night. Because I can't go another night without you." I put my heart out there to be crushed, giving away my most private desires. I didn't just want this man physically, I wanted all of him. I wanted him in a way I'd never had him before.

He rubbed his nose against mine. "Okay."

I closed my eyes in relief when I got what I wanted—without an argument. Maybe I should ask him to spare my life, but considering his gentleness, he probably didn't want to do away with me anymore anyway. "My brother is inside...please don't hurt him."

"I won't."

My heart softened again, turning into melted butter. "It took you a long time to find me."

He pulled away so he could lock his gaze on to mine. "Baby, I always knew you were here."

———

THE HOUSE WAS way too small for Cato. The man was over six feet tall and could barely fit through the doorway. He crossed the threshold and examined the living room and kitchen, which were scrunched together into a single room. He didn't give a false compliment, but he didn't insult it either.

"Landon is taking a nap."

"The countryside has made him lazy."

I stared at him awkwardly, unable to believe he was there. "Can I get you something to drink?"

"A beer is fine."

I grabbed a bottle out of the fridge and carried it back to the table. Cato sat on the wooden chair, but his weight seemed like it might be too much for the old chair. He relaxed and took a drink.

I sat across from him, looking at the blue eyes that were always the focus of my dreams. Whether they were sex dreams or just dreams of us talking, they were always present. Beautiful like the sea, they were his most gorgeous feature.

"I'll wait here while you pack your things."

"We're leaving right now?" I asked in surprise.

"Why would we stay?"

"First, I should tell Landon. And second of all, I have a lot of stuff to take care of."

Cato tried to hide his look of irritation, but he wasn't doing a good job.

"My brother bought this place so we would have somewhere to live. I feel guilty for just taking off."

"I'll reimburse him for it."

"That's not what I meant… I'm sure he could sell it."

"And I could be the buyer to speed up the process."

"That won't be necessary." I'd never wanted his money. I didn't want it then, and I didn't want it now.

He set his beer on the table and he watched me, his eyes glued to mine. His shirt fit his sculpted shoulders nicely, along with his chiseled arms and powerful chest. I hated to think about all the women who had been under him since I'd been gone. I refused to ask, unable to hear the answer. "How are you?"

I could have given him a generic answer instead of a sincere one. But I chose the latter. "Lonely. Empty. Cold." I lowered my gaze and looked at the table. "I thought this was the best thing for both of us, but I've never been so miserable. My life is the same lame activities on repeat. The heater in this house is even worse than my old one. Landon never complains, but I know he hates it too. I thought leaving would allow me to give a better life to my child…our child…but I realize there's nothing for them here. And even if I moved, we would still be alone." I lifted my gaze from the table to see his reaction.

It was exactly the same. "You left because you thought I couldn't provide a good life for our child?" There wasn't an edge to his tone, just general curiosity. His fingers wrapped around his bottle, but he didn't take a drink.

"You executed five people in the driveway…the answer is obvious."

"I wouldn't do that in front of our kid, Siena. Are you kidding me?"

"They would still hear the gunshots from their bedroom."

"You need to give me more credit than that. You're judging me on my ability to be a father before the kid is even here. No parent knows how to be a parent until the baby is born. And when that day comes, it always changes you. I don't know how my life will be different when our kid is here—but I know it won't be the same. So, no, I wouldn't execute people anywhere near our kid."

A weight lifted off my shoulders. "People will still try to hurt them all the time. They'll be the number one target of your enemies."

"Which is why I would give them the greatest amount of protection. I'm not stupid, Siena. I know what people will try to do to any child I father. I'm the most protective and paranoid man on the planet. I think about these things all the time."

He'd talked me off the ledge once again.

"You should have talked to me about all of this before you ran away."

"I feel like I can't talk to you sometimes…"

He leaned forward. "Baby, you can always talk to me."

"Like when I asked if my brother could come over, and then you whipped me?"

His eyes narrowed. "And then I said yes, and you plotted against me? My answer should have stayed no." He took a drink from his beer. "Learned my lesson."

"I just worry about our baby. I don't know them, but I already love them so much. I just want to do the right thing for them. I don't want them to grow up in the same situation I did. I don't want them to be scarred by greed and corruption. All I've ever wanted was a simple life. Having you as a banker and a crime lord doesn't fit into that category. I don't want them to be exposed to that lifestyle. I just…I wanted better for them."

Cato didn't seem to take offense to that. He pushed the beer aside and rested his hands together on the surface. "There's nothing I can do about that. That's their legacy— and we can't hide it from them either. The best thing we can do is teach them to be smart, grateful, and humble. That's what parents are for, right?"

He spoke about me like I would be there to teach those life lessons, and that was the biggest relief of all. Maybe this time apart was exactly what Cato needed to get his head on straight, to understand that his threats were vile and unfair.

His eyes trailed over my neck and to the features of my face, like he was taking in my appearance for the first time. "You look so damn beautiful. I've seen pictures of you every day, but they don't do you justice."

I couldn't stop the slight smile from spreading across my lips. I couldn't stop the warmth from entering my heart either. "You look good too."

"I've been working out more than usual…since I had nothing else to do."

"Well, it shows." And I couldn't wait to make a more thorough observation.

He glanced at the stairs at the end of the hallway. "Talk to Landon about everything. I'll be back to pick you up tomorrow afternoon. Be ready—because I'm taking you with me even if you aren't." He rose from the chair.

I walked him to the front door, even though it was only a few steps. "Alright."

He turned around and faced me, his arms by his sides.

I couldn't believe I was looking into his face, and I couldn't believe it was the gentle side I'd missed for so long. It wasn't the cruel dictator who'd punished me. It wasn't the tyrant who'd whipped me with his belt. It was the man I adored…the one I hadn't stopped thinking about. "I'll see you tomorrow."

His hands moved to my lower back, and he pulled me against his chest before he kissed me. So soft. So gentle. His hand moved into my hair, and he fisted the strands as he kissed me good. It was the same embrace we'd had on our last night together, like we were picking up where we left off.

My hands moved underneath his shirt, and I immediately noticed the difference in his abs. They were even harder than before, hills of steel. I breathed into his mouth and felt my fingers tremble.

He ended the kiss sooner than I wanted and turned away. "I'll see you tomorrow, baby."

————

"ARE you sure you want to do this?" Landon asked as he set the box of clothes on the counter.

"Yes." My relationship with Cato didn't make a lot of sense. Maybe I was magnetically pulled to him because of the baby we'd made together. Or maybe I would feel this way whether we were having a baby or not.

"Do you even have a choice?"

"I think so. He didn't seem…like his asshole self."

"I've never met that side of him before."

"It exists. It's just…rare."

Landon continued to watch me, observing me and judging me with his green eyes.

"He said he wouldn't hurt you. You don't have to worry about him."

"I figured. I probably would have been dragged out of bed otherwise."

"I'm sorry about all of this. The house, everything you bought…"

"It's not a big deal, Siena. I have a lot of money from the family business. It's tucked away in various places, so it's not like this house put me out much. I just wanted something humble so no one would suspect we were here."

"Well, your plan backfired."

"How did he find us?"

I shrugged. "He didn't say. But he said he knew I was here the entire time."

"Then why didn't he come get you sooner?"

"I haven't had the chance to ask him."

He crossed his arms over his chest then came closer to me. "I'll sell the house and move back to Florence. France isn't my cup of tea. The women here are beautiful, but they talk too much."

"All women talk too much."

"You don't."

"Ask Cato that," I said with a chuckle.

"So, what's going to happen now? You're going to move back in with him, and then what? Is it going to be different?"

"I think so."

"Maybe you should ask him first. Because the whole prisoner thing is a little much."

"I told him I wanted to sleep with him from now on, and he said yes. So I think it's different."

"You weren't doing that before?" he asked incredulously.

"We had separate bedrooms."

He nodded slowly. "So he's giving you a real commitment now."

"And he told me how he intends to raise our child. How it won't be all violence and money…"

"And what about killing you?"

"He didn't specifically say, but he talked about the future like I would live long enough to see it."

He watched me for a long time, that brotherly affection in his eyes. He was protective of me, but he also understood I was an adult who could make my own decisions. "I just want him to treat you right."

"I know."

"Let me know if he doesn't."

"I will."

A knock sounded on the front door. When I opened it, I came face-to-face with Cato. I almost couldn't believe it. "Did you just knock?"

That handsome smile spread across his lips. "Landon lives here too, so different situation."

"Wow, I could get used to this."

He stepped inside the house then looked at my brother. "Landon." He didn't extend his hand.

Neither did my brother. "Cato. Thanks for not killing me."

Cato gave a sarcastic smile. "No problem. You were taking care of your sister. Can't hold that against you."

"Good. I would do it again in a heartbeat." Landon turned to me. "I need to stick around and finish up everything. I'll see you back in Florence in about a week or so."

"Sounds good. When I get a phone, I'll call you."

Cato pulled out his phone and handed it to Landon. "Save your number in there."

Landon typed the number and handed it back.

Cato called him then hung up. "Call that number if you want to talk to her."

I watched silently as Cato make another heartfelt gesture.

Landon turned back to me. "Let me know if you need anything."

I hugged him hard and held him close. "I love you."

"Love you too." He kissed my forehead before he released me. "See you soon."

———

CATO HAD COME HERE in his private plane, so we boarded it then flew back to central Italy.

When we landed, his entourage took us back into the

countryside where his three-story estate looked exactly the same. Even in the dark, it was still beautiful, with the landscape lights illuminating the architecture inside the gates.

Cato looked out the window and said very little to me.

We arrived at the front, and then the men carried my bags inside the house. I took my clothes and other necessities, while Landon would take care of the nonessentials. When I got out of the car and stepped inside, it smelled exactly as I remembered. The hardwood floor was smooth under my feet. The only difference was the temperature. Now it was nearly winter, so the feeling of summer was long gone.

But it still felt like I was home.

The men put my things in my bedroom and left the door open.

When Cato and I walked upstairs, he immediately guided me to his bedroom down the hallway. My old quarters were forgotten.

The door shut behind us, and Cato's clothes dropped to the floor. He kicked off his shoes then peeled away his socks until he was in nothing but skin—and a ton of muscle.

My eyes trailed over his even harder physique, seeing the way the grooves of muscle cut deeper into his body. His pecs were thicker, and his biceps were at least an inch wider. The cords down his arms were more prominent, and the muscles of his thighs were tight. While he looked beautiful, I was pregnant. I had a belly, more fat on my hips and thighs, and I'd forgotten to shave my bikini area. I hadn't done it in a long time because of my belly—and the fact that no one saw me naked.

He stepped toward me then lifted my chin so my lips would meet his. He kissed me softly on the mouth with his purposeful lips. His breaths deepened quickly, and then he dug his hands deep into my hair. The same fiery passion we used to have was still there, still beating with the rhythm of our hearts.

He grabbed my shirt and started to pull.

I kept his hands down. "My body is changing…"

He looked at me with a fierce look of frustration. "I know. I like it."

"I don't look like a porn star like you."

He cocked his head to the side as the smirk stretched across his face. "That's how you describe me? As a porn star?"

"I've been watching a lot of porn, alright?" I said without shame. "I just mean you're really fit. And I'm… not the same."

"Baby…" He tugged my shirt over my head and revealed my pregnant belly. "I've been looking at those pictures every day, wishing I were fucking you every night." His hands moved over my bare stomach. "You're fucking sexy." His hands snaked to my back, and he unclasped my bra. "I've never wanted you more." His mouth moved to my neck as he kissed me and worked my jeans. He unbuttoned them and dropped the zipper before he lowered himself and pulled my pants to my ankles. He grabbed my panties next.

"I forgot to shave…"

He wore the same aroused expression as he took them off. "I haven't had pussy in two months. You think a little hair is gonna stop me?" He rose to his feet then led me to the bed. He gently guided me back until I was lying on the mattress. Then he moved between my thighs and held himself on top of me. "Fuck, I missed you." He pointed his cock at my entrance.

I pressed my hand against his rock-hard stomach. "I haven't been with anyone."

"I know. I haven't either."

"I ran away, and you didn't sleep with anyone else?" I asked in surprise.

He held his face close to mine as he sank deep inside me. "This is the only pussy I want."

I felt inch after inch, along with the warmth his body smothered me with. I closed my eyes as I felt my body stretch to accommodate him like it was the first time. My cunt had shrunk in his absence and tightened back to its original size. Now he would have to stretch me out again, pop my cherry like I wasn't already pregnant with his baby. I gripped his arms and released a moan so loud it was embarrassing. "Cato…" Those two months in that remote village seemed like such a waste of time. I had been frozen to the bone and so lonely. My days were spent daydreaming about him. My nights were spent fantasizing about him.

He held still as he savored the feeling of being deep inside me. "Fuck yeah." He pressed my legs farther into my waist and slowly thrust inside me, taking me slowly the way he did on our last night together.

I brought his face to mine and kissed him, every inch of my body on fire. He made love to my mouth as well as he did to my pussy. His cock hit me deep before he pulled it out again, just to dunk back inside me once more. He was thicker than I remembered, like his size increased due to my longing.

I felt so full I thought I might rip. "I missed you…" I spoke against his mouth as I kissed him, my legs wide apart so he could take me. I wasn't self-conscious about my belly or my hair anymore. When he took me like this, it didn't seem like he cared about those things.

"I missed you too, baby." He thrust until he came to a stop. He closed his eyes like he had to concentrate on what he was doing, to force himself not to finish too soon.

"I'm almost there. Then you can come inside me."

He moaned from way in the back of his throat, the masculine sound so sexy. "Don't talk about me coming inside you, not if you want to come first." He pressed his lips to my forehead and kissed me before he started to thrust again. His deep and even strokes hit my button every single time, making my thighs tighten and my toes curl.

"Cato, I'm gonna come." I cupped his face and brought his lips to mine. My lips didn't move with his. His warm breaths fell on my face as mine fell on his. My subtle moans became louder and louder as my body prepared for the explosion.

"Come, baby. I need to come."

I finally hit my threshold and soared into the high. It was a better climax than the ones I'd given myself over the past few months. This was amazing, much more intense. My cunt gripped his cock with fervor, and my hips started to buck involuntarily. "Oh god."

He couldn't hold on a second longer and released, shoving his length deep inside me as he gave me his seed. He moaned with pleasure as he dumped everything he had, giving me a load bigger than ever before. "Jesus." He stayed still as he finished, his cock twitching with joy as it slowly came down from the high. Instead of pulling out when every drop had been spilled, he stayed idle on top of me, getting ready for the next round. "Again."

———

IT WAS the second time I'd lain in that bed in the dark. The first time we slept together, we did it in this very bed, taking up a small amount of space because it was much too big for just two people. At the time, I was just a conquest, another notch on his belt.

But now I was pregnant with his baby, and this hunky man had his powerful arms wrapped around me. We faced each other in bed with the blankets pulled up to our shoulders. My leg was hiked over his waist, and my pregnant belly was between us.

His bedroom was so much warmer than mine in France. That house had a piss-poor furnace that couldn't even supply heat to the bedrooms upstairs. As a result, I slept with five blankets, and I was still cold. Sometimes I was so desperate I thought about getting into Landon's bed, but I never did because that would have been weird. But this luxurious estate was always the perfect temperature, always the safest and most comfortable place in Italy. We didn't even need five blankets because Cato was a human furnace.

I'd never thought I would be so happy to be here.

His hand moved to my belly under the sheets, his large hand big enough to span across it entirely. His eyes were downcast as he concentrated on the life inside me, waiting for a kick or any sign of movement.

"It was so weird," I whispered. "They were so calm until you arrived. It was like they knew you were there."

"Or maybe they felt their mother's soaring heartbeat," he whispered back. "Felt her body get warm, felt her emotion in her blood." His fingers gently rubbed against the smooth skin. "Felt the happiness in her soul." His eyes flicked back to mine.

"Why didn't you come after me sooner?" He'd waited two months before he did anything. Two months was a long time to sit idly by and do nothing.

"I was pissed when you left. My pride was wounded. I

questioned everything you ever said to me. I do so much for you, and you seemed ungrateful. So my response was to let you have your way…in the hope you would regret it. I hoped you would miss me, miss the life I provided for you. I hoped you would question your decision and realize it'd been a mistake. That was my revenge. With little money and only your brother for company, I knew you would realize that a life with me was preferable to one you could have on your own. Our child is safer under my regime. You are safer under my regime. Despite your feelings about my situation, you would realize that I was the most powerful man you'd ever known….and being at my side was the safest place you would ever be. I hoped you would come back on your own, on your knees and begging. But then I remembered you were the stubbornest woman in the world, and you would never resort to that. After two months had come and gone, I couldn't take it anymore. So I decided to come get you."

"What if I'd said no? Did I have a choice?"

His fingers gently massaged my stomach. "When I saw the tears in your eyes, I knew I didn't have to worry about that."

He never answered my question, but I thought I knew the answer. "How did you know where I was?"

"When you first started living here, I put a tracker in your ankle. I figured you would try to run away eventually."

I had no idea. "I don't remember that…"

"I sedated you."

"That was presumptuous."

He shrugged. "Aren't you glad I did it? I made sure nothing happened to either one of you while you were on your own. I knew exactly where you were so I could come get you."

"Still a huge violation of human rights."

"No such thing as human rights in this house. Don't expect me to apologize for it. When our baby is here, I'll do the same to them. Just in case something terrible ever happens, I'll be able to find either one of you in a heartbeat. Told you I was a paranoid man." His hand slid up my stomach until he felt my rib cage. He moved farther up until he pressed his palm underneath my left breast so he could feel my heartbeat. "Baby, don't be mad."

"If you think I won't be mad, you don't know me very well."

He smiled slightly. "Then we're at a stalemate." He moved his hand to the center of my chest and rubbed his palm between my cleavage, soothing me with his affection. "Your tits are bigger."

"So are my hips, thighs, and ass."

"It's sexy."

"You are just saying that..." My body had already changed so much. By the end of my pregnancy, my body would look totally different.

"Do I ever just say things?" His blue eyes bored into mine. "No. I speak the truth—even when it makes me an asshole. You're sexier now than you were before you started to show."

"You think a belly is sexy?"

"Fuck yes." His hand moved back to my stomach. "I've never been attracted to pregnant women. I only like women of a certain fitness level. But your pregnant belly... gets me going. I guess because I did this to you."

"So, it's all about pride, huh? You're proud of your handiwork?"

He shrugged. "Maybe. I think it's deeper than that. But don't ever feel unsexy with me...because the last thing you have to worry about is being unsexy. The idea of picking up a few girls seemed anticlimactic, especially when I looked at those pictures of you walking around with that bump. It made me prefer my hand if I couldn't have you."

This dictator had turned into a soft and romantic man, the ideal man I never thought I would meet. He made me feel safe when the world was against me. He made me feel sexy when I was most insecure. "When I saw your shadow behind the towel, I was so happy. I'd been thinking about you so much, wondering if I'd made a mistake. When you didn't come after me at first, I was actually disappointed."

"Then why did you run in the first place?"

"I thought I was doing the right thing for both of us…"

"I hope you realized the safest place in the world is by my side. I would never let anything happen to our child. I would protect them more fiercely than anyone else I know. That's something you never have to worry about."

"I know…" My hand moved against his chest, and I felt his strong heartbeat.

"I want you to apologize to me."

My eyes flicked back to his.

"You heard me," he whispered. "You took my child away from me. You subjected me to loneliness. You betrayed me—again. And you should be sorry about that."

My fingers rested against his thumping heartbeat. "You're the one threatening to kill me all the time. Can you blame me?"

"And you're the one who believes I won't do it. So what is there to be afraid of?"

"Doesn't matter what I believe. Why would I want to be with a man who talks to me that way? No, I won't apologize."

His eyes bored into mine again, a subtle threat of hostility beneath this gaze.

I stood my ground and refused to give in. I refused to bow to a man, regardless of how much I'd missed him.

He didn't press me on it. Slowly, his anger died away and the tightness in his shoulders relaxed. His fingers moved back to my stomach and over my belly button. "I hate it when you pull that shit. But I also respect you for it."

———

I WOKE up the next morning with a beautiful man beside me.

His chest was pressed against my back, and his arm rested over my belly, like he was protecting it with his powerful arm. Our breaths were in sync. Every time his chest rose, mine did the same.

It was so comfortable, I wanted to stay there forever.

Sleeping alone in my bedroom here never felt right. My mind always drifted down the hall to the man who slept in an enormous bed alone. When I stayed with Landon in France, I always wondered where Cato was sleeping, if he was alone or with someone else.

It was a relief to know he'd been alone—thinking about me.

The baby started to kick, making my tummy vibrate. Without touching it, I could feel it. It was a visceral sensation, an incredible one. I'd been pregnant for a few short months, but it seemed like a real person was inside me, someone I already knew so well.

Cato must have felt it, because he stirred a moment later. His hand gripped my stomach to get a better hold of my belly. He sat up and propped his body up on one arm as he focused on the child we made together.

The kicking continued.

With sleepy eyes, Cato stared at his hand, enjoying the feeling of his baby alive and well. "Boy or girl, they're strong."

"I know. I'm only half way through the pregnancy, and they're so ornery."

"I wonder where they inherited that from…" He gave me a playful look.

I swatted him on the arm. "Both of us. Not just me."

"I'm just arrogant. You're ornery." He kicked back the sheets then placed kisses over my tummy.

As I watched him, I forgot what we were talking about. I watched Cato kiss me with those soft lips while his eyes looked so sleepy. His hair was pointed at odd angles because I'd fingered it so much last night. He went from being a cold dictator to being a loving father—and a gentle lover. Sometimes it didn't seem like he was the same person.

They said pregnancy changed you, turned you into a more selfless and caring person. It changed me dramatically, since I could feel my child inside me every single day. But it had started to change Cato too, turning him into a more human man than monster.

"We're going to the doctor this afternoon," he said as he rose on his arms and held himself on top of me.

"Really?" I'd tried getting in to see someone, but I had to wait weeks at every place I called. Cato got me in to a great doctor instantly. It was one of the luxuries I missed, having a man who could take care of my needs so quickly.

"Yes. Time for a checkup. But first…" He grabbed my arm and slowly turned me onto my side. "It's been a while since I've seen that asshole." He lifted me above the bed and put me on my knees. Unlike the gentle way he took me last night, he gripped me by the back of the hair and tugged until my neck curved toward the ceiling. As he pushed his dick past my entrance, he moaned. "There it is…beautiful as always."

———

CATO WAS IN THE SHOWER, so I went downstairs to visit Giovanni.

He was cooking in the kitchen, like usual, probably preparing lunch. "Miss Siena, it's so good to see you again." His eyes moved down to my stomach. "Both of you. It seems like that baby is coming along well."

"Yes, but they kick a bit." I patted my stomach before I hugged him. "I'm sorry about before—"

"Please don't apologize. I understand."

"How long were you in the car?"

"A few hours," he said. "I was surprised it took so long for Mr. Marino to look for me. You had a good plan."

Since Cato tracked my every move, it'd never been a good plan. There was no escape, not unless I cut myself and dug the tracker out of my body. While pregnant, that was a really dangerous idea.

"Mr. Marino was very unhappy while you were gone."

"He was?" I asked, trying to mask the happiness in my voice.

Giovanni nodded. "There was emptiness in his eyes. He worked out harder and spent more time at work. When he was home, he was usually in a bad mood. Never talked about you. I wondered why he hadn't gone after you, but I also knew he would do it when he was ready."

"Maybe the time apart was good for both us."

"Maybe," he said. "Mr. Marino is a grown man, but he still has a lot to learn." He turned back to the stove. "Lunch will be ready in fifteen minutes. Would you like me to bring it to your bedroom?"

We'd been in bed long enough. "We'll eat in the dining room. We're going to the doctor afterward."

"Alright. I'll have it ready soon."

I walked out of the kitchen and back into the entryway.

And came face-to-face with Bates.

He wore a suit and tie, looking like a man who belonged in a conference room. His watch shone like his blue eyes, and his dark stare was similar to Cato's. With his hands in his pockets, he stared at me. He didn't try to hide his disgust for me. His lip curled up slightly, and he flared his nostrils like my face was enough to piss him off. "The tramp is back."

If anyone else spoke to me that way, they'd have a black eye. But violence was the wrong choice with a temperamental man like Bates. He wouldn't refrain from hitting me back, even if I was pregnant. "I understand you don't like me—"

"Don't like you?" he asked incredulously. "You deserve stronger words than that."

"Whatever. I think we should put the past behind us and move on."

He raised an eyebrow and laughed sarcastically, like I'd just delivered a terrible joke. "You've betrayed him twice now."

"I left to protect myself and my baby—"

"That is so fucked up. You took a child away from their father. How sick is that?"

My eyes narrowed in ferocity. "He threatened to kill me."

"And that's his right. Let's not forget why you fucked him in the first place. It was all just an act to get what you wanted."

"And save my father's life. Yes...I'm such a terrible

person."

He stepped closer to me, his rage escalating with mine. "You're just a surrogate, and that's all you'll ever be. You may be poisoning his mind with your cunt and pretty words, but never forget that I see right through that—even if he doesn't."

I crossed my arms over my chest. "You really need to let this go. Nations at war have made peace quicker than this."

"I'm not gonna let my brother humiliate himself more than he already has. When that baby is here, I'll make sure you're gone. Our lives have been turned upside down since you walked in the door. You're a fucking pain in the ass."

"Your mother likes me."

"Only because you're having her grandbaby. And my mom likes everyone."

"Do you have any idea how disappointed she would be if she knew you were acting like this?"

Bates turned quiet, his lips pressing tightly together. "Are you threatening me?"

"No. But it's something to think about."

"I have no respect for you, but I have even less respect for snitches."

"I'm not a snitch."

"Sounded like it."

I knew Bates was so lost in his hatred that he couldn't see straight anymore. "You know what's sad? You're so blindly hateful that you don't even have the capability of changing your mind. You're so stubborn, it's borderline ignorant. If you stopped for a second, you would realize how happy I make your brother."

"But it's not real. You don't care about him."

I was so offended, it was like he'd slapped me. "I care

about him more than you could possibly understand. I missed him the entire time I was gone—"

"But you never came back. So who fucking knows?"

The best course of action was to abandon this conversation. Bates would always be my enemy because he would never give me a chance.

"This is why we agreed never to get married or have kids. When you're us, you never know anyone for who they really are. Women only want us for our money. Men only want to see us fall."

"I've never wanted him for his money."

"Then why did you miss him?" he countered. "You missed him because you lived in a big mansion with a private chef and Egyptian cotton sheets. You missed him because you could sit around all day and watch TV without worrying about paying the bills. You're no better than the rest of them, so stop pretending."

It broke my heart to think Bates actually thought that, actually said those words to Cato. "I'm never going to persuade you, so it doesn't matter. I admit it's nice being with a man who can protect and provide for me and our child, but that's not why I care about him. I care about him because—regardless of how many times he's threatened to kill me—there's no else in the world I would rather be with."

———

I LAY BACK on the table with the gown covering my body.

Cato stood beside me in jeans, a shirt, and a black blazer. His dark hair was a little shorter than it used to be. He must have had it cut recently, before he fetched me from France. He pulled back his sleeve and looked at his watch to check the time.

I watched all his movements, finding him to be the most fascinating man in the world.

"You and Bates got into it today?" He pulled down his sleeve and turned to me.

"We always get into it."

"What did he say to you?"

I shrugged. "Same ol' shit. I'm a tramp and a bitch. He sees right through me…blah, blah."

He couldn't stop the corner of his mouth from rising. "At least you have a good attitude about it."

"It's the same conversation I've had a million times. No matter what I say, he doesn't care. First, he says I'm a traitor for how our relationship started. But then he accuses me of only wanting you for your money. So, which is it?" I threw my hands in the air. "I understand he's protective of you, but he's so hateful and paranoid that he can't see straight."

"I've given up too. Just ignore him."

"That's hard to do when he's at the house all the time."

"I talked to him about it. He might get in your face from time to time, but he would never touch you."

Good. No more knives to the throat.

"Especially now that you're visibly pregnant." He moved closer to me and rested his hand on my bump. "Don't be afraid of him."

"I was never afraid of him. I just wish he wouldn't hate me so much."

"He's the most stubborn person I know, so I don't think his opinion is going to change."

"Hmm," I said. "I always thought you were the most stubborn person I knew."

He looked down at me and made an annoyed face that was only partially genuine. "You're lucky I can't whip you."

"But you can spank me a little bit."

His annoyed expression instantly vanished, replaced with a look full of desire. "I'll hold you to that."

The doctor came inside and flipped through his chart. "The results came back. Your baby is completely healthy and normal. You both are very lucky."

"That's so great to hear." I rested my hand on Cato's as we both felt the baby.

"It is," Cato said in agreement.

"So, would you like to know the sex of the baby?" He finished reading the paperwork and tucked the clipboard under his arm.

My hand instantly squeezed Cato's with excitement. Now that I was far enough along, I knew that learning the sex of the baby was possible today. But I had no idea if Cato was interested in that information. I looked at him and tried to read his expression. "What do you think?"

"It's up to you, baby."

"I think I want to know. That way we can pick out all the right clothes and stuff. Is that okay?"

"Whatever you want." He squeezed my hand again.

I turned back to the doctor. "Alright. We want to know."

He smiled before he gave his answer. "Congratulations, you're having a girl."

I yanked my hands away from my stomach and brought them to my face. "Oh my god. I knew it!" I covered my mouth with both hands and looked up at Cato, seeing the slight smile on his lips. "We're having a little girl…" Before I knew it, tears were running down my face.

The doctor stepped out of the room. "I'll give you two a moment."

The hormones made me far more emotional than I normally would be, but hearing that concrete news would have made anyone shed a few tears. Now I felt an even stronger connection to the baby, a bond that could never be broken. "I can't believe it."

He lifted up my gown and pressed his palm directly to the bump. "You were right, baby."

"I know." I put my hand on top of his. "I know this isn't what you wanted, but I'm so happy."

Cato hardly ever showed emotion, only with the occasional softening of his eyes. His expression was stoic like usual as he stared at my stomach, the cold man resuming his air of indifference. But then his breathing quickened slightly, and he looked at me again with new eyes. "We're having a girl—she'll be like you. She'll be strong, smart, capable...and beautiful. That makes me happy. Very happy."

22

Cato

IT WAS LATE FALL, SO THE AIR STARTED TO GET COLD fast. The nights came earlier, and there were fewer people on the sidewalks. I'd started wearing my heavy coat over my suit when I visited the office, a few cigars in my pocket to keep me warm.

I arrived at our main facility and headed to my office.

Bates sat in the armchair, smoking a cigar while he stared out the floor-to-ceiling windows behind my desk. He was in a navy blue suit with dress shoes, ready to make money at a second's notice.

It was the first time I'd directly interacted with him since Siena had returned. I knew he was livid that I'd fetched her. If he could have it his way, we would have forgotten about her entirely—the baby too.

I sat behind my desk then raised my hand. "Lighter."

He pulled his out of his front pocket and tossed it at me.

I lit up my cigar and watched the smoke rise to the ceiling.

Bates took a deep puff, the smoke lifting from the end

of the cigar and rising in front of his eyes. It made his ferocity even more potent. He looked like a serial killer when he wore a stare like that.

"It's a girl."

He let the smoke shoot out of his nostrils. "Congratulations." His voice was heavy with sarcasm, like he couldn't care less. I could have said I was having a giraffe, and he would have the same reaction. "Another little bitch."

I lowered my cigar because I'd reached a new level of anger. It annoyed me when he spoke of Siena that way, but to talk about my daughter…was a whole different situation. Saying that phrase in my head made this pregnancy more real.

I had a daughter.

The smoke rose out of my mouth. "Bates, say anything like that ever again, and I will shove my cigar so far into your eye that it'll burn your brain. It pisses me off enough when you speak of Siena that way. But my daughter…it's different."

He kept smoking his cigar.

"She's your niece, asshole. What the hell is wrong with you?"

"She's half my niece. The other half…I don't know what the other half is."

My brother had always been pragmatic and smart. Sometimes he was emotional and temperamental, but I'd never seen him this way. "Bates, this needs to stop. I know you don't like Siena, but you need to get over it. Who gives a damn how many times she betrays me? I own her. I fucking own her, and there's nothing she can do about it. What's the worst that can happen?"

"What's the worst that can happen?" he asked sarcastically. He let his arms hang on the armrests, his cigar burning smoke to the ceiling. "I'll tell you what's the worst that can happen. She persuades you to marry her. She persuades you to sign over half the business to her. Then she kills you in your sleep, and ta-da, half the company is hers."

It was so ridiculous that I wanted to roll my eyes. "That's never going to happen, Bates."

"She's manipulated you this far."

"She's never manipulated me to do anything. I've told you that."

He shook his head. "From the second you met her, you've been different. You don't fuck other women, and now you're living with her—in the same room."

"That's not manipulation, Bates. That's a man finding a woman. Simple as that."

He shook his head again, the disappointment in his eyes shining like two beacons. "She got pregnant on purpose."

I didn't believe that. "Even if she did, that's my problem, not yours."

He took another deep puff. "This is ridiculous. You're so far gone that you don't even see how much you've changed."

"I don't care how much I've changed, Bates. I'm happy, alright? Don't you want me to be happy?"

"With a real woman, yes. Not with this lying, manipulative—"

"Don't fucking say it." My hand balled into a fist.

He rested against the back of the chair, sighing in defeat. "Fine. If you want to waste your time with this woman who's used you from the beginning, I can't stop you. Since the dawn of time, good men have lost wars because pussy was involved. It fucks with our brains, and we can't think. I've warned you many times, but you don't listen to me. But this also directly affects me. I helped you build this company from the ground up, fifty-fifty. By being involved with this woman I don't trust, you're jeopardizing that. You're putting me in a position I don't want to be in —so you're choosing her over me."

"Bates, that's ridiculous. My relationship has nothing to do with our business."

"For now," he said. "But what about when you marry her?"

"I'm not gonna marry her."

"Really?" he asked. "You're shacked up together and having a baby. It's only a matter of time before she puts on the pressure."

"I already told her marriage wasn't on the table."

His blue eyes narrowed with anger. "You told her a lot of things are off the table, Cato."

The woman had moved in to my bedroom and shared every inch of space with me. When she asked me for that, I didn't hesitate to give her what she wanted. All I wanted was for her to come home with me. And honestly, sleeping with her was something I wanted too. "It's not like the things she's asked for aren't mutual."

"What are you going to do when she asks to marry you."

"She has too much pride to ask me to marry her."

"You know what I mean," he snapped. "She's gonna put on the pressure, and when you say no, she's gonna leave. You'll be so miserable without her that you'll cave— like you just did."

"Like I would let her leave."

"You let her do whatever the hell she wants." He threw his arm down. "If you want to make the biggest mistake of your life, fine. But I want to stay out of it."

"As long as I don't marry her, you get what you want."

"If you were still gonna kill her, then I would be relieved. But you aren't."

"Who said I wasn't?" I watched my cigar burn down to the halfway point. I rolled it against the brown ashtray and watched the ash spread in the bowl.

He cocked his head. "Are you?"

"I said I would."

"But you won't."

I shrugged. "She's betrayed me twice. My memory isn't as bad as you think it is."

"But your mood affects how sharp that memory is. Until she's dead, I'll never let this go. This company is worth billions, and there's too much on the table for me to brush it off. She keeps worming her way further into our ranks. She used to be part of a wealthy family. I'm sure she misses the jewels and the cash. By acquiring half this company, she would be the richest widow in the world. That's the kind of dream anyone would do anything to achieve."

———

I WAS on my way home when my mother called me.

During Siena's absence, Mother had inquired about having another get-together, but I always made an excuse to put it off. Now that Siena was back, I couldn't put it off any longer. "Hey, Mother."

"Hey, honey. How are you?"

"Good. Just finished a long day at the office."

"It wouldn't be so long if you took time off like a normal person."

She was such a delight. "What's new with you?"

"Nothing. That's why I'm calling. I would love to have

dinner with you and Siena tonight. I feel like I haven't seen her in months."

No one had. "That should be fine. Maybe in an hour? I'm twenty minutes away."

"That sounds good. I'm so glad you aren't blowing me off…for the twentieth time."

I ignored her comment. "See you soon." I hung up and called Siena.

She answered right away. "Hello?" She'd gotten a new phone recently, so she probably hadn't used it until now.

"My mother is coming over for dinner. She was very insistent, so I couldn't say no."

"That's fine with me. I'm hungry anyway."

"For cheese?" I teased, thinking of one of our first dates.

"You know me so well. When will you be home?"

Home. She considered my place home. "Fifteen minutes."

"How was work?"

"Bates was a little bitch."

"Isn't he always a little bitch?"

I chuckled, feeling my stress melt away just from talking to her. "Yes, he is."

"I guess we'll just have to accept the fact that he'll never like me. And that's it."

My brother would never change his mind. That much was true. "He thinks you're manipulating me to get half the company."

She laughed loudly. "That guy is seriously paranoid. How would I even do that?"

"By marrying me and getting me to leave you my half when I die. And then you murder me somehow."

Now, she didn't laugh. "Wow…he has a really low opinion of me."

"He has a low opinion of everyone, if that makes you feel better."

She turned quiet, considering everything I'd just said about my brother. "This is why I hate money. All people care about is holding on to it to the exclusion of all else. The happiest thing in his life has made him the most miserable. It happens time and time again. It's the same story over and over."

Maybe she was manipulating me, tricking me into falling for her games. But when I listened to her say things like that, I thought she was being genuine. She never asked me for anything, never asked me to buy her a new pair of shoes or a diamond necklace. The most she ever did was let me pay for her meals. She even ran away to start a new life—and hung up her clothes to dry.

If she really was after my money, she did an extraordinary job hiding it. "I'm about to pull up to the house. I'll see you soon."

———

I SAT down with Mother in the dining room.

She greeted me with a hug and let me kiss her on the cheek. "Where's Siena?"

"She'll be down in a bit. She's having a hard time deciding what to wear."

"Oh, she doesn't need to impress me." She waved her hand as she sat down. "I already like the girl. She's growing my grandbaby."

"She's having a hard time fitting into her clothes, so she's trying to find something comfortable."

"Oh…I understand." She sipped her wine and cleared her throat. "That's the worst thing about pregnancy—gaining all the weight. You're so uncomfortable all the time. But then when the baby comes, it's all worth it." She smiled as she looked at me, motherly affection in her eyes. "I'm sure she's as beautiful as ever."

"She is," I said immediately. In fact, I thought she was more stunning than ever before. That round belly did interesting things to my desire. There was a new glow to her cheeks, a new joy in her eyes. The difference in her hips and thighs did nothing to stifle my appetite. Her pregnancy turned me into a caveman and spiced up our love life.

Mother watched my eyes as I said those words, like she was looking for something deep in my gaze. "Are you two together yet?"

I didn't know what we were. I shared everything with Siena, but there was still an invisible barrier between us. I didn't quite trust her, but I'd stopped pushing her away. "No." If I told her there was anything romantic, my mother would pressure me to marry Siena.

Like she hadn't heard what I said, she followed up with another question. "When are you going to ask her to marry you?"

Stunned by the question, it took me several seconds to respond. "I told you we aren't together. I'm not asking her to marry me."

"Then why do you look like a man so deeply in love?"

"I'm just hungry."

She chuckled. "Cato, I've been studying your expressions since the day you were born. I've never seen your eyes so blue, seen that slight smile that you're constantly trying to fight. Even when she isn't in the room, you light up when you talk about her."

"Because she's having my baby."

"You're excited to have a baby but feel nothing for the woman delivering it?" She shook her forefinger at me. "I

236

don't buy that for one moment." She grabbed her glass and took a sip. "I don't know why you insist on lying about how you feel about this woman. But let me tell you something, that woman is stunning. She would have no problem finding another man to love her, even with a child in the mix. So, if I were you, I would get my shit together and make sure that doesn't happen."

I smiled slightly at my mother's bluntness. "I'm just not looking for that kind of relationship."

"Even though you love her?"

My voice came out as a whisper. "I don't love her."

She continued to stare at me with a slight smile, like she didn't believe a word I said. She drank her wine then licked her lips. "Whatever you say, honey. I just hope you realize what you want sooner rather than later."

———

SIENA and my mother were two peas in a pod.

They got along better than my mother and I ever did.

They made each other laugh, talked about cheese, and excluded me from most of the conversation.

Not that I minded. Watching Siena's face light up was entertaining enough.

When we told my mother we were having a girl, her eyes welled with tears just the way Siena's did. She would have been happy no matter what we were having, but knowing the sex made it more real.

Even to me.

Siena and my mother talked for hours, long after my mother usually went to bed.

I actually had to kick her out. "It's getting late, and Siena needs her rest, Mother. Let me walk you to the door."

We gathered in the entryway then said our goodbyes. Mother hugged Siena for a long time then squeezed her belly with her hands. "I'm so excited to meet her." She kissed her on the cheek then walked to her car in the roundabout.

My mother didn't even say bye to me.

"Your mother is so great." She rubbed her stomach as she headed for the stairs. "I love her."

"That makes one of us," I said as I walked behind her.

"Shut up. Yes, you do."

Not right now.

We made it to my bedroom. Once the door was shut, I dropped my suit and tie onto the floor. I'd been wearing it all day, and having the tie around my neck got old. I was rich enough that I didn't have to wear a suit at all—but it was part of my image.

Siena slowly peeled off her clothes and hung them in the closet, sticking to the side that I'd given her. I'd moved my suits to the other side and gave her enough room to hang up her essentials. She didn't have a lot of clothes. Actually, she had significantly fewer shoes and items than I did.

"Did your mother wonder where I was for the last two months?" she asked as she peeled off her bra and put it in the hamper.

"I just told her we were busy."

"For two months?" she asked in surprise.

I peeled off my clothes and placed my boxers in the hamper. "Yes."

"That must have pissed her off."

"I'm sure it did." But I had been too depressed to care.

She examined me with that observant gaze, like she caught something I never meant to produce. "What is it?"

"What is what?"

"You seem resentful."

I walked past her and headed to the shower. "Just something she said to me."

Siena followed me, her feet lightly tapping against the tile. "What did she say?"

I grabbed the towel and turned on the water. "Nothing."

"It wasn't nothing. It was something."

I set the towel on the hook and noticed the steam filling the bathroom. It had already begun to fog up the mirror. "Doesn't matter if it was something. I don't want to talk about it." I opened the shower door and stepped inside.

A minute later, she joined me.

Now I really did feel like I had a wife, a woman who nagged at me.

She tipped her head back and let the water fall into her hair until it was slick against her scalp and neck. Her hands found my stomach, and she lightly pushed her hands up the grooves of muscle.

I stared down at her and silently warned her not to ask me about it again.

"It's fine if you don't want to talk about it." She moved in and pressed a kiss to my chest. "But I'm here anyway." She placed my hand on her belly. "Both of us are."

———

WHEN I WOKE up the next morning, she was right beside me.

Wrapped around me like a pretzel, she snuggled into my side with her belly pressed against my rib cage. One of her legs was tucked between mine. Her deep breaths were light and gentle, and her hair was still damp from the shower we took together last night.

She'd ended up on her knees in the shower as she sucked my dick.

I came in the back of her throat, and we went straight to bed with nothing but a pat down with the towels.

Now the sheets were slightly damp, and the maid would have to wash them. My sheets were usually changed every other day or so because there was come and pussy juice everywhere. Siena was so wet all the time that it made a mess.

Not that I was complaining.

Careful not to wake her up, I gently moved away from her and got dressed for my workout. I hit my private gym then went downstairs to have breakfast.

Siena joined me even though it wasn't yet seven in the morning. She answered my unspoken question. "It gets too cold when you aren't in bed." She wore pajama bottoms and one of my t-shirts. She threw her damp hair in a bun, and even though she was dressed so casually, she still caught my attention.

"I'm sorry."

"No need to be sorry." She picked up the mug of decaf and took a drink.

Giovanni prepared breakfast, salmon with mixed veggies, and placed it in front of us.

Siena hadn't complained about the meals he prepared for her, knowing she needed powerfully nutritious meals and not a bunch of maple syrup poured over waffles. She ate her meal and sipped her coffee. "There's something I want to ask you, but I'm not sure if I should ask now or later."

"Depends on what it is." I set down my phone and gave her my full attention. The last time we'd had a conversation similar to this, I snapped at her and got syrup thrown in my face. I didn't care to repeat that.

"Well, I was wondering if I could go get my car. That way I would have something to drive if I needed to go somewhere."

I dropped my fork and ignored my food because this conversation wouldn't be solved with a simple answer. "What makes you think you're going to go somewhere?"

Her eyebrows rose immediately, provoked by my tone. "I already ran away and didn't like it. You think I'm going to do that again?"

"No. But I don't understand why you need to go anywhere."

"Well, I don't have a specific place in mind. But if I'm going to be here indefinitely, I thought I should have a car. I might have errands to run. Maybe I want to take the baby to visit Landon. Maybe I want to get you a birthday gift. When is your birthday, anyway?"

Like I would ever tell her. "You won't be driving anywhere by yourself. If there's anywhere you wish to go, my men will drive you."

"You don't think that's excessive?"

"You were the one who accused me of not being able to protect our child. So, no, I don't think it's excessive." I didn't want to be an asshole when I just got her back last week, but it was impossible for me not to be when she questioned me like this. I was used to barking orders and men following those orders obediently. "I'm not inhibiting you from going anywhere you want to go. But having my men escort you there in an appropriate vehicle with appropriate protection makes more sense. You don't need your car."

"So it's just going to sit there forever?"

"You want to sell it?"

"I don't know…haven't really thought about it."

"Well, now you can."

"You never answered my question."

I was certain we'd touched all the bases. "What question is that?"

"When's your birthday?"

I picked up my fork again and continued eating. "Doesn't matter."

"Yes, it does. How are we going to celebrate it if I don't know when it is?"

"Because we won't celebrate it."

"Cato—"

"Drop it." I silenced her with my tone, telling her I wouldn't change my mind about this. "I never celebrate my birthday, and I'm not going to start now. Even Bates doesn't acknowledge it. So leave it alone." I turned back to my food and ate like nothing had happened. I could feel her gaze on my face, feel her disappointment penetrate through my skin. "If you don't want me to be an asshole, don't make me into one."

"I'm not," she said quietly. "I care about the man I'm sleeping with, the father of my child, and I just wanted to do something nice for you…because you mean a lot to me. The only reason you're acting like an asshole right now is because you are an asshole. If you just dropped your guard, you would see that I'm on your side…that I've always been on your side."

————

WHEN I CAME home from the office, I had dinner alone in the dining room then made my way upstairs. Siena was in my living room, so I went into the shower right away and didn't greet her at all. After I showered, I pulled on a pair of boxers then stepped into the living room.

She was watching TV, wearing one of my t-shirts and a pair of white socks.

I knew she was mad at me, but I couldn't stop myself from thinking she looked cute. "Baby."

She looked at me over her shoulder but didn't flash me that pretty smile. "You're home late."

"I had a lot to do." I had branches all over the world, so I had to delegate tasks constantly. Bates and I crunched numbers more than anything else. Threatening people to pay us back was actually a very small part of our job. I moved to the spot beside her and noticed the gift bag with tissue paper on the table.

That must have been for me.

She grabbed the remote and turned off the TV. "I wanted to give this to you…" She grabbed the bag then handed it to me. "It's not for any special occasion or anything… I had Giovanni go out and get it for me."

I held the bag but considered not opening it. It annoyed me when she did nice things for me, although I had no idea why. I guess I wanted to be the one to do everything. "Then what is it for?"

"I thought we could hang it up. Just open it."

I finally reached my hand inside and pulled out something solid. It was flat and long, not heavy at all. I pulled the tissue paper off then looked at the picture frame. Inside was the picture of the sonogram. Siena had added the date in pink writing, along with the words "Baby Girl Marino." I stared at it and didn't know what to say.

"I thought we could hang it up in here. You know… since we don't have any paintings."

I kept staring at the picture of my daughter, when she was so small we had no idea if she was a he or a she. Now she'd grown so big, made such a bulge in Siena's belly that her presence was undeniable.

"We don't have to put it up if you don't want to," she said quietly. "I just thought—"

"I love it." Once again, Siena showed me how valuable things could be, especially when they were free. This gift meant more to me than anything she could have bought me. It meant more to me than anything I'd ever bought myself. It was thoughtful, meaningful, and it reminded me how big Siena's heart was. I hoped our daughter inherited all her good qualities—and very little of my own. "Thank you."

"Do you really like it?" she asked, finally smiling.

"I do." I looked at her and gave her a smile. "And I want to hang it up. I want to look at it every day."

"Me too. I looked at it every day I was gone."

"So, she can have my last name?"

"I figured I didn't have a choice in the matter…"

"We could hyphenate." If we would never be married, it didn't seem fair that Siena didn't have any presence in the name.

"Really?" she asked.

"Yeah. Russo-Marino."

She nodded. "I'll take that." She took the picture frame from my hands and admired it. "I'm so excited to meet her. I really hope she has your eyes. I remember the first time I saw them…I thought I'd never seen anything more beautiful."

"Really?" I asked. "I thought the same thing about you."

She lifted her gaze from the picture and smiled at me. "Do you have any first names in mind?"

"No. I haven't even thought about it."

"I have a few. Do you want to hear?"

"Sure."

"Martina. It goes well with your last name. Martina Marino."

I didn't know anyone with that name, and I liked how sophisticated it sounded. My daughter wouldn't be just anyone. She would be the daughter of the richest man in Italy. With a powerful father, she needed a powerful name. Martina Marino. "I like it. I really like it."

"That was easy," she said with a chuckle. "I thought you would reject all my ideas."

"Martina…I think that's her name."

"You don't even want to hear the others?"

"No." I was already settled on it.

"Alright…Martina, it is." She set the picture down on the table then placed her hand on my thigh. In her baggy shirt, her belly wasn't visible, but she still had that glow in her face that couldn't be ignored. "That's our daughter." She rose to her feet then subtly pushed me back against the couch.

I knew what was coming, so I got hard instantly. Her hormones made her horny, but her pregnancy had the exact same effect on me. My back hit the cushion, and I pushed my boxers to my knees so my cock had all the room it needed.

She slid her panties down her long legs then straddled me. She left her shirt on, which was a turn-off because it didn't hug her figure at all.

I pulled it up.

She pushed it down again. "Not like this…"

I gripped the cotton tight and shot her a venomous expression. I wasn't gonna fuck this woman while a wall separated us. I wanted to see those tits, that beautiful skin, and that belly I couldn't get enough of. "This shirt is coming off—whether you like it or not." I pulled it over her head and took in her beautiful figure. Her belly was sexy and her skin glowed. She didn't have a damn thing to be insecure about. "You're beautiful." I grabbed her hips and directed her toward me so I could slide my shaft deep inside that slit I was obsessed with.

She pressed her hand against my chest to halt my movements. "Cato…please tell me why you don't celebrate your birthday. You don't even have to tell me when it is. I just want to know why."

She slowed down sex to talk. I didn't love that. "Why?"

"Because I care about you." She moved her hand over my heart. "And I want to know you. I want to know the good stuff as well as the bad."

I was surprised I was even considering telling her this. I hadn't talked about it since the night it happened. My brother and mother immediately understood my feelings because they'd been there. Every year when my birthday came around, it seemed to be a moment of mourning rather than celebration. "It was the day my father walked out on my mother."

Emotion that she couldn't fake moved into her gaze. The moisture flooded her eyes so quickly, it seemed miraculous she could feel so much so quickly. But her heart seemed to beat for me, and it felt like she really did care about me. She liked me for the man I was, not the wallet in my back pocket. "Thank you for telling me."

I pulled her closer against me and moved my hand into her hair. "Now fuck me, baby."

23

Siena

CATO WAS ALWAYS AWAKE HOURS BEFORE I WAS. I WAS wrapped in his warm sheets when he got up and hit the gym for two hours. I was so comfortable that when he returned and hopped in the shower, I still didn't crack open an eye.

The only reason I finally got out of bed that morning was because a nausea attack hit me. They'd become less frequent, but I still got them at least once a week. As I left the bed and walked to the toilet, I put my hair in a bun automatically since I'd done this procedure so many times. I reached the toilet and let everything out before I flushed.

Cato came out of the shower with the towel wrapped around his waist. "Baby, are you alright?"

"Yeah. This is a normal part of my life now." I moved to the sink and washed my face and rinsed out my mouth. "But I do resent you because it's entirely your fault."

"My fault, huh?" He stood behind me and looked at me in the mirror. "I guess I can take the blame, especially when I don't feel sorry about what I did." He tugged on the sleeve of my shirt to expose my shoulder. He placed a soft kiss there, the whiskers from his beard rough against my body.

I watched him walk away in the reflection and finish getting ready.

I brushed my teeth in the sink then pulled my hair loose from the hair tie. Now that I didn't have a job, I had nothing to do with my time other than think about giving birth to Martina. Childbirth was one of the most painful things a human could ever experience, and I wasn't looking forward to it. I'd rather have Damien shoot me in the shoulder again.

I returned to the bedroom and watched him put his suit together. "Any exciting plans for work?"

"I'm going out tonight with a few clients."

"Like to dinner?"

"No. A bar."

I raised an eyebrow. "You're going to a bar for work?"

"A lot of my criminal partners prefer to avoid the office. Too public, especially when the sun is out. It's not unusual."

Whenever I saw Cato in a bar, women threw their asses in his face. They stuck their tongues down his throat and helped themselves to his lap. The idea of Cato returning to that atmosphere made me feel nauseated again. "Will Bates be there?"

"Yes."

That made it worse.

He sat in the armchair and finished tying his shoes. "What is it, baby?"

"I'm not thrilled about you doing business in a bar."

He tied the other shoe then rose to his full height. "Why?"

"Uh, because I've seen women hump you right in the middle of the room."

"So?" he asked. "I humped them too."

My eyes flashed with rage. "You aren't helping."

"I don't know what you expect me to say. I'm meeting my clients for drinks, and there's nothing I can do to change that. Yes, there will be women there. And yes, they'll probably try to sit on my lap. I could go to a bowling alley, and that would still happen." He walked to the dresser and grabbed his watch and wallet. "I'm going to be out late, so I'll probably just sleep at my place in Florence."

The place where he took me to fuck me the first time. I remembered the beautiful woman lying beside me with no opposition to a threesome. So now he would spend the evening at a bar and not bother coming home. "Is this a joke?"

"You aren't laughing, so I don't think so."

There was so much back-and-forth with Cato. One moment, he was sensitive and loving, and then the next moment, he was incredulous of my feelings. "How would you feel if I went to a bar to meet an art client and said I wouldn't be coming home."

"You're pregnant, so I would say you're a terrible mother."

I smacked his arm. "I'm being serious."

"What do you want me to say?" he snapped. "This is happening, and there's nothing I can do about it."

"You're Cato Marino. You could do anything you wanted to." Playing to his ego was the best way to manipulate him. Like all powerful men, it was his downfall.

But he didn't take the bait. "For two months, I had every opportunity to fuck as much pussy as I wanted. Instead, I drank in my office and stared at your pictures. Now that I have you back, you think I'm gonna fuck a woman in a bathroom stall at a bar?"

My jealousy clouded my judgment until I couldn't think straight. "I know how women are with you. I've seen it with my own eyes. No offense, but I don't want to be home alone wondering if they're trying to get into your lap. I've seen women sit on your lap and let their dresses slide all the way to their waists to flash everyone in the bar. And most of them weren't wearing underwear."

He adjusted his watch on his wrist as he looked at me. "I'm not ashamed of my life before you. If you're waiting for an apology, you won't get one. I enjoyed every second of that period of my life—until I found something better."

As touching as it was, it wasn't enough for me. "Then come home."

"It'll probably be three in the morning."

"I don't care."

He slid his hands into his pockets and shook his head. "I'm surprised you don't trust me."

"It's not about trust. It just makes me jealous picturing you out at a bar…with those women fighting for your attention. If this situation were reversed, you wouldn't be okay with it."

"Completely different situations."

"Because I'm a woman?" I asked incredulously.

"Exactly." He turned away from me and headed to the door. "I'll call you when I get to my place in Florence tonight."

I followed behind him. "Couldn't I just come with you?"

He stopped and turned around. "Come with me?"

"Why not?"

His eyes darted back and forth as he looked into mine. "You want to come to work with me today, and then stay out until two in the morning listening to me talk about business, all so you can keep an eye on me?"

"I'm not keeping an eye on you," I snapped. "I just want to keep those gold-digging skanks off my man."

The second I used the possessive phrase, his eyes narrowed farther and his eyebrows rose. He held my gaze for a long time, still digesting the statement. A second later, approval entered his gaze. "Your man?"

"Yes." He was the man I slept with every night and the father of my child. To say I was possessive of him was an understatement. Even if Cato turned down all their offers, I didn't want them to have the opportunity to make a pass to begin with.

"Then let's go."

———

I RECOGNIZED the building because I'd seen him walk into it several times. When I had been gleaning as much information as possible, I'd followed him to various locations to determine his schedule. It was interesting to actually walk inside when I'd only stared at the front doors.

The second Cato was in the building, everyone waited on him hand and foot. The secretaries all greeted him with a smile and over-the-top enthusiasm, and the other employees inside the bank went out of their way to say hello and compliment his tie or his watch.

We moved to the top floor, which seemed to be a restricted area just for Cato. It was two enormous offices along with two assistants. Cato checked in with one of them, received his messages, and then introduced me. "Shelly, this is Siena." Then he headed to his office.

Siena? That was it? I didn't consider myself to be his girlfriend or his wife, but I felt like I was more than just my first name. I followed behind him and entered his office. "That's it? I'm Siena?"

He sat behind his desk and got to work, hardly looking at me. "She already knows who you are."

"Which is?"

"The woman I'm fucking."

And that was it? "Does she know we're expecting?"

"She has eyes, doesn't she?" He grabbed his laptop and typed in a few passwords before he finally accessed it. "I have a lot of work to do, so no more talking."

I raised an eyebrow.

He didn't need to look at me to know I looked pissed. "You wanted to come, Siena. I told you I couldn't entertain you." He stared at his screen and then his fingers hit the keyboard fast. He was typing at lightning speed, better than a typist. Then he flipped through his stack of folders and made notes.

So this was what a billionaire did all day?

The door burst open, and Bates walked inside. "I've got another live one—" He halted when he saw me, and his horrified expression quickly turned into a livid one. His eyes burst with rage, and it seemed like he might strangle me right then and there.

Cato looked up from his work and examined his brother. "You were saying?"

He couldn't take his eyes off me. "What the fuck is she doing here?"

Cato quickly matched his hostility. "Shut the door if you're going to act like a maniac."

He slammed it shut and then spoke louder. "What the fuck is she doing here?"

"She wanted to come," Cato said. "We have that meeting tonight, and she wanted to be the woman on my arm. You know, bug repellent. Apparently, I have a jealous woman on my hands." He tried to stop the corner of his mouth from rising in a smile, but it was too hard to ignore.

"Or a bitch that's just trying to learn everything she can. I told you what she was after, and you still don't believe me."

Cato rose to his feet. "Enough with the bitch bombs, alright? And no, that's not what she's doing."

"Really?" he snapped. "Open your damn eyes. She saw an opportunity and took it. I used to think you were the smartest guy I've ever known, but now that I've seen how far you've fallen, I don't even know you anymore. This business is everything to us—and you're throwing it away for her." He walked out and slammed the door again.

Cato stared at the closed door for several seconds before he sighed.

I didn't realize how much my presence would ruin Cato's day. "I'm sorry…I should have stayed home."

"No." He looked back at his computer. "He's just unhinged. Don't worry about him."

I'd seen the progression of their relationship, from their strong alliance to their broken friendship. Now they were falling apart right in front of my eyes. Cato had few family members, and the last thing I wanted him to do was lose another. "I have an idea." I rose from the chair and walked to the desk.

"Yes?" He leaned back in his chair and looked at me.

"If Bates is that concerned about me plotting to take your business, then let's give him some reassurance."

"And how do you propose we do that?"

"Legal paperwork." I'd never done anything like this before, but I assumed it existed. "We meet with a lawyer and draft up a contract stating that I will never have any ownership claim to this company. Even if we married and you died, your share of the company would return to Bates or would be passed down to the baby. We can indicate in every way imaginable that there's no possibility I can ever get my hands on it." If that was what Bates needed to sleep well at night, it was fine by me.

Cato stared at me incredulously, as if he couldn't believe what I'd just said. Seconds passed and he didn't blink. All he did was look at me, his hands coming together in front of his chest. He repositioned his legs under the desk and shifted in his chair. "You would do that?"

"Of course. Bates has been such an asshole to me, but I know he's only trying to protect you. The last thing I want is to drive you two apart. When Martina gets here, I want her to have a close relationship with her uncle. I want her to see you two happy together. I don't want her to see family fighting over money the second she comes into this world. The first thing she would see is how important money is to people…and that's the last thing I want."

He continued to stare at me in disbelief.

"And even if we never got married, but you died, you could have it written that Martina couldn't have access to anything until she was in her twenties or something—and I wouldn't get a dime." If that settled the beef between Bates and Cato, then it sounded like a good idea. I'd never cared about Cato's money, and I was willing to put my money where my mouth was.

"I think that would make Bates feel much better, actually."

"Then let's do it. Problem solved." I could finally be comfortable in Cato's house without fear of running into Bates—and being screamed at. I could come to the office again without being accused of being a gold digger. Maybe Bates and I could even have a nice relationship…in time.

Cato didn't show an emotional expression, but he seemed touched by the gesture I'd made. Unable to put his thoughts into words, he stared at me as the silence surrounded us both.

There was no need to be surprised. I'd told him I never cared about his money—and I meant it. If anything, I despised the ego he had based on that wealth. I disliked the way he treated other people just because of the size of his wallet. The qualities I admired about him had nothing to do with his wealth. I actually liked him in spite of his riches.

Cato finally brushed it off. "I'll make some calls."

———

I WORE a slimming black dress that hid my baby bump fairly well. It was backless, distracting stares away from my front. I wore black pumps and a few pieces of jewelry that Cato's assistant picked up for me.

I was grateful I'd come along because the second we were inside that bar, every single woman looked at Cato as a target. His handsome features were impossible not to recognize. He was a beacon to all women, the rich and handsome man every woman wanted for a husband.

Too bad. He's mine.

Cato had his arm around my waist as he guided me to a private seating area. With leather couches curved into a circle and a table in the center, it was raised above the rest of the bar so visibility was clear.

I sat beside Cato and crossed my legs.

He rested his hand on my thigh with his knees apart. He had his signature drink, scotch with a single ice cube, and I sipped a glass of ice water.

My arm was hooked underneath his, and I snuggled with him on the couch, claiming my territory so none of the other bitches would think they had a chance.

Bates said nothing to Cato. He was still livid from that

exchange in the office. Now he was so mad he wasn't on speaking terms with his brother at all.

Two women joined us a moment later, both tall and beautiful.

I squeezed Cato's arm harder. The tough thing about Cato was he was known to have multiple lovers, so seeing me grip his arm like this didn't matter at all.

The brunette came to us, her eyes on Cato. As if I weren't there at all, she addressed him in a sultry voice. "Cato Marino, I heard you and I have similar tastes. Care to find out?" She helped herself to his lap, about to straddle him without even introducing herself.

"Whoa, sweetheart." Cato put his hand out and steadied her. "As flattered as I am, I'm giving monogamy a try."

"And we're having a baby together," I added, even though it was unnecessary information. "But Bates it totally available and just as rich."

"She's right," Bates said. "And I've got two arms."

The woman took Cato's rejection in stride and decided to join Bates instead.

I couldn't believe women were that forward with Cato. I'd seen it with my own eyes but still couldn't believe it. Did they really think being kinky would bag them the richest husband in the country? Cato needed something more than another night of good sex. That was exactly why he was a hollow shell—because nothing really meant anything. My jealousy faded away, and I actually pitied him. One-night stands were fine, but they weren't even based on a real connection, a true lustful attraction between two people. It was just sex in its most basic form, like a lion with a pride of lionesses.

Cato turned to me. "That would have gone the same way whether you were here or not."

"I thought I would be a better bug repellent. Guess I'm not."

"No. They think I've found one woman for the night— and now I need a second one."

"Well, you do have two women for the night. Just not in the way you're used to." I moved his hand to my stomach.

He looked down at my bump as he felt it over my black dress. "I prefer this way."

———

CATO DID business with shady people, I'd leave it at that.

The guys seemed to be part of some organization called the Skull Kings. I'd heard the name before, but I didn't know much about them. Apparently, they'd borrowed money from Cato for an arms deal, and now they were asking for more.

I got to see a different side of Cato, the cold-hearted moneymaker. If I thought he acted like an asshole to me, it was nothing compared to the way he treated others. He iced down his alliances and his enemies with the same frost.

I was absolutely silent for the entire exchange, not making eye contact and holding on to Cato's arm for balance.

Bates complemented Cato's coldness with his fire. He was more aggressive than his brother, pushing Cato's state-ments to solidify them. He might be pissed at his brother, but he didn't let his personal feelings affect the deal they were making.

Three hundred million was on the table—including the five hundred that had already been borrowed.

Geez, that was a lot of cash.

Once the interest rate had been decided, they came to

an agreement. There was no paperwork or contracts to sign. It was a gentleman's agreement, with the promise of death as collateral.

How did Cato live this life every day?

Was the money worth it?

———

WE ENTERED the penthouse he had in the city. The living room was exactly as I remembered it. The building seemed to belong to him exclusively because there was no one else around.

I stepped inside and examined the windows, noting how thick and dark they were. They were probably bullet-proof. I stripped off my jacket and hung it on the coatrack by the door. The last time I'd stepped inside this place, I had decided to bed Cato to save my father. Once I'd kissed him, I didn't have to talk myself into it anymore.

But when I'd spotted Christina on the bed, the mood had been destroyed.

What if I had slept with him that night? What would have happened? Would I be pregnant now? Would he have forgotten me by morning? Would my father be dead and I would be a prisoner to Damien?

Cato came to my side by the window. "What has you so deep in thought?"

I'd been staring out the window at the cold city. It hardly snowed here, but it definitely seemed like an unusually cold winter. The air was chilly to the skin, and I could feel the coldness slightly when I stood right next to the glass. "I was thinking about the last time I was here."

"A night I'll never forget."

"I'm sure you had fun anyway..." I didn't mean

anything to him at the time. He'd probably forgotten about me the second I left.

"I did," he said honestly. "But I didn't stop thinking about you. Those last words you spoke to me stayed with me. I'd wondered if I'd made a mistake. I'd wondered if I actually lost a real woman." He moved closer to me then stood at my back. His head bent toward my neck, and he pressed a kiss to the top of my spine. His fingers moved up my bare back to the slender straps over my shoulders, then he pushed them off, watching them drop down my arms.

I let the dress fall to the floor.

His hands gripped my tits and then moved over my distended stomach as his breaths caressed the back of my neck. "Even if it was all a lie. Even if it was all bullshit. I'm glad it happened. You're the real woman you vowed to be." His arm slid under my stomach and rested there, as if he were supporting both of us.

He kissed the back of my neck before he lifted me into his arms. My dress was left behind on the ground as he carried me to the bed where he'd bedded all those other women, all the women who'd meant nothing to him. He gently laid me on the bed before he peeled his clothes away. His watch was left on the nightstand, his jacket resting over the armchair in the corner, and the rest of his clothes were dropped into a pile on the floor.

I watched him strip down to his bare skin, to his muscles and his strength. With wide shoulders, powerful arms, and narrow hips, he was over six feet of perfect man. I'd always imagined starting my family under very different circumstances, with a nice man who was sensitive and kind. We would date, fall madly in love, and after a small wedding outside somewhere, we would start our family. My reality was nothing like my fantasy, but now I wouldn't have it any other way.

I didn't want anyone else to be the father of my child.

I didn't want to share my nights with anyone else.

Even if I weren't pregnant and he would let me go, I didn't want to be anywhere else.

I wanted to be right here.

He left my heels on and went for my black thong. He slowly pulled it down and over my shoes before he left it on the foot of the bed. Then he moved on top of me and widened my legs, taking the position he usually took when he screwed me. He used to do it this way so he could see my tits and face, but now he wanted to see my belly instead. He got the head of his cock inside me and slowly slid deep into me, pushing through all the moisture my body produced for him. He released that sexy moan I always looked forward to hearing. It was a moan of pleasure, a moan that showed he wasn't thinking about anyone else but me. He could have any woman he wanted, but he only wanted to be with me.

My palms planted against his chest, and I stared into his eyes as he moved inside me, feeling that big dick take me all the way. Now that I'd had a real man like Cato, I couldn't go back to anything else. Now that I'd lived with this man and slept beside him every night, I knew I never wanted to be without him. The one time I'd tried to cut him from my life, it ended up being the biggest mistake I'd ever made. When his shadow appeared behind that towel, I hadn't been able to keep the tears back.

Because he was home.

I'd lost everything to greed, but I found everything in him. Now I was starting my own family, rebuilding all that I'd lost, and I was doing it with a man I respected and admired. Our relationship was built on a lie, but that lie turned into the truest feeling in my life.

My hand cupped the back of his head, and I brought

his lips to mine for a passionate kiss, full of tongue and longing. We breathed into each other's mouths as we enjoyed each other, our bodies so deeply intertwined, we were one person.

My heart ached for this man in a way it never had before. Watching him reject that woman in the bar tonight showed me how much he had changed. He was an arrogant asshole who had fucked anything that moved. He was stubborn and egotistical. But once he let some of his walls come down, he showed a beautiful side he shouldn't be afraid to hide. He buried my father when he didn't have to. He shot Damien so I could have my revenge. He let me go because he knew I would only want to come back. He'd turned into my protector, my partner. It wasn't the future I'd planned, but now it was the future I wanted more than anything else. "Cato…I want to make more babies with you."

He kept thrusting into me, his intense eyes focused on mine.

I wasn't afraid to say how I felt. I would have said it sooner if I'd known what was in my heart. "I want to spend my life with you." I cupped his face. "I love you." Everything spilled out of my lips, like warm caramel pouring over ice cream. The passionate ignited me, but the love in my heart gave me the courage to tell him how I felt. He wasn't the man I'd pictured myself with, but now I couldn't imagine my life with anyone else. Maybe he was wrong for me, but I didn't care. With Martina, we were already a family.

Cato slowed down his pumps then unexpectedly came inside me. His dick got extremely thick as it buried farther in my body. He gave his hips a swift buck and dumped everything into my cunt, releasing a moan at the same time.

It was the first time we'd made love and he didn't make me come first.

Maybe my words aroused him so much that he couldn't keep it in. Maybe my confession was so sexy his body didn't know how to react.

He pressed his forehead to mine as his heavy breathing continued. No words were forthcoming, but he seemed to gather his bearings. His cock softened inside me, but within a minute, it was hard again. He moved his mouth to mine and kissed me, giving me a slow and sexy embrace.

But he didn't say it back.

And it didn't seem like he was going to.

When he was at full mast, he started to thrust inside me again, this time a little harder. He pulled his lips away and looked into my eyes, the desire burning white-hot like an inferno. He clearly wasn't angry by what I said.

But he didn't reciprocate either.

My hands rested against his chest, and I felt my tits shake up and down. My eyes locked on to his, and I tried once more. "I love you so damn much."

There was another flash of desire across the surface of his eyes, like we were making dirty talk and I'd said something particularly kinky. My whispers aroused him even more, made him thicker than he'd ever been.

But I got silence in response.

———

HE WENT to sleep right when we were finished, but I stayed up most of the night. When the sun came up, Cato woke up and immediately got into the shower. He didn't kiss me good morning or try to fuck me again.

Most mornings, he didn't, so that wasn't too unusual.

But I wondered if we would talk about last night.

Or pretend nothing happened.

Cato wasn't the kind of man to shy away from anything, so I doubted he would ignore the tension between us indefinitely.

Or maybe he would. He'd looked me in the eye and listened to me say I loved him twice. And he said nothing at all.

When he was finished with the shower, he came back to the bed and kissed me. "Morning, baby."

Whenever he called me baby, that was usually a good sign. "Morning."

He opened his closet and pulled out a new suit to wear. "We are meeting my lawyer this morning."

"What for?"

"To sign all the paperwork we talked about." He grabbed my clothes that I'd brought with me and set them on the bed. "It shouldn't take more than an hour."

Everything seemed normal, except for the big elephant in the room. "Okay." I grabbed my clothes and got ready before I headed into the bathroom to do my hair and makeup. Flashbacks of last night came to me, our sweat rubbing together and our breaths deep and powerful. Those words had rolled off my tongue so easily. I'd never told a man I loved him before, and when I did it for the first time, it felt so right. It felt like a burden had been lifted from my shoulders.

When I walked back into the bedroom, he was ready to leave. In a navy suit with a black tie, he looked like the corporate dictator he was. He owned every room he stood in, including the bar last night when he cornered the Skull Kings into giving in to his ridiculous interest rate. With one hand in his pocket, he scrolled through his phone.

"I'm ready." I wore my black jeans, blue sweater, and my black jacket.

He looked me up and down appreciatively. "You look beautiful." His arm circled my waist, and he kissed me.

Like everything was normal.

We went down to the car waiting for us and then drove to his lawyer's office.

I couldn't figure out why Cato was behaving this way. Would he continue to ignore it until I believed it never happened in the first place? It had happened, right? "Are all your business dealings like that?"

"Like what?" He looked out the window.

"Hostile. Aggressive. Kinda scary."

He chuckled. "That's how you have to be to survive in this world."

"Not survive. Triumph."

He nodded in agreement.

"I thought you were an asshole to me, but now I realize you can be much worse."

He chuckled quietly. "Much worse."

I stared at the side of his face for a while and wondered what he was thinking. I remembered how thick he felt inside me when I said those words. I felt how hard he came inside me when I whispered my feelings. He'd obviously enjoyed what I'd said even though he didn't reciprocate.

When I looked back on everything he had done for me, I refused to believe he didn't feel the same way. He rescued my father from an oil drum and buried him where he belonged. He protected me against his brother's fists. And then he came to France and asked me to come home... because he missed me. He slept with me every night now, had been faithful to me during those two months we were apart. Would a man do that if he weren't in love? No, I didn't think so.

I knew Cato loved me.

But maybe he wasn't ready to say it.

———

HIS LAWYER PRESENTED ALL the paperwork to me, along with an intimidating pen to add my signatures. "According to these documents, in the event of Cato Marino's unlikely passing, one-third of his personal assets would be divided between his brother and mother. The other two-thirds would be given to Martina Marino. She would inherit most of the holdings in Cato's trust. But she will not receive this inheritance until she's twenty-one years of age."

"Alright." I read through the paperwork and added my signature.

He pushed another paper toward me. "This states you have no legal rights to his company, even in the event of marriage. If Cato Marino passes away, all of his holdings in the company will pass to Bates Marino."

I added my signature. "Anything else?" Signing paperwork was boring.

"One more." He pushed another paper toward me. "In the event of termination of a marriage by death or divorce, you're waiving your right to Cato Marino's personal assets. Everything will fall to Martina Marino when she's of age."

"How is this any different from what I already signed?" I asked.

Cato sat beside me, his legs crossed and his face stoic.

The lawyer explained. "This relates to his personal assets, such as his home, the money in his bank account, and his investments."

I understood we were doing this to protect Bates, but this was a personal clause Cato had specifically asked for. I didn't care about his money, but I thought it was in poor taste that a husband would make sure his wife didn't get a penny if he were hit by a bus. But since it didn't matter anyway, especially since he wouldn't tell me he loved me, I signed it and handed it back. "Anything else?"

"No, that's it." The lawyer gathered all the papers and then walked to the copy machine. "Once I give you a copy, the two of you can be on your way." He quickly made them and handed the folder to Cato before he shook his hand. "Until next time, Mr. Marino."

"Thank you." Cato moved his arm around my waist and walked with me down the hallway. Once we were back on the street, we got into the car. The car headed for his office a few blocks away.

I didn't know I would be spending the day with him at work again. I was hoping we could go home and have some privacy to talk.

The car pulled up to the sidewalk.

Cato didn't get out right away. "The car is going to drop you off at the house before it returns to pick me up. I'll be home at the usual time. No bar stops, I promise." He smiled like the last twelve hours had been perfectly normal, like I didn't tell him I loved him and signed off on everything that kept his money out of my hands.

"So…are we just going to pretend that didn't happen?"

His smile fell, the light slowly leaving his eyes.

"Because you don't strike me as the kind of man to ignore problems. I thought you were a man who faced them head on."

He looked out the window for a few moments as he considered what he might say. He eventually turned back to me, his blue eyes cold as the sea. "What do you want me to say, baby?"

"You know what I want you to say." It was pretty obvious what I wanted, to tell him I loved him and hear him say it back.

He looked out the window again. "Well, I can't."

"But you enjoyed it when I said it to you."

"Why wouldn't I? The beautiful woman who's having my baby is in love with me. Yes, it fucking turned me on. But that's it." He released a quiet sigh when he finished speaking, as if this conversation was a nuisance.

"You would take a bullet for me, Cato."

"Because you're carrying my daughter—"

"That's not the only reason. You can pretend burying my father was just a humane act of kindness. You can pretend that stopping Bates from hurting me was just instinct. You can pretend that the only reason you don't want to fuck other women is because you don't want to wear a condom. But when you came to France to get me, you would have done anything to get me back. You were distraught without me, just as much as I was without you. So you can say you don't love me all you want. Because I know that's bullshit. I know you do, Cato. And I can be patient until you grow the balls to say it."

24

Cato

I GOT OUT OF THE CAR WITHOUT LOOKING BACK AND stepped into my building. The folder was gripped tightly in my hand, the paperwork I needed to get Bates to calm the fuck down. Instead of riding the elevator to the fifth floor, I took the stairs just so I had extra time to cool off.

When I was deep inside Siena, she'd said the sexiest words I'd ever heard a woman speak.

I love you, Cato.

Those words would have been a nightmare coming from anyone else. I would have stopped what I was doing then and there and gotten rid of her.

But from Siena, the words were the trigger to the best orgasm of my life.

My entire body was set on fire. I didn't even let her finish first. As if she'd pressed an invisible button, I was forced to climax, like my body needed to do it, otherwise, it would shut down.

It wasn't just the words that she whispered to me, but the passion that fueled them, the sexy look in those green eyes. It was everything, including the baby growing inside her, the baby I put there.

I knew she meant it.

And that was the biggest turn-on of all.

But, no, I didn't feel the same way. I thought my silence confirmed that. It was the kindest way to reject her, to let her down easy. I was still rock hard between her legs and committed to what we had. A confession of love wouldn't change that. But I didn't want to talk about it either.

I assumed we could just move forward and forget it ever happened.

For her sake.

But then she threw all of my gestures in my face. She argued that I felt the same way, but I didn't have the balls to say it.

I had bigger balls than anyone else in this world.

Trust me, if I loved her, I would say it.

I didn't.

She was the only woman who had my fidelity, but that was because I enjoyed our chemistry so much. She was the only woman who slept beside me every night, but that was because it'd been one of her demands. She was the only woman who'd met my mother, but that was because it'd been out of my control. She tried to see the love in my actions, but in actuality, they meant nothing. I buried her father because it was the right thing to do. I shot Damien because that asshole shouldn't have shot her in the first place. I bent over backward to take care of her because she was growing my daughter inside her. I could admit I felt something special for her that I felt for no one else. But that didn't mean it was love. It was lust, friendship, respect, admiration…but not love.

I made it to my floor and headed to Bates's office.

He was on the phone when I walked inside. "Hang up."

His feet were on the desk, and he was smoking up a cloud. "I gotta go. Cato just walked in, and he looks like he's gonna throw a hissy fit." He hung up and tossed his phone on the table. "I'm surprised your little spy isn't here."

"She's on her way home."

"Thank god," he barked. "If I had to look at her face every day, I would just head to another branch."

Hopefully, his attitude was about to change. "After your little outburst in my office yesterday, Siena offered to do something."

I tossed the folder at him, and it slid across his desk.

"She strikes me as a woman who offers to do a lot of things…" He grabbed the folder and opened it.

"Sometimes I wonder if you're suicidal."

"I am when she's around." He flipped through the pages. "What the hell am I looking at?"

"Do you not know how to read, asshole?"

He lifted his gaze and glared at me.

"She offered to remove herself from any possibility of inheriting anything from me—in any shape or form."

His finger slackened on the papers, and he almost dropped them on the floor.

"In regards to the document, if something happens to me, whether we're married or not, my share of the business would be transferred back to you."

He flipped through the pages until he found that clause and her signature.

"She also signed off on giving Martina all of my assets in the event something happens to me. The trust will hold on to it until she turns twenty-one."

"Who's Martina?" he blurted.

"My daughter, idiot. That's what we decided to name her."

"Martina Marino…it's cute."

"I know. On top of that, Siena removed herself from ever inheriting any of my personal assets in the event of my death. There's no wiggle room around it. There's never any possibility of Siena getting a dime from me personally or getting anything from the company. If I die, it's all yours."

He flipped through the pages and read the sections Siena had signed.

"She and I aren't getting married, but that's included in the unlikely event it happens, a glorified prenup. So will you calm the fuck down and give her a break? That woman doesn't want anything from me but me." As I said the words out loud, I thought about last night. I pictured the way her lips moved when she told me she loved me, the way her breath fell across my skin. Her sultry voice made my skin break out in goose bumps.

Bates finished reading it and returned the folder to the desk. His feet were still up on the surface, and his cigar had been abandoned. He picked it up again and took a few puffs, slowly letting the smoke release from his mouth.

"You have nothing to say?"

He shrugged. "Maybe I was wrong."

"Maybe?" I asked. "No, asshole. You were wrong. I denied her access to my personal assets just to see what she would do. But she signed it anyway and didn't blink an eye over it. No other woman would have done that, even if they weren't a gold digger. It's totally fucked up."

He held the cigar between his fingers and let the smoke rise to the ceiling. "Alright…maybe she's not as bad as I thought she was."

"She's nothing like you thought she was."

"Let's not forget how this fuck-a-thon started, alright? She lied to you. Lied to your fucking face."

"But she's never been after my money."

He sucked the tip and let the smoke escape his slightly parted lips. "Alright, I'll chill out. Maybe she's not the manipulative thief I thought she was. I'll be civil to her. I'll even ask her how her day is going. But I still don't think this woman is right for you, Cato. The entire beginning of your relationship was a lie. If she were a man, she would be dead right now. Maybe she doesn't want your money, but that doesn't mean she didn't play you for a fool." He turned his head and looked out the window. "We've had this same conversation a million times, so I'm not going to have it anymore. But as your brother, I have to be straight with you. I think you deserve better." He held up both of his hands. "That's all I'll say about it." He took another hit of his cigar until he reached the butt then dropped it in the ashtray.

I sat in the leather armchair and rested my ankle on the opposite knee. Since Siena had come into my life, we hadn't talked the way we did before. Bates resented me for being so merciful to the woman carrying my child. A distance had developed between us, but it'd grown so much in the last few months. He used to be my closest friend. Now he was just…Bates. I missed that bond. "She told me she loved me last night."

He stared at me blankly, like he didn't know how to process that. He opened his left drawer and pulled out two cigars. He tossed me one. "You need one of these." He tossed the lighter next.

I lit up and let the smoke enter my mouth. "She said it twice, actually."

"Like you didn't hear it the first time," he said with a chuckle. "I'm guessing you didn't say it back."

"No." I didn't smoke at the house anymore because Siena was there all the time. I tried not to smoke at work either because it stuck to my suits and I brought it back into the house. But right now, my need to relax outweighed Siena.

"She must have been pissed."

"No, actually."

"No?" he asked in surprise. "That's the most awkward thing in the world—tell someone you love them and listen to crickets. When did she tell you?"

"While we were fucking."

He nodded slowly. "More awkward."

I didn't tell him how much I'd enjoyed it, how I came harder than I ever had.

"And you just kept going?"

"Yeah."

"And then what happened?"

I shrugged. "We went to sleep. Woke up the next morning, and I pretended nothing happened. But when we were in the car, she cornered me. Said she knows I love her even if I won't admit it. And she can wait until I grow enough balls to actually say it."

He lit up his second cigar and took a long puff. "Well, do you?"

"No." I'd said it many times, especially when my mother asked me.

"You've made a lot of exceptions for her. I can't blame her for thinking that."

"She misinterprets a lot of things I say and do."

He shrugged. "I don't know, man. I'm not calling you a liar, but a man doesn't remain celibate when a woman is gone because of lust...there's needs to be something besides lust to keep him faithful. You didn't fool around once in two months, even when I dragged you to the bars and the women dropped in your lap. You always left. How do you explain that?"

My arms sat on the armrests, and the cigar hung between my fingers. My gaze turned to the painting on his wall, something someone must have hung a decade ago. Without really looking at it, I stared at the dull colors of the flowers.

I didn't have a logical counterargument against my brother's words. Those two months were difficult for me. My dreams were filled with her beautiful face, and my broken heart never seemed to heal. It was in a constant state of pain. I had every right to fuck whoever I wanted, but returning to that lonely lifestyle made me sick to my stomach. Now that I had something meaningful, something that actually made me happy, going backward would just be painful. I hadn't desired another woman in the first place. I hadn't desired anyone because I was numb.

My brother kept staring at me. "If the woman already loves you, what's the harm in saying it back?"

"I told you I don't feel that way."

Bates gave me a sad look, like he didn't believe a word I said. "If you do all those things for her, but still don't love her...then what does love actually mean to you?" He cocked his head as he examined me.

My mouth was immobile because I didn't have an answer. We slept in the same bed every night, we were having a baby together, and I was committed to someone for the first time in my life. She was the only person I'd ever met who wasn't impressed by my money, and I think that rare occurrence made me feel poor rather than rich. She saw me for what I really was, all the good and all the bad. I didn't like someone having that kind of hold over me. This woman had more control over me than anyone else in the world, more than all my enemies combined.

She knew exactly who I was.

That terrified me.

I didn't want to give her any more power.

Because it would destroy me.

Also by Penelope Sky

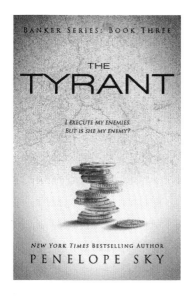

Order Now

Made in the USA
Monee, IL
31 October 2019

16156538R00164